JOHN EVERSON

VOODOO HEART

This is a **FLAME TREE PRESS** book

Text copyright © 2020 John Everson

FLAME TREE PRESS
6 Melbray Mews, London, SW6 3NS, UK
flametreepress.com

US sales, distribution and warehouse:
Simon & Schuster
simonandschuster.biz

UK distribution and warehouse:
Marston Book Services Ltd
marston.co.uk

Thanks to the Flame Tree Press team, including:
Taylor Bentley, Frances Bodiam, Federica Ciaravella, Don D'Auria,
Chris Herbert, Josie Karani, Molly Rosevear, Mike Spender,
Cat Taylor, Maria Tissot, Nick Wells, Gillian Whitaker.

The cover is created by Flame Tree Studio with
thanks to Nik Keevil and Shutterstock.com.
The font families used are Avenir and Bembo.

Flame Tree Press is an imprint of Flame Tree Publishing Ltd
flametreepublishing.com

A copy of the CIP data for this book is available from the British Library
and the Library of Congress.

HB ISBN: 978-1-78758-512-6
US PB ISBN: 978-1-78758-510-2
UK PB ISBN: 978-1-78758-511-9
ebook ISBN: 978-1-78758-514-0

Printed and bound in Great Britain by Clays Ltd, Elcograf S.p.A.

JOHN EVERSON

VOODOO HEART

FLAME TREE PRESS
London & New York

For Geri

PART ONE
BLOODY BEDS

CHAPTER ONE

Tuesday, June 18

Honey Moon

I see them every day. They come here by the thousands looking for a good time. Drinking themselves into oblivion on Bourbon Street. Laughing and gorging and lifting their shirts to strangers in the ridiculous ritual of beads. Waking up in strange beds with partners they don't recognize in the hard morning light. Walking through the voodoo shops and taking home Love Potion and Tranquility Tea.

As if these things were spells to be toyed with.

They have no idea.

Voodoo is not a toy. I can't really blame tourists for not understanding; it's taken me my whole life to realize that. Most of them will never be given any reason to think otherwise. Because they'll pack up their suitcases and pop a pill for their hangovers and head to the airport and whatever transgressions they've enjoyed in the Crescent City will be a blurred memory.

Those of us who stay here, however, often grow to know better.

My name is Detective Lawrence Ribaud. My friends call me Cork. But I don't have many friends.

What I do have is problems. New ones every day. Dead ones.

Because that's what you get when you're a detective in New Orleans. Sweat and blood and booze...and death.

And lately, a lot of missing bodies.

Case in point: the bed in front of me was unmade, the sheets twisted and draped on the floor near its foot.

There were two deep dents in the mattress; it was not a new bed by any means. The woman who slept on one side stood next to me, still in her nightgown, an old blue robe hastily sashed over it. Mary Mendel was talking, fast and animated, but I barely heard a word.

She'd already said it twice before.

When she woke up early this morning and got up to go to the bathroom, she'd realized that her husband wasn't lying in bed next to her. When she'd come back to bed, she'd realized the sheets beside her were wet.

That's when she'd turned the lights on.

That's when she'd seen the blood.

That's when she'd screamed.

That's why I was here now.

★   ★   ★

There was no body.

The sheets were drenched in blood on half the bed. Right around the area where Mr. Mendel's shoulders would have been.

But Mr. Mendel wasn't there.

A lump of something dark and crimson lay in the center of the stains. I bent over the mattress and nodded. The killer had cut out Mr. Mendel's heart. And left it behind while stealing away the rest of him. A quick search of the small one-story house did not turn up a body.

I wasn't surprised. I've been through this before and knew it wouldn't. Not that I could say that to Mrs. Mendel.

Bloodstained beds, missing bodies and broken hearts (not to mention disembodied ones) had become a regular occurrence of late.

"I'm not a sound sleeper," Mrs. Mendel sobbed. "I don't understand. How could someone have hurt him so bad and I didn't hear it? Oh, my Lord, look at the blood. Could he be okay still after all that?"

She clearly was ignoring the significance of the lump of flesh that lay in the center of the stain. "I don't know, ma'am," I said. "Let's talk about what happened exactly."

It was a pointless but necessary process question. I knew the answer – I'd heard it in too many cases now.

All unsolved.

There was one commonality in all of them.

Woman or man woke up. Spouse was missing. Their place on the bed was drenched in wet blood. There was no body.

"I already told you, I woke up and Bert was gone. I thought maybe he'd just gone to the bathroom or maybe the kitchen to get himself something to drink. Bert gets insomnia sometimes and it isn't unusual for him to be up wandering the house while I'm sleeping. But when he didn't come back after a few minutes, I got up myself."

I put up my hand to stop her. "We've talked about this already," I said. "But what I'm wondering is, did Bert have anyone who was angry with him? Had he had a fight earlier that day maybe?"

Mrs. Mendel shook her head quickly. I was clearly frustrating her.

"Bert is the nicest man alive," she said. "There isn't a soul who dislikes him. He makes friends with everyone he's ever met."

I nodded and made a note in my case notepad. *Occasional insomnia. Charismatic type.*

"Was he funny?" I asked. "Class clown type?"

She grinned. "Bert can always make you smile," she offered. "He can walk into the middle of a fight and have both sides laughing in two minutes flat and wondering what they'd even been arguing about in the first place."

"So, you're not aware of anyone who wished him harm," I reiterated. I knew the answer, but I had to ask all the standard questions.

She shook her head violently. "No sir," she said. "My Bert stops folks from getting hot, he doesn't start fires."

Peacemaker and comedian, I wrote.

"Was he away from home much?"

She shrugged. "Not too much. He works at a shop just off St. Bernard Avenue. Sometimes they keep him late when it gets to be the busy season, like a couple nights this week, but mostly, he's home by supper time."

We were interrupted by a metallic knock on the rickety front screen door. I glanced over my shoulder and saw a shoulder clad in uniform blues. It wasn't often that I scooped the boys on their regular beat. But I'd been just a couple blocks away when I heard the radio call. They'd probably be annoyed.

Mrs. Mendel was already at the door ushering the two beat cops into the small sitting room. I held my badge up over my head so they could see.

"Detective Ribaud," I announced. "Heard the call and was nearby."

I got a curt nod from what I assumed was the senior partner given the sprinkle of gray in his short brown hair. He didn't say a word to me, but instead pointedly only addressed Mrs. Mendel. Yep. He was annoyed.

"Officer Metaine," he said, introducing himself. Then he gestured at the squat dark-haired man at his side. "And this is Officer Jarousch. Can you tell us what happened?"

I listened to the story of Mrs. Mendel's rude awakening for the third time and followed them into the bedroom. Eventually, they told Mrs. Mendel to go sit down while they looked things over closer. The short guy – Jarousch – moved all around the bed, shooting photos of the bloody mattress from every angle. When he was finished, he set down the camera, pulled a pair of rubber gloves from a pocket and gingerly picked up the red hunk of flesh that lay in the center of the crimson stain.

"What do you make of this?" he asked, holding it up between thumb and forefinger. It was larger than my fist, and blood dripped from the end of it to soak back into the bed.

"Looks like a human heart," Metaine suggested.

"Who would do such a thing?" Jarousch said, clearly disgusted.

"That is the question, isn't it?" I said.

The two of them looked at me as if they'd only just noticed that I was in the room.

"We've got this," Metaine said.

I nodded. Beat cops hated it when detectives they didn't normally work with turned up to cramp their style. I filled them in anyway.

"We had some cases just like this last month. And a few the month before. We've been able to keep it out of the media so far, but I'm guessing this won't be the only one we get a call for today. The number seems to be increasing each time it happens."

Jarousch opened his mouth to say something and then thought better of it. The silence between us grew uncomfortable.

"Put everything you find in your report," I said. They both rolled their eyes...*as if*....

"And be careful with that heart," I warned. "Somebody might want it back."

Jarousch realized he was still holding the thing between his thumb and forefinger and dropped it instantly.

The orphaned heart made a soft splat as it hit the sheets.

CHAPTER TWO

I walked in on a vampire joke at the Two-Headed Horse. It happens a lot here, thanks to Anne Rice. Raymond was sitting at a low round table and holding up a glass that I bet, after knowing him a long while, held more bitters than alcohol. He could 'drink anybody under the table' because the reality was, there was barely any liquor in his drinks.

"Three vampires walk into a bar...." Raymond was saying. "The bartender looks them over and shakes his head. 'We don't serve the likes of you,' he says. 'No problem,' the first vampire says, and grabs one of the patrons who already looks close to dead. The guy is leaning against the bar rail. 'I serve myself,' the vampire says, and takes a deep drink from the man but then abruptly stiffens and his eyes bug out.

"'That guy's been drinking martinis with garlic olives all night,' the bartender announces. 'You should really pay a little closer attention to what you drink when you're in a bar.'

"The first vampire falls to the floor.

"The second vampire shakes his head. 'You really do have to be a little more selective when you're out on the town.' He moves to a woman sitting alone at a table with a glass of red wine in front of her. After talking to her for a moment, he leans in closer to her as if to whisper a secret. But just as his fangs extend and touch her neck, he screams. Smoke is suddenly billowing from his face and hair as if he's just been set on fire. The woman reaches into her handbag and shakes something in her hand all over his head. He scrambles away from her on the floor as if he's escaping from a fire.

"'She doesn't wear the habit, but that's a nun,' the bartender notes. 'She doesn't have many friends, but she always has holy water. You should really pay a little closer attention to the kinds of friends you make when you're in a bar.'

"That left the third vampire," Raymond continued. "Noting the fate of his friends, he takes a long look at the bartender. 'If you were me, what would you suggest I do to have a good time in a bar?'

"The bartender shrugs. 'Pick out a good spot with the wall to your back so nobody can sneak up on you, and then pay attention.'

"'Good advice,' the vampire says, and suddenly lofts over the bar and plunges his teeth into the bartender's neck. 'You've got the best seat in the house,' he says as he draws a sip of warm, sweet blood.

"And then his eyes pop wide and he gags and clutches at his heart. A wooden stake protrudes from the center of his chest. The bartender releases his hold on it and brushes his hands together as the vampire falls to the floor.

"'And I don't intend to give it up,' the bartender says. 'You should pay a little closer attention to what your victims have in their hands when you decide to have a drink.'

"The bartender raises a glass. 'Bloody Marys are on the house!' he says and the whole bar cheers."

"And the point of all that is?" I asked.

Raymond looked surprised. "Well, I thought it was obvious." He shook his head. "When you're in a bar you need to watch what you drink, watch who you kiss and watch whose stick gives you a prick!"

I shook my head in despair, but the three men around him broke up in loud guffaws. They'd clearly been matching Raymond drink for drink...and he was going to win.

"So how was another day wearing the uniform?" he asked after taking a sip from his glass.

I pulled up a chair and sunk into it with a loud sigh. "Just another day in paradise," I said, looking around the bar. I hadn't come here for Raymond's meandering, pedantic stories. "Is Gen working tonight?"

"What, four drunken fat men aren't enough to keep you entertained?" Raymond laughed.

"Not on the best of days," I said, refusing to play his game.

"I'm hurt," Raymond said.

"I'm not fat," Caldwell said, the import of Raymond's comment dawning on him after a moment.

"And I'm not working the armpit of the Gulf of Mexico," I said. "Is she here?"

Stu piped up then and pointed across the room at a table with two silver-haired men and a dark-haired waitress leaning with one arm on their table.

"She's been trying to take their order for fifteen minutes," Caldwell said.

"And you couldn't get up and give her a hand?" I asked. "Chivalry is dead."

"I don't work for tips," he drawled and lifted a glass with a shaky hand.

"Pathetic lot, you all are," I said, and pushed myself back up and out of the chair.

Genevieve and I went back a long while. She had been a friend of my wife's, but I didn't hold that against her. Though if she'd been more of a friend to me, Amanda might still be alive today. I tried not to think too much about that, though it was never far from my mind.

"Is there a problem with the order?" I asked, sidling up to the table she was working. The men traded guilty looks and then smiled.

"No sir, we were just enjoying a little conversation with the lady. I hope we didn't get her into any trouble."

"Not at all," I said. "Just so long as she's served you well, that's all we care about here at the Two-Headed Horse." I played it up further and looked directly at Gen. "If I could see you by the kitchen when you're done here?"

She nodded, a faint smile tilting the edge of her pouty lips, and I walked away before they could pull me into further conversation. She'd be along.

And a couple minutes later, she was.

"Ever the knight, aren't you?" she asked as she turned the corner and found me in the dark hallway between the bar and the kitchen.

"Someone's gotta tilt at windmills," I said.

She snorted. "Careful you don't fall off your horse," she said.

Then she curtseyed. "Thank you, good knight, for saving me from the knaves. How may I repay the favor?"

I ignored the drama and cut to the chase. "Tell me who Amanda was sleeping with."

She dropped the hem of her skirt and stood up straight.

"Let it go," she said. "I've told you a hundred times, I don't know."

"And I know better," I said. "She was with him the night before she was killed, wasn't she?"

Gen clenched her eyes closed for a second before reopening them with a look that was intense and final. "I don't know. I only know she's gone and nothing you can do will bring her back. So, stop. Just… stop."

"I can't stop," I said. "There's been another murder. Or, as the official police reports say, "a disappearance." Actually, when I left the station an hour ago there had been a half dozen *disappearances* reported today. More hearts left on the bedsheets like pieces of discarded clothing. The chief has managed to keep this thing fairly quiet up to now – the papers have reported most of the incidents as "missing persons" and haven't connected the dots. But with that many in one night…I think it's about to hit the fan. I need to know who Amanda was with that night. This all started in March, the night she was killed. And I'm not saying disappeared. I know better. I also know that she was cheating on me with someone. Whoever she was with could be the key to all of this."

She shook her head, and a hint of moisture glinted from the corner of one eye. "He didn't kill her," she said. "He didn't do any of this."

"How do you know?" I asked.

She looked away from me, and then stared at the ceiling, trying to regain her composure.

"How do you know?" I insisted. "People are dying. Just like she did."

She turned her face back to me then and there was a look of anger there that I'd never seen before.

"I know because the guy she was seeing is dead too. His wife found a bloody piece of meat in her bed instead of her husband on the same night that Amanda disappeared."

"You *did* know," I said. My voice broke. The fact that the man was dead hadn't sunk in yet. I was still stuck on the fact that Genevieve had known who my wife was sleeping with and had kept it hidden from me for weeks. "I knew there was no way that she would have kept it from you. Did you help her sneak around behind my back to meet him?"

Gen threw back her head and laughed. It was a bitter sound. "What need to sneak? You were never home. The poor girl had to do something. She didn't deserve you." She choked then and turned her head away. "She didn't deserve to die for it, either."

"I'm going to find the man who did it," I said. "And when I do...."

Gen looked at me sideways. "What makes you think it's a man? Hell, what makes you think it's one person?"

"All of the killings have been the same. Bloody bedsheets. A heart left behind. And we've kept the details out of the papers so far, so it can't be a copycat. There have only been a couple minor stories about disappearances because the first couple months it happened, the police were able to keep them quiet. They're missing persons, not murders, and so the papers aren't really picking up on it. But from the way these have happened, we know it's got to be the same guy behind them all."

"I might have bought that the first couple times it happened. But do you really think one guy snuck around to all those houses last night and killed all those people and stole their bodies without help? No way. And why all on the same night? You haven't had any of these for weeks and then...bam. A slaughter? And it was the same thing the last time...just not as many people died."

I nodded. She was right. It was weird before, but now?

"I'll find him," I promised. "Who was the guy she was sleeping with?"

Gen shook her head. "Let it go. It doesn't matter. His wife doesn't need you to make her feel worse. I've gotta get back to work."

She turned and disappeared into the kitchen.

I frowned. "Fine," I said. "I can just look up whoever else was killed that night."

CHAPTER THREE

Wednesday, June 19

There was a note taped to the computer monitor at my desk. *See me. ASAP.*

It wasn't signed, but I knew the writing. It was the chief. And I knew what he wanted to talk about. The problem was I didn't have anything to tell him. I took a deep breath and walked down the hall to the door that said simply, *Fontenot.* Looked like any other office...but it wasn't the one you wanted to be called down to.

"Hi Chief," I said, poking my head in the door. "You wanted to see me?"

Chief Peter Fontenot had been on the force as long as I've been alive. But he looked anything but old and feeble. He stood six feet tall and probably weighed in at about 250. His hair was mostly gray but still showed some pepper in the salt. He looked up from the paperwork strewn across his desk and scowled at me from behind his trademark black plastic glasses.

"There were nine murders Monday night, and an equal number of missing bodies."

"Nine?" I said.

He nodded. "Another one was just found. Tell me you've got some leads this time because the media is going to be all over this any minute now."

I hesitated a minute and then shook my head. Negative.

"What do the victims have in common? There must be something that ties them together."

"It's hard to say since we don't have bodies for any of them," I began.

Chief put up his hand. "I don't mean how they were cut up. I don't care about that. There must be some reason that the killer – or killers, I'm inclined to think this is a gang at this point – is targeting these people. Did they all work at Entergy or Tulane or something? Were they all related to someone? Did they all belong to the same social club?"

I shook my head. "They come from all backgrounds and races. I haven't run checks yet on all of today's victims, but you know from last month and the month before that we haven't seen anything that connected them. They don't even live in the same sections of the city."

"So, when Randy Tidaris shows up from NBC, I should just shrug and say, 'Yeah, it's a mystery and we don't have a clue'?"

"No, of course not," I said. But I honestly had no idea what to tell him to say. That was his job and I knew he'd handle it perfectly. Whatever Chief Fontenot said, people ate it up. He had the steel eyes and deep voice that just made him come across as the unquestionable authority. It served him well in his current job. Hell, it was probably why he got the job.

"While you were out, I put Aubrey and Tarrington on this case. And we've got every cop on the street looking for bodies. They have to be somewhere. Connect with Tarrington and make sure you three divide and conquer. Let's get some leads this time. There's going to be panic if the full scope of this gets out and we need to get ahead of it."

I didn't say anything. Inside I breathed a sigh of relief. Part of me was sure he was going to take me off the case completely. But instead, he was just giving me some help. Lord knows I needed it.

"If he's dumping the bodies in the swamps, we'll never find them," I said.

He looked up at me and raised a single eyebrow. "Even gators leave evidence," he said.

Then he looked back down at his papers and began marking something up with a pen. I took that as my cue to get back on the case.

*   *   *

Back at my desk, I pulled the ancient PC back from sleep mode and navigated to the unsolved cases directory. I'd get with Tarrington shortly, but first, I needed to look something up for myself.

I needed to see which men had died on March 20. More particularly, which men had gone missing, leaving behind a shriveled red organ on the bed.

There were two in the downtown area.

Fernando Ortiz, aged twenty-three, Seventh Ward.

James O'Brien, aged thirty-two, Lakeview.

I lived in Lakeview. So that made James O'Brien my prime suspect. Plus, the age seemed more likely. I couldn't see Amanda messing around with a kid just out of college.

I wrote down the addresses of both, and then went to O'Brien's case file.

It was basically empty. Victim's wife discovered a bloody bed in the morning. She'd been sleeping in the other room and claimed to have heard nothing. The bedroom showed no sign of struggle. Just an empty bed. I wrote down the wife's name and tucked the information in my pocket. Then I went to find Tarrington, to see about how we were going to divvy up this investigation.

CHAPTER FOUR

I pulled up in front of a small green frame house. The brown shutters were missing a couple of their slats and one of them hung crookedly away from the window. The number 6438 was pinned above a brown door. I let myself in the low wrought-iron gate and walked up the patched cement steps to knock on the front door.

I waited a minute or two and then knocked again. There was a car parked in front, but that didn't mean it was hers. I heard the creak of floorboards inside before the door opened and a short, heavyset woman stood before me. She had short curled dark hair and tired eyes. "Can I help you?" she asked before I could introduce myself.

"Are you Florence O'Brien?" I asked.

She looked guarded. "Who wants to know?"

"Detective Ribaud, New Orleans police, ma'am."

Her eyes perked up at that. "Did you find something out about Jimmy?"

I shook my head, still trying to think of how I wanted to bring this up. "Not exactly," I said. "Do you mind if I come in?"

She stepped back from the door to allow me to step in out of the heat. But her air-conditioner wasn't much of an improvement over the ninety-degree afternoon. Beads of sweat dotted her forehead. She didn't offer me a seat, but stood with her arms crossed over a pale pink robe.

"I work the late shift," she said. "It's the middle of the night for me, and I'd really like to get back to sleep."

"I'm sorry, I'll make it brief," I said. "I needed to ask you about a delicate matter. Would you say you and your husband had a strong marriage?"

She snorted. "You woke me up to ask me that? You have got to be kidding." She turned away from me and walked three paces toward the kitchen, then turned and moved toward me again. "Jimmy was a lying, cheatin' sack of shit. Why d'ya think we were sleeping in separate rooms when he was killed? I didn't even know he was missing for who knows how long? Sometimes I'd go a couple days without seeing him. But like I told the other officers, that don't mean I killed him. I still loved the bastard."

"So, you know he was cheating on you?" I said.

"Of course I knew," she said. "Jimmy didn't like to sleep alone, and I work nights. There were a couple times I came home and he didn't even have the decency to make sure his sluts were gone before I got off work. I can tell you those girls never made *that* mistake twice."

"So, you had an open marriage?" I asked.

She laughed. "Not by choice," she said. "But he couldn't keep his hands to himself. That's how we got together in the first place, so I shoulda known back then that he'd do the same thing to me."

I reached into my pocket and pulled out a picture of Amanda. It was a shot of her holding a glass of white wine and smiling. We'd been sitting at Leveau's one night after dinner. It was one of my favorite pictures of her. The glint of the chardonnay brought out the humor in her eyes.

"Any chance you'd know if this woman was a friend of Jimmy's?" I asked.

She snorted. "That bitch? What is her name...Amy? Audrey?"

"Amanda," I said.

"That's it. I knew it was an *A* name. Why do you care?"

"She was my wife," I said.

Her eyes widened a moment, and then she started to snicker. Finally, she shook her head. "Jimmy was messing around with that one for quite a while. Is that what you wanted to hear? Because you can't do much about it now. You can't beat Jimmy up until you find him. And at this point, I don't have a lot of hope for that."

"Me either," I said. "Amanda disappeared on the same night, in the same way as Jimmy."

A frown crossed her forehead.

"You think they ran off together?"

"With all that blood?" I said. "No. Somebody took them. And others as well."

"You think they want them as slaves or something?" she asked.

I shrugged. "I have no idea. But Jimmy and Amanda aren't the only ones who have disappeared this way. This isn't just about them."

"I don't know what they'd want with Jimmy," she said. "Man didn't work an honest day in his life. But he sure could talk up a storm."

"Do you mind if I ask why you stayed with him?" I said. "It doesn't sound like a good situation."

"Probably for the same reason your wife came sniffing around his bed," she said. "When you had Jimmy's eye, well, he made you feel like nobody else. There was something about him that could just make a woman melt when he wanted you to."

She yawned then and looked me straight in the eye. "Is that all you came for? To see if your wife was sleeping with my husband?"

"Pretty much," I admitted.

She nodded. "Well, now you know. I don't see what good it does you, but...maybe you'll sleep better tonight. I doubt it though. Me? I need to go back to bed and get some more sleep myself. So, if you don't mind...."

I didn't really know what else to say. I thanked her and let myself back out the old screen door. When I settled into the driver's seat, I didn't start the car immediately. Instead, I looked up and down the old street lined with ramshackle houses. This was where my wife had come when I was working late. To cheat with a cheater. The thought gave me a stabbing sensation in the middle of my chest.

So, there it was. I knew who Amanda had been with. But Mrs. O'Brien was right. I didn't feel any better about it.

★   ★   ★

I started the engine and slowly drove home. When I walked in, the place felt eerily quiet, with early evening shadows cloaking the corners of the room. I still hadn't grown used to Amanda being gone. Every night when I got home I still half expected to hear her lilting voice from the back bedroom. But it never came. Needing something to fill the gap, I flipped on the television to make some noise. The six o'clock news was on, and the sound of people talking eased the emptiness just a little as I traded my damp shirt and slacks for shorts and a T-shirt. The background noise made it seem a little more like a home than an empty drywall box.

Then it occurred to me what they were talking about.

"...a rash of disappearances that might have set a New Orleans record for the highest number of people killed in a single day, if these turn out to be murders and not abductions...."

The shit had hit the fan. This was not going to be good.

"...Police Chief Fontenot has confirmed that there are similarities between the missing persons cases, which suggest that they are all linked, though the police have released no details about what they believe ties these victims together. However, we have talked to several spouses and friends of the missing people and all have confirmed that in each case, there was blood found in the victims' beds, though no trace of the victims' bodies."

I sat down on the couch just as the co-anchor called on a remote reporter. The camera switched to a twentysomething blond girl holding a microphone in the face of a dark-skinned woman. The lines of several decades were etched into the skin around her brown eyes.

"I'm here with Jacqueline Tobarres, at the corner of Fifth and Balm, just a few yards from where one of the victims disappeared. While theories already range from this being a mass cult suicide to slave trade abductions, Mrs. Tobarres believes that something even more sinister is at work."

She held the microphone closer to the old woman's face. The camera zoomed in.

"There is only one thing that could have caused this," she said. The lines in her forehead deepened. "This is voodoo. There is a curse at work here, a bad one. You people aren't paying attention. I've seen the back pages of the newspaper. Things like this have happened the past couple months on the night of the full moon. And now it's happened again. Mark my words, when the moon is full once more, more people will vanish."

The reporter smiled patronizingly and pointed at an old house just down the sidewalk as she launched into her segment wrap-up. "Whether it's voodoo, abduction or something worse, the family of Labelle Montrose just want their wife and mother home again. I'm Caitlin Currales for NBC *Stories at Six*."

I had stopped listening by then. One thing the old woman said had stuck with me. Something I'd never considered before. Could it be true? Where did I have a calendar?

Amanda always had one hung in the den and so I walked down the hall to that small room where she'd put in bookcases and a recliner chair. I pulled the Dogs of Summer calendar off the wall. Last night had been a full moon.

I flipped the pages back to March.

I had a feeling about what I would see, but that didn't stop my heart from jumping when I looked at March 20, the night Amanda had disappeared.

The icon of a full moon sat at the bottom of the square.

I pulled out my phone and looked for my notes on the April disappearances. The date had been April 19. I flipped the calendar to the next page and put my finger on the box for April 19.

The full moon icon was there too.

Holy shit.

I looked at May and the same thing panned out. A rash of bloody beds on the 18th.

Full moon on May 18.

Okay. The old woman on the newscast might have been a bit wack when it came to the voodoo thing – everyone in New Orleans wants voodoo to be the culprit – but there definitely was something to the full moon connection. I kicked myself for not picking up on that before.

There had been disappearances reported in March, April and May, as well as this month. I'd never noticed that they had all occurred on the day of the full moon. Could there really be a connection?

I walked over to the fridge, pulled out a Hopitoulas IPA and took a hard swig. The soft bitterness went down easy but at the same time brought a tear to my eye. It was cool and hard and made me have to blink and breathe. Sometimes you could gulp a little too much of a good thing if you allowed it.

Chief wanted leads, and now I at least had something to consider as a tie-together bit of fact on these cases.

People all disappearing on the night of the full moon. What did it mean? The truth was, maybe nothing. But it probably did mean something to the person who was orchestrating the killings...or,

as we were still referring to them to the media...disappearances. I
had to stop myself when I talked about the case every time. I *knew*
these people were dead. I knew Amanda was not coming back to
me. Beds were not left sodden with blood when someone got up
and walked away. Especially if their hearts were left behind. We still
hadn't acknowledged that last bit to the press. Nor had we proved
conclusively that the hearts did indeed belong to the victims, though it
was a good bet. We needed to find the bodies, and I had a hunch that
they were in the bellies of alligators at this point, having been dumped
in the miles of river and swamp just outside the city.

But why?

There were people I knew who could theorize. And there
were people I knew who really *knew* things, even if those things
did not correspond to what was taught at university about how the
world worked.

In this instance, I thought the latter type of person would be the
most useful source. And so I looked up Eleanor's Arcana on my phone.
As I thought, the shop was open until at least 11 p.m. tonight. Eleanor
would likely be there. It was past peak tourist season but still busy,
and she would be in the shop most of the time it was open these days.
They needed every hand they could get. I knew that she'd know some
potential reason why someone might pick the night of the full moon
as a time to steal people from their beds.

That didn't mean that the reason was valid...but she'd know all of
the lore that might lead someone to pick the event of the full moon as
the right time for whatever ritual they were messing with.

I didn't believe in voodoo or magic or any of that shit. But I knew
that plenty of people did. Especially here in New Orleans. We were
like a fucking beacon to crazies who thought that they could pinch an
herb or put the blood of a frog into an absinthe potion and come out
with some weird change in the natural world because of it.

I always thought voodoo was the result of an impressionable
mind that has latched on to a cure for an ailment that can't be cured.
Impotency. Loneliness. Fear. Those were the things people bought
spells and potions for. Whether or not *you* believed for a minute that
the combinations of herbs and blood and chicken sacrifices could
change the course of real life for better or worse, other people did.

There were plenty who felt that spirits could be called into the service of the living with the right mix of aromatics and sacrificial blood.

Whatever.

I knew a woman who knew about those things. And if someone was counting on the full moon as a trigger for...a curse...well...she might know the lore that led them to whatever causal end result they were gunning for.

The rest of the Hopitoulas went down fast. For the first time in months I had a lead that might tell me what had happened to Amanda. Not to mention a long list of other victims on my caseload.

I threw the can in the trash and slapped water from the sink on my face.

Then I went to the bedroom and pulled on a pair of pants to meet the night.

I had places to go and a voodoo priestess to see.

CHAPTER FIVE

Thursday, June 20

Litha Eve

The French Quarter was already coming alive though it was only just after seven. People wandered down the center of Bourbon Street holding tulip-shaped plastic cups filled with electric green and blue drinks. I shook my head quietly as they laughed and danced with manic energy down the street. These were the ones who would be puking before it was even fully dark. The alcohol they put in those things *had* to be masked with Kool-Aid and sugar to hide how nasty it really was. You want to see double fast? Or maybe just go blind? Drink grain alcohol. Me? I appreciate a good buzz and good bourbon; I avoid crap.

Eleanor's Arcana was just off Bourbon Street. That immediately made it suspect. Some might say, 'Well, if she's got a store in the Quarter then she's not a real voodoo priestess. That place is just for scammers and tourists.'

But the truth was, Eleanor was the real deal. That is, if you believed people could influence the world by putting together potions and calling on invisible forces to reshape the world to your whims. There were plenty of scammers who were only in business to rook tourists looking for charms. But even though I was a skeptic, I knew that she truly believed. She wasn't scamming anyone – she created charms and spells that she thought could help people, so I respected her for that. She also maintained a private shop outside the city for a limited clientele. I'd been there once or twice in the past. After Amanda had disappeared, she'd insisted that I come to see her there. But that shop was never going to bring in the kind of money that a shop in the Quarter would. Eleanor was more than just a voodoo priestess; she was a savvy businesswoman. She promoted her spells and potions and religion here to the gawking visitors hungry for spooky, kitschy souvenirs; people who thought voodoo was just a silly superstitious belief system informed by horror films. I assume she actually made converts, in addition to socking away a good wad of cash that went back into her private chapel. No matter what your religion, everyone understands the importance of free enterprise.

I parked in a garage a couple blocks away from her store and walked through the mob until I found her door. As soon as I stepped inside and moved across the wooden plank floor, I felt the falseness. Air-conditioning. Incense. T-shirts with price tags on the wall. I had to smile. A real voodoo shack would have none of these things.

But as Eleanor had told me many times, "I do what I need to do. And I do it well."

"Hey stranger," a voice whispered in my ear. I turned and faced the smooth brown face and startling white teeth of a beautiful girl in a black Eleanor's Arcana T-shirt.

It was Renee. She was one of Eleanor's right-hand girls, and I talked to her almost every time I came in here. In fact, Renee was one of the reasons I'd come back to Eleanor's Arcana before I knew Eleanor. She was the kind of girl that made a guy need to find a reason to walk a few blocks out of his way just to see if she was around. We'd gone out a few times to talk (and drink) when she needed a friend. Because…she really did need a friend. Her husband was an asshole, if you believed her side of the story. Which I did. I'd seen the bruises. Nobody would just make up the things she'd told me over the course of many nights while tilting back one more barrier against reality. I never could fill the hole she had in her heart, but I always was honored to be the person she chose to talk to on those nights when she needed to hide out.

"How's the magic potion business?" I asked.

Renee rolled her eyes. They were wide, deep brown eyes, the kind that drew you in instantly with one look. She wore her hair today in tight, thin dark braids, pulled back behind her ears, accentuating her high cheekbones and heavy lips. No matter how Renee wore her hair, she was always striking.

"You should joke less and believe more," she said.

"So you've told me," I said. She folded and placed a New Orleans T-shirt that featured a crucifix with a single all-seeing eye in its center on a stack of like shirts. Then she turned and motioned for me to follow. We walked past a handful of customers picking up magic tea bags and other gris-gris until we reached an employees-only door just beyond the store altar.

"What brings you in so early?" she asked. "You know I can't leave for another three hours."

"It's not actually you that I came to see," I said. When she frowned, I quickly added, "Although, I hoped you would be here."

She raised a thick dark eyebrow. "Nice recovery. Are you here for a love charm then, or did you want to talk to Madame Trevail?"

"I've had enough of love, thanks," I said. "Is Eleanor around?"

Renee looked disappointed, but pointed at the door behind us. "She's putting together some orders in the back. You know the way. I have to mind the store."

I thanked her and turned the knob on the old wooden door. It swung inward easily and I stepped into the small room that doubled as both a storeroom and a business office. This was where Eleanor kept all of the ingredients for the potions she mixed on-site. It was also where the employees had lunch and dinner. Unlike the customer side of the store where everything was old wood planks and garish painted symbols, this room was sparse and utilitarian…and fairly modern. The floor was faded linoleum and the walls a dull pale blue. There was a laptop on a small wooden desk and a shelving unit that held a tumbling variety of plastic and cardboard boxes against the far wall. Eleanor was rolling something up in a square of bubble wrap. She taped it closed and set it gently into a cardboard box on the desk before looking up to meet my gaze.

"Cork," she said softly. "It has been a while. Are you here for business, or pleasure?"

She always spoke with a near-formal cadence that belied the fact that she could drink most men under the table.

"Eleanor, it's always a pleasure to see you," I said. "Though tonight, it's about business."

"Your face told me that story without speaking."

I laughed. "You have always been able to read me."

She gestured to a small round table. "Sit down and tell me what troubles you."

I pulled out a padded folding chair and did as she suggested. Eleanor pushed the box she was preparing to the side and rested her elbows on the desk. I had her full attention. I didn't waste it. I knew she would be needed up front sooner or later.

"You know about my wife, Amanda, and all the other disappearances these past few months," I began. "One night each month more and more people vanish, and the only clue we have is a bed full of blood."

She nodded.

"There were more this week," I said. "And tonight on the news, a woman suggested that voodoo was behind it all."

Eleanor laughed. It was a deep, hearty sound filled with equal parts humor and bitterness. "Of course it is voodoo," she said. "All bad things in New Orleans come from voodoo, do they not?"

"I know, I know. And I wouldn't have come to you except for one thing. She also said that on the night of the next full moon, more people would come up missing. So I went back and looked. I don't know why we didn't notice it before, but all of the disappearances have happened on the night of a full moon."

"And because of this, you are now convinced that some mambo or houngan is dancing in the swamps somewhere and using black magic to abduct all of these people? Lawrence Ribaud, are you telling me that you now believe in voodoo?"

Her face beamed with amusement. We had had many conversations over the years about the religion she practiced. She knew that I respected her beliefs, but also did not share them.

"I believe someone might be trying to stage a ritual of some kind, and isn't the night of the full moon considered a night of power?"

"You *do* listen to me when we talk, don't you? I'm shocked."

"Sometimes," I said.

"The night of the moon is a night of power," she agreed. "I suppose someone could be trying to use it for some dark purpose."

"Is there a ritual that you know of where bodies are taken on that night and their hearts cut out and left behind?"

Her eyes widened. "Is that the state of all of those who have disappeared? Not just Amanda?"

I nodded. "Every one of them. A bloodstained bed and a lump of flesh. Maybe it's a psychotic who believes he's performing some strange dark magic, but I don't know what the goal would be."

"Nor do I," she said. "Whether or not it has to do with voodoo, that *does* sound like ritual."

"You've heard nothing from any other priestesses about this then?"

Eleanor pursed her lips in amusement. "It didn't come up at our weekly voodoo priestess meeting over coffee and beignets."

I couldn't help but smile with her. "Touché. Can you think of anyone who might be involved in such a thing?"

Eleanor stood up. "Someone with delusions of dark magic grandeur? No."

She picked up a packing tape gun and began to seal the box she'd been working on when I came in. "Let me think on it some," she said. "I will look through my books at home and see if I can find any writings about a ritual that looks like this. It does not sound like anything that I have heard of, but every priestess brings her own spirit to the table. I will let you know if I find anything."

I could tell that our meeting was done; she had work to do. "Thanks, Eleanor, I appreciate your help."

"You realize that this is probably the work of some serial killer who wants you to think it's black magic?"

"I do. But if it is, and if they're mimicking some ritual... knowing what it is might help us track down who's behind it."

"I will do what I can," she said and then looked up from her box to hold my gaze. "It is always good to see you, Cork."

"Likewise," I answered. Then I stood and let myself out.

I wound my way through the small tables covered with T-shirts and mock voodoo dolls and mugs that said *Madame Trevail's Voodoo Shop. We have the cure for life.* The words wound around an ornate skull.

"I'm off at eleven," Renee called from behind the counter.

"Thanks, but I have to work in the morning," I said. I appreciated the offer, but was not in the mood for company tonight.

"Suit yourself," she said. "Keep this until next time."

She lifted her arm to toss something from behind the cash register and I instinctively reached up to catch it. When I opened my hand, there was a small black satchel in it. There was a label attached to a string that said, *Cupid Spell: Find True Love.*

I grinned and stuffed it in my pocket. "Thanks," I said. "This may come in handy."

CHAPTER SIX

Tuesday, June 25

Last Moon

Chief was really not happy with us. Seven days had passed since the last round of disappearances, and we still didn't have a clue. Aubrey and Tarrington and I had all looked into the backgrounds of the missing and found no obvious connections between them. And since they'd all disappeared from their beds – with no foreign fingerprints found in the rooms – we couldn't even try to run phone traces to see if we could find one through a cellphone check-in.

It was the perfect mass abduction scheme.

We ran blood tests on all of the spouses and significant others left behind, looking to see if there was any evidence of drugs in their systems. We theorized that they'd been knocked out during the event, because it made no sense that none of them had woken up during the abductions, which from the evidence left behind, couldn't have been without some sound and struggle. It would seem like people having their hearts ripped out would be fighting and screaming enough to let the person next to them know something was amiss. Even if the first stab came in their sleep, they'd surely come to consciousness for a minute or two before bleeding out.

Unless the hearts and blood left behind weren't theirs. But blood types on file for the victims matched with the blood and organs left behind suggested otherwise.

All of this led me to now.

And I hated now.

I was crouching in a low-floating barge, slowly threading our way down one of the main riverways that spidered through the swamps just outside of the city. This was a popular place for killers to dump the evidence of their crimes. I'd been called out here a half dozen times when bodies were sighted near the shore, one arm sticking out of the water, or a head staring sightlessly back to land after it had lodged on a fallen tree branch in the shallows.

We were dragging the myriad fingers of the river as best we could and watching the shore for any evidence of bodies or discarded clothing.

It was tedious work, and the sweltering humidity of the swamp in summertime made it an experience comparable to boating through hell. We were all covered in mosquito spray, but that didn't stop swarms of them from buzzing in my ear. We'd been out for over three hours now, and I was more than ready to go back. The sweaty heat and reek of Bourbon Street was nothing compared to this.

"Hang on a minute," Armand called. He was handling the drag hooks at the moment as Thomas steered. They were a couple of bluecoats who'd been unlucky enough to draw shit-show duty with me. Thomas cut the engine and I moved beside Armand to help him pull up whatever he'd snagged.

Whatever it was, it was heavy. I leaned down and grabbed. Together we both pulled. Sweat ran off my forehead to drip into the water while we dragged whatever we'd caught toward the surface. I could feel it shift and roll beneath the boat as we pulled it in. The line moved, drawing up through the thick green water slowly but steadily.

You could only see a few inches into the muddy water, and then everything just became a brown and emerald soup. I peered into the thick water, struggling to see...anything.

Just below the surface, something pale began to come into view. My stomach clenched; it had two dark circles and a shadow not far below them. Like a skull...was it really a human head?

An instant later it burst through the surface of the river.

"Goddamn it," Armand complained.

"Should have known," I agreed.

We'd hooked ourselves a big rotten log, with holes near the top. I reached down to dislodge one of the hooks, and something moved in those holes. Something black and dirty yellow. It swirled and disappeared into the heart of the wood.

A snake.

Probably poisonous.

"Watch your hands," I warned Armand, and we gingerly finished loosing the thing to slip back into the murky depths.

My pocket vibrated. I sat back on the low bench and wiped the slime of the rotten log off on my pants leg, and then pulled out my phone. I'd missed a call from Eleanor.

I thumbed the screen open. She hadn't left a message, so I dialed her back.

"Hello there," she answered on the second ring. "That was quick. I didn't expect you to call back so fast."

"I just couldn't pick up right away," I explained. "Slimy hands."

"Do I dare ask why?"

"We're dragging the river for bodies," I said. "So...nothing fun, trust me."

"I see. Sorry to disturb your fishing trip. I was just checking in. I'm afraid I don't have any news to give you so far. I've been looking through a lot of old texts and I've not found any rituals that revolve around stealing bodies on the night of a full moon and leaving the heart behind. There are certainly spells where the heart must be removed, but those typically are a single instance and related to some vendetta against a whole clan. There is a spell called 'The Deadly Connection' where you cut out the heart of an innocent to punish their parents or spouse, and use its life force to bring down ruin on all who were tied by threads of love to that dead heart. This doesn't seem anything like that, plus the hearts in that instance are not left behind, but instead pinned to a cross above the priestess's altar."

"Yeah, no altars in any of the places that this has happened," I said.

"I will keep looking and talk to some friends who might know more than I do," she promised.

"Thanks," I said. "I'd like to get out of river duty as soon as possible, so any clue that would lead us to a suspect would be appreciated."

"I don't think you're going to find them in the river," she said. "I feel as if there is another purpose that these bodies are being used for."

"Well, even if they *are* in one of these canals, it's a wild-goose chase," I said. "We're never going to stumble on them. We've gone to the main places that people have used to dump bodies in the past, but...these rivers and channels go on forever. Still, we have to try."

"I'm getting together with some friends who may have thoughts about this over the weekend. I'll let you know if I find out anything that might help," she said. "And if it comes to it, perhaps the next time this happens, you could bring me in to one of the victims' homes. I could try to use a spell to tell you if voodoo had been worked there."

"Well, I'm hoping that we're going to have some leads before another couple weeks goes by, but I'll keep that in mind," I said.

We said our goodbyes, and as I slipped the phone back into my pocket, the engine's drone suddenly slowed.

"We're at the Cumberland Fork," Thomas announced. "Do we want to start a new branch of the river, or call it a night?"

"It's after six and we're a half hour from town," Armand said. "I vote we cash it in for the night."

I looked at the moss-covered banyan branches that flanked both sides of the *V*. Their shadows were already covering large swaths of the water in shade.

"This is as good a spot to stop as any," I agreed. "Let's call it a day."

Thomas didn't need any more encouragement. As Armand began to pull up the hooks, the boat suddenly did a tight U-turn and as soon as the last line came over the side, Thomas opened up the engine and we shot back up the river toward the place where we'd left our vehicles.

It had taken us hours to wind our way down the river, but we were back to our starting point in fifteen minutes. This was a fool's exercise if there ever was one. And we'd be back at it again tomorrow unless I could come up with some more useful lead to track down.

But I didn't have the faintest idea of where to look for one.

CHAPTER SEVEN

Saturday, June 29

Moon enters Gemini

The days slipped by at a gruelingly slow pace. We found garbage bags, a television set that looked to be vintage 1950s era with old rusted tubes behind the busted glass screen, and a car tire among other junk while combing the various fingers of the river, but no bodies turned up. In a way I was glad of that, because there is nothing quite so bad as a waterlogged decaying corpse when it hits the air for the first time in days. But that also meant we were not a single step closer to solving the mystery of 'The Missing'.

Little by little, the news reports on the last disappearance faded from the public consciousness, replaced by the latest scandal in Washington, D.C. I started taking on other cases again, because without clues, there really wasn't much we could do. I could spend a lifetime pulling garbage out of every side channel of the swamps around New Orleans, but that was likely never going to fish out a corpse. You had to have some idea of where the bodies were buried if you really were going to try to dig them up. Throwing your shovel into the earth randomly wasn't going to turn up results. Throwing your net into an endless stretch of waterways wasn't going to catch a body.

I had slowly come to realize that we were going to reach the night of the next full moon, and we were going to be called for a whole new rash of missing-persons investigations. It was unavoidable, because we were not going to find any of the bodies of the previous groups. Unless someone called with a 'Hey, we've just opened this warehouse and there are a ton of reeking corpses here' kind of clue, we were stuck.

So, what would we do different next time? Next week?

I didn't know. But I pulled up a chair on the corner of the long bar nearest the windows to think about it. I'd wandered down Decatur and ended up at Turtle Bay, as I often seemed to. There were tons of crappy bars in the Quarter, and most locals avoided them if at all possible, but I liked this one. It was away from the main tourist funnel of Bourbon Street and they had a good selection of taps. Plus, Maria worked on Saturday nights, and I always looked forward to talking to her. It was fascinating to watch the place cycle through customers over the course of a couple hours. It would fill and then empty in waves, and when things thinned out, Maria would come to my corner of the bar and talk with me for a while, watching the street to see if new customers might be dropping in.

You heard some strange stories if you sat there night after night. I once talked to a priest from Alabama who swore that he had seen the Virgin Mary one night in the back corner near the jukebox, and hence, he came back here every year on the same night. He admitted that he'd never seen her again, but he refused to chalk the apparition up to one too many Hurricanes.

Tonight, I settled down next to a young black couple from Baton Rouge. They were ordering takeout, and when I asked about why anyone would do takeout from a beat-up bar that specialized in cold beer, not amazing cuisine, she smiled. "We met here back in 2010 and had the strip steak. So, we come back every year on our anniversary. It's really good. But I want to enjoy it back in our hotel." She winked at me, and then stroked the shoulder of the big guy next to her. I did not have a follow-up question for that.

"NOLA IPA?" Maria asked.

"You know me too well," I said.

"It's my job," she said.

I frowned. "So, I'm just another customer to you?"

"Never," she laughed. I watched the dragon on her shoulder flex as she pulled the NOLA Brewing tap for me. "Hunting down any bad guys tonight?" she asked.

"Only in my mind," I said.

She set the overflowing pint down in front of me and I lifted it and sipped off the top layer. "It's the weekend," I said. "All the bad guys are out getting drunk."

"And you should do the same?" There was a sparkle in her eyes that I could not resist. She made me want to be twenty-five again more than any girl I'd met in the ten years since I'd been that age.

"If I'm lucky," I answered.

"We make our own luck," she said, and then with a smile moved down the bar to help a new couple who had walked in off the street.

I raised my glass and stared at the tiny bubbles moving in the golden liquid within. How could I change my luck?

When Maria came back, I took my stab. "What time do you get off tonight?" I asked.

She grinned. "Nice try," she said. "But you know the answer."

I shrugged. "I know, but a guy's got to try. You know, make my own luck and all that."

"A guy also has to know when to admit defeat," she said.

"Touché."

"Maybe I can set you up though," she offered. Then she pointed down the bar at a dark-haired woman sipping a martini at the opposite end of the room. "You might have better luck with her. That is, if you don't mind dancing with snakes and cutting the heads off chickens once in a while."

I snorted. "What are you talking about?"

Maria rolled her eyes. "She's always in here whispering about voodoo and shit with her little clique. You know the type. Black fingernails, weird tattoos. Not real social."

I nodded. I did know the type.

"She's alone tonight though, so maybe you should buy her a drink?"

"Why not?" I said. Maria looked pleased. She loved setting people up. A minute later she was handing over a second martini at the end of the bar, and then pointing in my direction. I waved, hesitantly. This was *not* how I met people.

The woman held up the glass in my direction and took a deep sip. Then she turned her attention to the bar in front of her and didn't look my way again.

"This is your chance," Maria said. She tilted her head. "You need to go talk to her while she's still drinking your drink."

I sighed and pushed back the bar stool. *What the hell,* I thought. I had nothing else going on.

"How's your night going?" I asked when I reached the woman. She turned to meet my eyes and shrugged.

"Well, I'm not drunk yet," she said. "But thanks for your help."

"I do what I can," I said.

"What can I do for you?" she said.

"Tell me your name, for starters?"

"I could do that," she said. "Or I could stay anonymous and mysterious."

"I'm Lawrence," I said, holding out a hand. "Cork to my friends."

She took it with a slim hand. She wore a ring of silver entwined snakes, and, as Maria had promised, her long nails were glossy black.

"Nice to meet you, Lawrence." Her fingers slipped out of my grasp, and I waited a beat for her to give me a little more. She remained quiet.

"It's traditional for you to tell me your name now," I suggested.

A wry smile spread across her lips. "I'm not a traditional girl," she said. "Tell me why you are named after a bottle stopper."

I shrugged. "I had some friends once who said if you put a bottle to my mouth, you'd never get any liquid out of it again. They started calling me the Cork."

She raised an eyebrow but didn't comment.

"What's your name?"

"Tell me why you wanted to meet me first."

So, it was going to be a game. I pulled out the empty stool next to hers and took a seat beside her. "Maria said you were into voodoo."

"Did she now?"

"I have friends at Eleanor's Arcana, so she thought we might get along."

"I see." She took a sip of her martini, studying me over the rim. "I don't have any friends there," she said.

"I could introduce you."

She shook her head. "No need. I have my own circle."

"So, you do practice voodoo yourself?" I asked.

"I have danced naked around a fire at midnight a few times," she said with a wry grin. "If that's what you're asking."

I felt her watching me to measure my reaction.

"Were there snakes?" I asked. She took a breath and launched into a recitation.

"With the serpent shall you commune and invite the loa into your midst. With the loa you shall entwine, and experience all of the pleasures of existence in the eye of the midnight sun."

I couldn't tell if she was putting me on or serious.

"That sounds intense," I said.

"The best things are."

This was getting me nowhere. I wasn't really in the mood for games.

"Do you ever hold ceremonies on the night of the full moon?" I asked.

She looked at me with a new curiosity. "That's the best time. When the moon is closest to the earth, the doors can be opened."

"Opened to what?" I asked. "What would you want to come through?"

"The loa and their children," she said. "They can walk through the worlds and be present with us on those nights."

I knew a little bit about the loa. It would be hard to know a voodoo priestess like Eleanor and not know about the spirits of the voodoo religion. There were many types of loa, who were typically called to earth in ritual ceremonies by a priest or priestess to receive gifts and perhaps provide advice or some kind of magic to the voodoo circle in return.

"What do they want? Why do they come?"

"On those nights, we welcome them into our bodies and they soothe our souls until we can pass through."

"So, it's about possession?"

"The best feeling in the world is to be ridden," she said.

I'd heard of the ceremonies she spoke of. A priestess would call the loa within a defined ritual area called a peristyle, and one of the spirits would 'ride' a human horse at the center, often driving its human vessel into epileptic seizure-like convulsions. It had never sounded like 'the best feeling' to me.

"Have you been ridden often?" I asked. As I said it, I realized how foolish – and personal – the question sounded.

"There is a Ghede that comes to me often," she said. "He never wants to leave."

Thanks to Eleanor, I knew about the Ghede too – they were a

family of loa connected with the powers of fertility, and conversely, death. Papa Ghede is supposedly the first man who ever died.

"If you love it so much, why don't you let him stay?" I asked.

"Oh no," she said. "They can't be allowed to leave the peristyle or the balance would be broken. Who knows what kind of trouble they could cause?"

That idea gave me pause. I had always approached voodoo with a great deal of skepticism, but I couldn't help but ask, "If a loa were to possess those outside of the peristyle, could they hurt their horses? And disappear with their bodies?"

The woman looked at me strangely. I wasn't sure if it was because she thought I was nuts or because I was treading too close to guarded secrets.

"The loa mean us no harm," she said. She took the last sip from her glass and abruptly slid off her barstool.

"Thanks for the drink," she said. "But I have to go now."

"You haven't told me your name," I complained.

She turned and flashed me a smile. "No, I haven't."

And then she was walking past the bar and out the open door onto Decatur.

"I can't do it all for you," Maria's voice mocked from behind me.

"Do you know her name?" I asked.

"Really? You didn't even get that far? This is worse than I thought."

"Never mind," I said. A sudden feeling of hopeless irritation possessed me, and I lifted the pint and emptied the last half in one long gulp. I set that and a twenty-dollar bill on the bar and began to walk out myself.

"Désirée," Maria called from behind the bar. "Her name is Désirée. She works at Mythologica, the occult bookstore on Second Street."

I didn't know if I could convince her to talk on her home turf more than here in a bar, but I stopped and made a note on my phone. Then I waved my thanks and walked out onto the bustle of the street.

CHAPTER EIGHT

Tuesday, July 2

New Moon

"We got one!"

I had to pull the phone away from my face for a second. It was Aubrey, and he was excited. So excited, in fact, that my right ear was now ringing. I shook my head for a second, and then returned to the call. "You've got what, exactly?

"One of the bloody bed people," he said. "Tarrington and I just pulled him up from the swamp."

"Are you sure?"

"Ninety-nine per cent," Aubrey said. He was breathing heavily. "He weighed a ton and he's got a tattoo on his right shoulder of a nude girl tangled up in a bunch of rose stems. We remembered that as a unique identifying mark from one of the missing. We need to pull the case file and compare the pictures. Can you grab it and meet us down at the morgue?"

"Will do," I promised, and hung up. I had been hoping to clock out early today, but apparently that was not to be. On the plus side, I hadn't been the one to pull up the body. I've said it before but there is nothing on this godforsaken earth worse than the stench of a body that had been rotting in swamp water.

★   ★   ★

An hour later, I was watching them cart the bloated body down the hallway in the underbelly of the city hospital. I had a photocopy of the tattoo in hand but did not look forward to getting a close look at the body. If it was who they thought it was, the guy had been underwater for weeks. This was not going to be good.

Aubrey and Tarrington followed the two ambulance workers into the long room of steel beds. Thankfully, they were all currently empty; it must have been a slow week in death-land.

"Did you find the file?" Aubrey called as soon as he saw me.

I nodded. "Yeah, I got it. Peter Maytree, fifty-two years old. Missing since April. Adult-themed tattoo on his right shoulder. But if he's been in the water this long, I don't think you're going to be able to see it."

"That's where you're wrong," Tarrington said. His voice was calm but...with an edge. "This guy should have been gator food a long time ago, but he barely looks like he's been in the water more than a couple days. And take a sniff."

"I'd rather not."

"Right," Tarrington said. "It should be awful. But do it. Tell me if you smell anything."

I realized as he said it that the ungodly gagging cloud had not appeared when the body had rolled by. I could smell the body now – the room smelled swampy and rank now that we were all inside – but it wasn't terrible. The stench of cigarettes that followed Tarrington around everywhere he went was stronger.

"Someone keep the body on ice?"

Tarrington shrugged. "Let's check the tattoo."

I walked over to the right side of the corpse. He was a big guy. Still wearing a ragged pair of old shorts, though his upper body was bare. He had a lot of tattoos – but then again, he had a lot of skin to tattoo. Ink wrapped in vibrant swaths of skulls and demons and thorns all around his chest and arms. I pulled out the picture of the right arm tattoo and then walked to that side of the table to compare. There was definitely something similar on his biceps. When I held the print out next to it, Aubrey whistled from just behind me.

"That's fuckin' it," he said.

"Sure looks like it," I answered. "But where has this big boy been hiding? Couldn't have been in that swamp all this time or he'd be jelly on this table right now."

★   ★   ★

The next few days were a blur. The coroner confirmed that the body was, in fact, Peter Maytree. Oddly, he also suggested that the body did appear to have been submerged for several weeks based on the growth he found inside the man's organs. Which made no sense at all. He was holding on to the corpse to do further tests, because something wasn't normal. The widow was not happy; she wanted him buried.

Meanwhile, we stepped up our search of the swamp in an ever-increasing radius around the point where Maytree's corpse was found, hoping that this was just the start of locating the rest of the missing... but as the days went on, the nets didn't drag in any more stiffs.

All in all, it was one of those weeks where on Monday, you feel like it will take forever to get to Friday, and then all of a sudden you're closing up shop on Friday afternoon and wondering 'how did I get here?'

I hadn't heard from Eleanor all week, so I decided to make a stop at her shop on the way home. And...maybe have a drink or two in the Quarter while I was at it. This was a prime people-watching night, if you were in the mood for watching drunken fools. Things were already busy as I walked the strip and it was still before seven. That meant the night was going to be nuts. There'd be lots of police calls to the station tonight, but thankfully, I was off the clock.

I decided to stop in at Redfish for a gumbo and a beer before heading deeper into the Quarter. Redfish was right at the mouth of Bourbon Street, next to the Hustler store. You'd never expect it from the location, but it seriously is one of the best places there is for a quick bowl of spicy stew or a plate of perfect white fish. And they always had NOLA Brewing on tap, so it was a win-win for me.

They were hopping as always on a Friday night, but I was able to get a single seat at the bar. A couple guys were arguing about the merits of Pappy Van Winkle bourbon just down the way from me, and I couldn't help but eavesdrop. That used to be my go-to sipper, before bourbon got trendy. For a few years, I always had a bottle on hand, but now...you couldn't lay your hands on one for less than a hundred bucks, and you'd be lucky to get one for that. Redfish actually had a bottle on their huge mirrored back bar, but you'd pay sixty bucks for a single shot. Too rich for my blood.

Apparently, though, not for the yahoos who were arguing about it. One of them was insisting that Four Roses was better (and more accessible) and to make his point, he ordered a shot of each. It killed me how money just *flowed* in the Quarter.

"Find any stiffs lately?"

Rudy, the head bartender, had just come over to rinse out a glass at the sink in front of me.

"No, but I'm still looking for a bunch of them."

He nodded. "The big bloody bed case, huh?"

"Yeah. Hard to track down a suspect when you don't have any actual victims."

"I bet. Especially if it's all because of a curse. You might not have a murderer at all."

"What do you mean?" I asked.

He shrugged. "I hear all sorts of crap," Rudy said. "Latest is that someone got on the wrong side of some voodoo priestess and she's put out some kind of crazy curse on the whole city. Hard to fight something like that. You can't even keep your head down cuz the voodoo eye sees all."

Again with the black magic crap.

"You really believe that shit, Rudy?"

He grinned. "I don't know what I believe, but what I do know is that there are plenty of things I don't know, so I don't pretend I know any better. It's a strange, strange world, my friend."

"I'll second that." I picked up my pint and took a deep pull. A month ago, if you'd told me I would be listening to people talking about voodoo being responsible for murders, I would have laughed out loud. I still thought the idea was ridiculous, but there was something weird about the whole situation. Maybe it wasn't magic that had stolen dozens of bodies…but it could be related to magic. Some group picking out victims and using them in rituals during the night of the full moon. That I could believe. But that also meant there wasn't one perpetrator, but a whole gang of perps. And so far, they'd been remarkably clean; we hadn't turned up a single unusual fingerprint or item left behind.

Rudy filled a drink order for a couple sitting a few stools to my right, and then he stopped back with a concerned look on his face.

"Hey, have you talked to any of the voodoo groups in the area to see if they know what might be going on? I know of a couple people who are into that scene, if you need an introduction."

"Thanks," I said. "I'm actually on my way to meet one just as soon as I finish up here. But I'll take any references you've got."

The older man squinted, as if he were trying to think of something, and then nodded.

"Don't go anywhere," he said. "I have a card from one of them in the back. I just need to do a couple things out front here before I get it."

A waiter appeared behind me with a steaming bowl of gumbo and my stomach jumped at the smell. I could be stuffed to the gills but let my nose smell that Redfish bowl of shrimp and andouille goodness and I'd find room for it.

I dipped a crust of fresh bread in the brown roux and smiled. For a few minutes, I was insanely happy, and without a care in the world.

I was using a hunk of bread to sop up the last of the gravy from the bowl when Rudy slipped something into my hand. It was a black business card, with a snake, a cross and a skull on it. The edges were accented with filigree patterns and next to them was a name:

Mythologica.
Rare Books. Hidden Magic.

Beneath the tagline was a street address.

That was all. I recognized the name; it was the place Maria wanted me to go, to chase down the voodoo girl from Turtle Bay. So that was twice now I had been pushed to seek out that store.

"Where did you get this?" I asked.

"A woman who comes in here now and then," Rudy said. "One of those black fingernail, black lipstick, heavy eyeliner types. All I know is that she's connected. But she might be worth talking to."

It was my turn to shrug. "You never know."

I pocketed the card, and then pulled out my wallet to pay the tab. It was getting dark, and I didn't want to be down here when things got really wild. It was time to go see Eleanor.

★   ★   ★

The air was thick with lavender as I stepped off the broken sidewalk and into the warmth of Eleanor's Arcana. There were a half dozen people browsing in the bins and aisles of the store, and Eleanor herself was at the cash register checking someone out and explaining the particular powers of whatever charm she was wrapping up for them.

"Hey stranger," a familiar voice whispered at the back of my neck. "You never came back for me."

I turned and Renee stood just inches away, hands on her hips and lips pursed in an exaggerated sad face.

"It's been a busy couple weeks," I said.

"Too busy for me? I'm hurt."

"I'll try to make it up to you."

"You'd better." She reached out to stroke my shoulder. "I'm guessing you're not here to see me tonight though, either."

I shook my head. "No. I just had a few questions for Eleanor."

She curtsied. "Always the lady in waiting." Then she pointed across the store. "She's over there."

"Thanks," I said. "We'll go out again soon."

"Uh-huh." She rolled her eyes and faded back into the next aisle. She picked a small bag out of the customer's hand and shook her head. She set the bag back on the counter and selected a different one. I had no idea what charm the person was looking for, but Renee seemed to know right away what the need was. I needed that kind of help with my case.

Eleanor's face lit when she saw me walk toward her counter. She pressed a bag into her customer's hand and immediately moved to the side to greet me.

"I was hoping you'd come this weekend," she said. "I have been talking to people since I saw you last, and I might be onto something."

"Onto what?" I asked.

"People talk," she said. "No matter how much someone wants to keep something a dark secret, someone else always knows. And then someone else and someone else. We aren't good at staying silent all our lives, you know?"

"What are you talking about, Eleanor?"

She waved for me to follow her to the side room of the store, where the walls were covered in bones and crosses and painted figurines meant to represent the different loas. Each was distinct, with different colors and expressions.

"There is a rumor that I heard," she said. "A powerful voodoo priestess was wronged, and in return, she swore vengeance on everyone in the city. She cursed New Orleans."

"Interesting," I said. "And apparently lots of people are spreading that rumor because a bartender literally just told me the same story. Suppose there's a curse on us all. What does that have to do with missing bodies?"

"I don't know yet," she admitted. "But I know that the person who pronounced the curse is very powerful. This is not the work of a novice. Or even most experts. To cause so much death...or disappearance...she must be very strong."

"So you really think that this is dark magic stealing bodies, not people? I've been thinking that this is a group who are abducting people for some dark ritual."

Eleanor shook her head. "I don't think so. But I'm not sure yet. I need to talk to someone this weekend and I may know a little more after that. It's big, whatever it is. Maybe the biggest curse New Orleans has ever known."

"You know how dramatic that sounds."

"How many people are missing?" she asked. Her voice was steely and quiet.

"There were a dozen last month alone."

She widened her eyes. "You know how dramatic *that* sounds?"

I nodded slowly. "Point taken. But...a curse? Black magic stealing people from out of their beds?"

"I know it's hard for you to believe this, but there are spirits beyond where your eye can see. They *exist*, Ribaud. You may deny them but that doesn't make them not real. It just means you may never open your eyes wide enough to see them for what they are. You don't have to take my word for it, but leave yourself open to the possibility. And then make your mind up only when you know more."

"And when will that be?" I asked.

"Tuesday is the night of the full moon," she said. I'd known that. It was circled on the big calendar that covered the surface of my desk. "I suspect that we'll have more to consider on Wednesday morning."

"More missing bodies doesn't mean we have any more evidence about voodoo," I said. "We haven't had any clues or evidence in any of the past disappearances. So, I don't suppose this week will be any different if it happens again."

"Do you have any doubt that it will happen again?"

"No."

"Well, there you go. You've taken the first step down the road of belief. You believe that an impossible thing will happen on Tuesday."

"I believe that something horrible is going to happen to a bunch of people on Tuesday if I don't find out who's behind it," I said, correcting her. "That doesn't mean I believe that spirits are going to come and steal away the living."

"You've always been stubborn, Cork," she said. "You see what you want to see. If you saw more, you would have seen your wife slipping away from you before she was gone."

Her words were like a slap in the face.

"Not fair," I whispered.

Eleanor looked at me hard in the eyes.

"There is fair, and there is true."

I opened my mouth to say something, but realized that I had no words.

"Wait," Eleanor said. She walked to the back of the room and opened a door to slip into the office behind the store. She was gone only a moment, and when she came back, something dangled from her hand. It caught the light of the overhead fixtures and glimmered faintly.

"I made this for you," she said, and lifted it up so I could see. A silver pendant hung from a black woven cord. The center of the talisman was a silver star with a circle in the middle. But between each of the points of the star, five pitchfork-like symbols emanated outward.

"The star is the image of endless light," she explained. "It will help you to open your eyes to the hidden worlds that surround you. The protection symbols emanating from the light will ward off evil spirits and curses and protect you from harm. Nothing can keep you safe from everything, but I have put as much power as I know how into this amulet."

Eleanor reached up and over my head, and draped the necklace down my chest. "Keep this close to you now. I know you don't believe. But believe in me. Do this for me. Something evil is awake in this city, and you are chasing it. That can only lead you into danger."

I fingered the amulet, marveling that she had poured and shaped it herself. And I knew she had. And it probably had tiny bones or herbs or something mixed into the mold. She was truly an artisan, whether you believed her religion or not. I undid the top button of my shirt and slipped it inside.

"I'll wear it always," I promised.

Eleanor nodded. "Good."

At that moment, the front of the store erupted with laughter as a rowdy bunch of twentysomethings came staggering inside. There were four guys and three girls, all of them flush with an evening of drinking. One of the women was particularly striking, with long gently curved black hair and perfectly smooth pale skin. She wore short shorts and a ripped T-shirt with a particularly low-cut *V*. She'd apparently made use of that *V* on the street tonight – her neck was thick with necklaces of beads. The other women had strands as well, but the black-haired girl was loaded.

"How about we find us some Love Potion Number Nine?" one of the more heavyset guys called out. He began picking up satchels of herbs from one of the tables, and tossing them in the air for his friends to catch.

"I need to leave you now," Eleanor said. "Call me on Wednesday morning when you make your rounds. I'll be ready."

"I'd rather find a way to stop this from happening again on Tuesday night," I said.

Eleanor put out her hands in a gesture of helplessness. Then she pressed a finger to my forehead, and then to my chest. A moment later and she was across the store, rescuing her gris-gris bags from the thoughtless hands of the drunks. I lingered, waiting to see if she needed my help in evicting them, but in moments she had them separated and quieted down. She was pointing out the meaning of a painted figure to one of the girls – not the beaded one – when I decided to slip back out. I wasn't in the mood for Renee tonight, and Eleanor had said what she had to say.

I hated to admit it, but for the past two weeks I'd really just been on a countdown to Tuesday. And Eleanor had cemented that. There was really nothing I was going to do to stop it at this point. It was just an inevitable landslide waiting to fall.

I stepped back out onto the street and the neon-tinted darkness never made me feel more alone.

CHAPTER NINE

Tuesday, July 2

Buck Moon

The rats in New Orleans are the size of squirrels in other cities. You don't have to stay up late to see them, but on Tuesday night, I did. Everyone at the station was on edge. We all knew it was the night of the full moon, and we knew the last five 'mass abductions' had happened on the night of the full moon.

The chief called me in at one point to ask what my plan was.

What kind of plan can you have for something like this?

"We're ready for a lot of emergency calls and no bodies," I said. "So…really no plan at all. What do you expect us to do?"

He didn't have an answer to that. I hated having to ask the question.

The day went by uneventfully, and after work, I stopped by Turtle Bay for a beer. Which turned into five or six. I don't know. Maria kept my glass full, even when I didn't ask for a refill.

I was a little unsteady when I walked the street at 1:30 a.m. And I considered the rats, who had no fear of one shambling human headed in their direction. A pack of them tore at the garbage in front of one of the restaurants and paused only to turn their long heads to look up at me for a moment as I passed by. Some people were creeped out by the things, but I just took them in stride. Every creature has to eat. And as long as they weren't eating *me*, I didn't care if they roamed the streets like packs of wild dogs.

And they kind of did.

I hadn't heard any traffic yet on the police band, but I knew it was only a matter of time. I looked up at the sky and could see the moon like a white blinding brand in the sky. It was full and bright… somebody was going to die tonight.

I don't know what I thought I was going to do, walking the streets in the middle of the night. Stop the voodoo curse from striking because I was out and about? Tackle the body snatchers as they walked down the pavement with corpses thrown over their shoulders?

I did nothing of the kind.

The streets were dark and empty, except for the rats. And when I arrived back at my house, I stabbed a key in the door, and managed to fumble my way up the stairs and into bed without an issue.

The issues would come in the morning.

★   ★   ★

And they did.

My phone went off at 5:45 a.m.

I wasn't receptive. I hit the 'deny' button twice before its incessant buzzing made me finally hit the answer prompt.

"Ribaud?" a voice asked.

"Yeah?"

"We've got a missing person reported at 153 Parkside. Can you cover? It's another bloody bed."

Fucking A. It was all starting again. Just as I knew it would.

My head was pounding and my eyes didn't want to stay open, but I staggered into the shower and turned the water to hot. I'd scald myself awake if need be. The morning was going to start early, and the day was going to be long. I knew it without a doubt.

I dragged the razor across my stubble half-heartedly in the shower, and dragged the towel across my body with equal distraction when I stepped out. Back in my bedroom, my socks wouldn't pull on because my feet were still damp.

Nevertheless, I managed to get dressed by 5:57 and strapped on my gun just before picking up my keys. Then I thought for a moment, and reached for my phone. I hit speed dial, and in a few seconds Eleanor's voice, raspy but clear, echoed through the speaker.

"Is it time?"

"First call of the day," I said. "Do you want to meet me there?"

"No," she said. "But yeah. Where is it?"

I gave her the address, and then hung up. At six in the morning, traffic was still light and I was at the scene in ten minutes. My head was still swimming a bit from the night before, but I pushed through it. I pulled up alongside a broken curb and forced my eyelids open after stepping out of the car. New Orleans was already breath-heavy and armpit-sticky humid at the start of the morning. It was going to be a sweltering day.

The house I pulled up in front of was a nondescript two-story with a small wrought-iron gate at the front walk. A small sign that read *153* hung next to the sidewalk, and I brushed past it barely noticing before I rang the lighted oval doorbell.

I'd only just touched the button when a balding older man in a white T-shirt and blue jogging shorts answered the door. He looked to be at least two hundred and fifty pounds and sweat from the day's fledgling humidity already stood out on his forehead.

"Mr. Feldner?" I asked.

He nodded, and pushed the door open to let me in.

"It's back here," he said. "Our bedroom. She was there when I went to sleep. And now...well, you'll see."

I walked down a narrow hallway and into the dimly lit bedroom. The scene was exactly as I had expected. I'd seen it too many times.

Top sheets rumpled at the foot of the bed, gathered away from the point of concern – a heavy red stain on the bedsheets that shone in the low light like fresh red paint. A hunk of flesh dotted the middle.

"I've looked all over the house," Mr. Feldner said. His voice trembled. "I can't find her anywhere. And there's no trace of blood anywhere else. But...it doesn't seem like she could get very far after losing that much blood, does it? Where could she be?"

I shook my head. If I lost enough blood to make the bedsheets sodden, I didn't expect I'd be able to go very far at all.

When I didn't answer him, Mr. Feldner paced to the other side of the bedroom and looked out the window.

"Do you think she could be all right?" he asked. "Maybe she went to the hospital?"

I didn't suppose Mrs. Feldner had her heart ripped out, bled all over the bed, and then got up and walked out of the house to hitch a ride to the hospital. No. I didn't suppose that at all. But I said nothing. My phone vibrated in my pocket and I pulled it out to see a text from Eleanor. She was waiting out front.

"I'll be right back," I promised and went to the front of the house to let her in.

Eleanor wore a strapless dress that wrapped and sashed around her middle with multiple folds. The material looked tribal; black and green and magenta stars and geometric shapes interwove in a mind-numbing blur of patterns and motion. Her hair was braided in a dozen or more small braids, all gathered at the back of her neck. She looked the part of a mambo.

"Morning," I said.

She nodded and stepped inside.

"You don't exactly look like a police officer," I murmured.

She held up a knapsack with the symbol of the moon outlined in sequins on one side. When she pulled it open, I saw an array of small candles and bottles inside.

"That's because I'm not," she said. "You wear the uniform of your trade, and I'll wear mine."

Fair enough.

I led her to the back bedroom, and I heard her take in a fast breath when she saw the bed.

"This is Eleanor," I said to Mr. Feldner. "She's going to be helping me with some investigative work."

Feldner raised an eyebrow at her costume, but said nothing.

"I'll need you both to leave me for a time," she said.

"Do you need anything?" I asked.

She shook her head as I knew she would. "Just quiet. No distractions."

I led Mr. Feldner out of the room. When I sat down on an old beige sofa chair in his living room, he continued to stand. "Has the police department resorted to voodoo now to solve cases?" he asked.

"No," I said. "I know this seems a little unusual, but Eleanor has her own way of approaching these things. She looks at things differently than I do, so her insights can be useful."

"Sounds like doublespeak to me," Feldner said. "You brought a voodoo priestess to my house. Does that mean you think there's some kind of black magic going on here?"

I took a deep breath before answering.

"There have been several cases like this one," I said. "So I'm investigating all angles."

The other man paced back and forth in front of his couch without sitting down. After the fourth or fifth turn, he stopped. "Shouldn't you be doing something? Dusting for fingerprints or looking for clues somehow?"

I stood up with a sigh. My head swam just a bit.

"Yes. Show me the rest of the house?"

He led me from room to room. I knew it was a pointless exercise, but I wrote down a couple notes on the house layout and the lack of any blood outside of the bedroom. Then I had him lead me outside. I walked the perimeter, and again found nothing unusual. The house was surrounded by small shrubs set in beds of gravel. I checked the windows for signs of forced entry, and looked at the back door as well. It was an old reddish-brown painted wood door with cracks where the humidity had caused it to expand and split. But there was no evidence of tampering. We walked back around to the front of the house once more.

The air was already heavy with moisture, and I could feel sweat trickling down my back just from the brief slow walk. If it was like this now, it was going to be a miserable day.

Eleanor was waiting when we stepped back inside. The smell of incense now colored the musty air of the house.

"Can I show you something?" she asked.

"Wait here," I told Mr. Feldner and followed her back to the bedroom.

She closed the door behind us, and then reached into her pack for a small jar of powder the color of lima beans.

"Watch," she said, and pulled me close to the bed. She held the jar out in front of her, and gently blew on its surface. A small cloud of pale dust leapt up and into the air over the bed...and then cascaded left, right and forward. I could smell something faintly bitter above the scent of whatever incense she had burned here a few minutes before. But I barely noticed it as I stared at the way the faint cloud of powder rained and drifted in any direction but down to the center of the mattress. It was as if the dust had landed on an invisible dome over the area where Mrs. Feldner's heart lay. The powder would not fall in the bloody area of the bed.

"That's bizarre," I said. "Is it a draft? What does it mean?"

"The air is still," she said. To prove her point, she lifted a small, stubby black candle that she had burning on the nightstand, and lifted it over the bed. The flame burned straight and tall in the air, without flicker.

"There are forces at work here," she said. "The burut powder will not fall on a cursed place."

"So, you're saying that the bed is cursed?"

"You saw for yourself," she said. "Something has touched this place and still lingers."

I had seen it for myself. I found it difficult to believe that it had anything to do with a curse, though. The powder had looked as if it had struck a surface and slipped off. Or as if it had been repelled by a magnetic field.

"What's the powder made of?" I asked, considering the magnetic idea. "Does it have iron dust in it?"

"This is not science," she said, and gave me a dark stare. "You will try, I know you. But it cannot be explained that way. The burut powder is derived from a mixture of roots and leaves. There is nothing of metal or man in it. I would typically use it to create a ward against curses, but it is also, as you saw, a good indicator where one exists."

"All right," I said. "Then what does this mean?"

"There is a strong force here. Dark magic. A spell, a curse… someone very powerful has called the body of this woman to them."

I held up my notepad. "I can't exactly write that in my report."

Eleanor smiled thinly. "No, I suppose not."

"Speaking of which, we should get your things out of here. I'm sure we won't be alone here very much longer."

She agreed, blew out the candle, and began to gather up other small implements that she had placed in the room. A tiny statue at the foot of the bed. A feather at the head. A stick of slowly smoldering incense in the corner.

"Where's my wife?" Mr. Feldner said from the doorway. He was not addressing me.

Eleanor turned to him and answered.

"She is in a place that none of us can reach."

"Will she come back?" His voice quavered.

"I don't think so," she said.

She put a hand on his shoulder for a minute, a gesture of comfort and empathy. Then she slipped past him out the door. I followed.

"We'll call if we learn anything," I said.

Mr. Feldner nodded, and then leaned against the wall and buried his face in his hands.

CHAPTER TEN

"This is the work of someone very disturbed," Eleanor said, as she emptied the contents of her bag into the desk. I had followed her back to the Arcana to talk.

"That's a given," I said. "So how do we find them? This has to be stopped."

"Whoever is behind this will not be easy to find. And they are clearly very dangerous. I have spent my entire life learning the power of voodoo and making relationships with the mystères, those spirits who go between. Some of them can be very difficult and unpredictable to work with. But I do not know of any who would do something like this. I do not know of any priestesses who are so powerful and so evil that they would try to do something like this. Whoever it is does not practice the work of the light."

"What does that mean?"

"I trained in how to work with herbs and the loa to heal and help others. There are many different churches and varieties of voodoo practice, but healing is at the core of our belief – that by working with the sacred power inherent in all things, we can bring positive light to a life. Whoever has launched this attack has subverted that. They have only darkness in mind. They are speaking to spirits and invoking forces that I don't know...and don't want to know."

"So again, how do I find them?"

"They are more likely to find you," she said. "That's why I gave you the amulet of protection. You must wear it at all times."

I nodded and showed her that I still wore it. "I won't take it off. But you can't make one of these for everyone in New Orleans. So how do we track the source of this...curse, if that's what it is?"

"I will talk to some people and put out the word about what I have seen today. There are many priestesses throughout the city and the swamps. We don't typically work together, but I will see what I can learn. If there has been a new group focusing on dark rituals, there may at least be a whisper of who and where."

"Thanks," I said, just as my phone buzzed. I knew what it would be about before I picked it up.

"Another bloody bed reported on Wharton Street," the dispatcher said.

"Text me the address," I said, and hung up."It's going to be a busy day, I think."

She nodded. "Every month has been more, right?"

"Yep."

"It is growing. Each harvest fuels more."

"Harvest?" I said.

"They are using the bodies for something. And only discarding the heart. Which is not at all what I would expect."

"Why not?"

"The heart is the core of all of our life energy. It's the seat of love and health."

"And you said this curse is not about healing and life. So maybe that's the one part our priestess doesn't need or want."

She agreed and opened the door to the back of the store. A figure knelt in the shadows at the foot of the Arcana altar.

"Renee, what are you doing here so early? We won't open for a couple hours yet."

The girl looked up and shook her head. "It was a bad night," she said. "I just needed to be gone." She met my eyes and her lips split into a surprised smile. "Cork, what are you doing here? Do you want to buy a girl a beignet?"

"I wish I could," I laughed. Then I held up my phone. "But duty just called. I've gotta go. You'll call me later if you hear anything?" I said to Eleanor.

"Promise," she said. "Be safe."

I clutched at the chain near my heart and smiled. "I've got protection."

Then I hurried out of the store and back to my car.

There were missing bodies to add to my growing list.

CHAPTER ELEVEN

I wasn't back to my car yet when the phone rang. The screen said it was Aubrey, so I thumbed the connection open.

"Yeah," I said. I may not have sounded the most receptive, but I knew if he was calling me that nothing good was afoot. Turned out, I was right.

"Ribaud," he said. "We've got a problem."

"What kind of problem?"

"You know how people keep disappearing from beds?"

"Very funny."

"Well, last night, someone disappeared from the morgue."

"What are you talking about?" I asked. Aubrey was starting to aggravate me.

"You know that guy we fished out of the swamp – Peter Maytree?"

"Yeah. Haven't they buried him yet?"

"No," he said. "And now they can't. Because someone took the body overnight."

"That's ridiculous," I said.

"God's own truth," Aubrey countered. "The coroner came in this morning and found the locked entry door was smashed open – from the inside. He did an inventory and found the big man's body had up and disappeared. How do we put an APB out about that?"

"I dunno," I said. "I don't think 'be on the lookout for a large zombie just escaped from city morgue' is going to win anyone a promotion."

"But that's the truth."

"Maybe," I said. "There are always other answers."

"I'd love to hear them," he said.

"You guys are sharp, you'll come up with something."

I hung up. But I kept seeing the image of a big, fat, half-naked, rotting man with a naked girl tattoo roaming the side streets of New Orleans.

A missing corpse from the morgue was the least of my concerns right now, though; I was backed up with five different calls about overnight disappearances of people who had gone to bed alive and woken up missing. Those problems took priority over a stiff.

★   ★   ★

Have you ever wanted to claw your way out of your skin? You yearn to leave the shell of your body standing in place, while you slip out a rip in your backside, free to find another place, another life?

That's how I felt all day on July 16. New Orleans was a sweltering urban swamp of sweat and bad smells and crying men and women. Every hour I visited a new victim's residence, taking down their accounts of the night and morning, how they'd awoken without their lovers, and how they'd either slept through the apparently deadly event, or come home to find the ghastly mess.

After the fourth or fifth case, I think my mind glazed over and checked out; my body just walked through the afternoon on autopilot, moving from one sad story to the next. One rain of tears to another shower. I wrote down my notes and nodded and asked the same questions over and over, but the anger and heartbreak of these people didn't really get to me. I couldn't have been on the force in the position I was in if I was a bleeding heart.

I've always been good at keeping my distance there. So I moved through the day and finally checked out after twelve hours and instead of going home, walked straight down Decatur back to Turtle Bay. The first two pints went down in about fifteen minutes.

I'll be honest. I've never been a very emotional guy. It's not that I don't care about things, but most of the time I just can't see the point in 'crying over spilt milk'. Life happens, it is what it is, and you just have to accept it and move on. It doesn't mean you have to like it, but when I can't change things, I've usually been able to just shake my head, pound my fist into a table (or wall) and then move on. When people go on and on about things, wringing their hands with drama and emotion, I usually just want to slap them and demand, 'Get over it. Move on.'

You can extrapolate from that that I've had problems with relationships. But honestly, I really haven't. Maybe because I've never cared deeply enough for most of them to be too upset whether things continued or ended. I've always enjoyed talking with women, some would say flirting, but I've never personally felt that I was the 'flirtatious' type. I do enjoy joking and sparring a bit. And I'm not a dedicated introvert where all I want to do is be alone. I know some cops like that, and honestly, I think they're dangerous. If you're not connecting with the community you serve, then you're not part of them. And if you're not part of the community, then the way you serve is going to change. You'll take more chances, or not take any chances – because you really don't care at all.

I care about New Orleans. It's my home and the way the air smells at nine-fifteen on a summer night or at six-thirty on a cool November morning is unlike the way it smells anywhere else. For better or worse.

I've been in relationships where I cried when it was over. I'm not a rock. But I've also been in plenty where I have felt a brief circle of loneliness at the end, and then after a deep breath, a feeling of freedom.

At the end of the day, you're the only person you ever have to live with. And sometimes, just being with yourself is really all you need.

All this is a long way of saying I wasn't prepared all those years ago for Amanda. She came into my life like a force of nature. She brought out a spring of love from my heart that I didn't know existed, and for a long while, I was happier than I had ever been. She *fit* with me. When I couldn't remember the words, she finished my sentences. When I wanted to take a trip to just get out of town for a while, she had already looked up a half dozen options.

She was stronger and more thoughtful and funnier than me. And maybe in the end I was a little jealous of that – knowing that she was better than I could ever be in so many ways. I argued with her and spent more time at work chasing leads on cases that didn't matter, instead of being home to cement the bond that meant more to me than anything ever had in my life.

Of course, we never admit some things until it's too late. I didn't know that her life had come to mean more to me than my own. I didn't know that life would become an empty hell that made me consider turning the barrel of my service revolver toward my head every day that I was forced to find a way to live without her.

She'd given my life a meaning that I didn't understand until she was no longer there. And then I understood it in a sickening, sorrowful way that I had never wanted to feel.

Amanda has been gone over four months now, and I still find myself suddenly needing to turn away from people because the tears have welled up in my eyes after someone said a phrase like something she would have said. Or because a song like Pink's 'Learn to Love Again' came on the radio and I heard the words and knew that I could never learn that lesson. No way. Not in a million years.

I've loved and lost. And will be forever a broken man because of it. Maybe I was better off sleeping with women when I felt the need, but never really connecting in the way I had with Amanda. Because those morning afters never really hurt. They were sometimes awkward, but a day later they didn't cross my mind anymore.

Amanda was still on my mind every single day. And every bloody bed that I saw today had reminded me of the morning I'd woken up without her.

The raw end of that memory, though, was the knowledge that I had not been enough for her. She had gone on to someone else, either out of anger at my insensitive nature, or just because I was not, in the end, the man who could fully fill her heart.

You can spend hours running around a mental maze chasing thoughts like that.

It doesn't do any good. But I still do it.

I've always been good at picking myself up and moving on. But not this time. Oh, I'm still moving on. I get up every morning, and walk the streets, and ask questions and try to solve cases. But there's an empty spot where there used to be satisfaction at the end of a good day. Instead, there's just a stillness and an empty bed to fall into, before getting up to go through the motions all over again.

Because that's all my life had become.

Going through the motions.

I needed something. Someone. To make me whole again. I had never been an emotional guy…but I had never been numb either.

I needed to feel something again.

The cold beer trickling down my throat on a sticky night was a good feeling, but it wasn't what my chest craved.

I pulled out my phone and texted Renee.

"Feel like a drink tonight?" I asked.

I'd already had three, but I figured I was good for three more. I took a sip while I waited for her to answer, but I didn't need to wait long. I saw the three dots appear on my text window in seconds, letting me know that she was answering.

"Where are you now?" she asked.

I told her and her response was almost instant.

"Store is quiet tonight. I'll be there in a half hour."

★   ★   ★

I moved to the far end of the bar at Turtle Bay near the window where a couple stools had opened up and staked our space while waiting for her. Someone put a stream of R&B songs on the jukebox, which was a little annoying since this was usually a classic or modern rock kind of atmosphere. But then with a jarring transition, Led Zeppelin's 'Heartbreaker' suddenly boomed from the speakers, and I instantly relaxed. Almost on cue, Renee appeared in the doorway and stood there framed by the dark street behind her and the yellow bar lights inside. She looked around for me before coming all the way inside, and in that moment I remembered why I had spent so many hours talking with her about 'her old man'.

She was a quiet force of nature. Her cheeks were high and smooth, and thick dark eyebrows arched above wide, expressive brown eyes. Her nose was not slim, but was still elegant, and her lips were heavy, always with a hint of a smile at the edges.

Renee always looked as if she knew a secret.

She'd pulled her hair out of the usual braids tonight and it was wild as a storm cloud around her shoulders and across her back. Maybe the humidity had puffed it up. Whatever the reason, she ran one hand through it absently, trying to tame it.

And then her eyes lighted on me, and her lips split apart.

"Cork," she cried and quickly closed the gap between the door and me.

"I saved you a seat," I said, and she threw her arms around me for a fast, hard hug.

"It's about damn time," she said. "How many hints does a girl gotta give?"

"I know, I know," I said. "I'm bad at follow-up. What can I buy you to make up for it?"

"How about a condo near the Garden District?"

"How 'bout a vanilla vodka and soda?"

She shrugged. "Or that, sure."

"So how have you been?" I asked. "I didn't expect to see you so early at the store this morning. Did something bad happen with Levar again?"

She rolled her eyes. "I didn't expect to see you, either. I mean, coming out of the storeroom with Eleanor at seven in the morning? People could talk."

"Please. You know us both better than that. It was business."

"Umm hmmm. That's what they say. Just business."

"Cut it out. I asked her to help me with a case."

"The police are now using voodoo to solve murders? Why Inspector Ribaud, I am surprised at you."

"No," I said. "You're not, because you know better."

"I know it's not usual for a cop to take a mambo out to a murder scene," she said.

"Yeah, well, there's something really weird going on with these murders."

"And you think black magic is involved?"

"I don't know what to think anymore."

She ran a hand over my shoulders. "You could call on me for help too, you know. I've been studying voodoo all my life."

"I appreciate that," I said. "Today was a special case, though. I wanted to see if the way these crimes were committed was something that might have been part of a ritual."

"The bloody beds and the hearts," she said, elaborating on what I wasn't saying. "I know what you've been investigating. I've heard you talking to her about this when you came by the store before. And I heard some of what you said this morning. The store was pretty quiet after all."

"Well, yeah," I said. "Please don't repeat what you've heard. Nobody is supposed to know all the details of these disappearances."

"Murders," she interjected.

"Probably."

"It does all sound like a crazy voodoo ritual gone bad," she said. "Blood and hearts and missing bodies."

"I didn't want to ever see anything like it again after I woke up and Amanda was gone," I said. "But now, every month, it happens again and again. And there are more cases each time."

"An army of the dead is growing."

"I sure hope not."

"An army of the heartless," she said. And then she laughed and took a sip of her vodka.

"So you know about my problems," I said, changing the subject to bring it back to her. "How are yours? Is Levar hurting you again?"

Her husband had beat her up several times in the past, but she refused to press charges. Nevertheless, I had seen the bruises and spent a lot of late nights talking through the aftermath.

She shrugged. "He is who he is. Been working a lot, so I really haven't had to deal with his bullshit that much. When he is home, well...he gets what he wants, let's just say that and let it die."

I took the last sip of my beer.

She noticed that I was at the end of a glass and raised hers and took a gulp until her drink was as empty as mine.

"Wanna get out of here?" she asked.

"Where do you want to go?"

"Your place."

"It's a mess."

"Just like you."

"Fair warning."

★   ★   ★

I tried not to assume things; it's unwise for a cop to be in the habit of making assumptions. But I'd known from the moment I texted Renee that we'd probably end up at my place. She was unhappy, strongly sensual by nature and enjoyed my company. I was unhappy and she took my mind off that for an hour or two.

It had been a few months, but there was no difference in the intensity between us. She was a force of nature and I was just the earth she moved over. My typically stoic nature meant that I could play the anchor to her tempests very well.

When we reached my apartment, I poured her a vodka on the rocks. I didn't have much in the way of mixers for her.

"Orange juice?" I offered.

"Do you have maraschino cherries?" she asked. When I nodded, her face lit up. "I like to turn the glass sparkling red."

I handed her the cherries from the back of the fridge and she poured in a shot of red syrup.

I poured myself a NOLA Brewing IPA into a pint glass that I kept frosted in the freezer, and then led her back to the living room. She sat on my sofa and I eased down next to her with a groan. It had been a very long day.

Renee instantly leaned in against me, and tapped her glass to mine. "Cheers," she whispered.

"Cheers," I answered and took a deep swig. "What time do you have to be home?"

"I don't ever have to go home," she said.

"Let me rephrase that. What time do you need to leave by so that Levar doesn't come pounding on my front door with a gun in his hand? I'm not up for a shootout tonight."

"On busy nights, I don't get home from the store until after one in the morning," she said. "So, we've got plenty of time."

"For what?"

"For you to remind me of how much I enjoy your company." She motioned for me to lean closer, as if she was going to tell me a secret. Her lips were just inches from my face, and her eyes wide and dark as pools.

"I have missed talking to you," she said.

"Just talking?"

Her eyes flashed. "You know I've missed more than that."

"Every time you see me, you take your life in your hands," I said. "You've told me how Levar is. If he finds out that you've been with another guy, he'll strangle you."

Renee's eyes rolled back until I could almost only see the whites. Then she looked at me and whispered, "Sometimes I wish he'd just strangle me and get it over with."

A tear leaked from her left eye, and I couldn't resist. My arm slid behind her head and I pulled her in closer to me. I cared about this girl, I did. I'd started talking to her about her troubles at home almost a year ago. Probably about the same time that I'd realized Amanda was thinking about another guy, actually. Funny how that sort of thing works. Doors close and others open. Or something like that. Or maybe you open new doors because others close. I don't know. But I'd connected with Renee because she needed an ear, and a warm shoulder. And a warm body, if truth be told. She was not the celibate type, and she didn't want to screw her abusive husband anymore.

Her hand began to trace a slow route from my chest to my crotch. Her fingers were soft, and deceptively gentle. She pinched, and traced circles and then kneaded. After a few silent moments of groping, I gently put my hand over hers, and moved it away from my belt. She pouted, and set her drink down on the coffee table. A moment later, she was straddling my lap and looking down into my eyes with an undeniable hunger.

Her lips touched mine and I wrapped my arms around her in a hug. Her eyes spoke silent words that I understood and answered. I knew the dance she asked for. I yearned to dance.

"I've missed you so much," she whispered.

"I know," I said. With both hands, I eased her back off my lap to the couch. "I've missed you too. But…we shouldn't do this. Not like this. Not in secret."

It took everything in me to say those words. It felt right having her next to me here. Her skin burned dark against mine; hot and smooth chocolate as she slid her leg over mine. But I worried about her. Specifically, what would happen to her if her husband found out. We'd strayed before, and I'd vowed not to again. Not unless she got herself free of him.

★   ★   ★

"I want to be here again," she said after the silence drew out.

"You need to decide where you want to be long-term," I said. "I love being here for you, but if you want to have a real life, you're going to have to leave him. You can't have guys on the side, or he'll kill you. Hell, if he knew you were here, he'd kill both of us."

"I know," she said. "But Eleanor gave you a protection charm. I saw it. You'll be okay."

"And what about you?"

"Don't worry about me. Just watch yourself."

I frowned. "Why?"

"For the reason you were at Eleanor's this morning. You are poking at things that you should stay far away from."

"People are dying, and I'm a cop. I have to try to find out why. And stop it."

"I know," she said, slipping her hand across my chest. She grabbed on to the flesh around my right nipple and squeezed. "I want you to still be here when I need you. And if you keep looking for the reasons behind the curse of the full moon, you won't be."

"Curse of the full moon?" I asked, moving to prop myself up on one elbow. "Is that what it's called?"

"You can call it whatever you want," she said. "I know you're trying to find out why all of those people have disappeared the past few months. And I'm sure there's a reason that people are disappearing the way they are. I just don't want you to disappear too. I need you to be here for me."

"I don't intend on going anywhere," I said.

"Neither did any of those people you're trying to find."

I didn't have a response to that.

She didn't wait for me to have one; instead, she covered my mouth with hers.

This time, at least for a little while, I didn't argue.

PART TWO
SNAKES & SKINS

CHAPTER TWELVE

Thursday, July 25

Last Moon

The buzzing of my cellphone woke me from a dream about ghoulish masks and a knife dripping blood. Lots and lots of blood.

Not really the dream you want to have after a night of heartfelt connection with a beautiful girl.

But there were things on my mind.

I slapped at the phone on my nightstand, but instead of palming it, I just succeeded in moving it to the floor.

"Goddamn it," I swore, and hung over the edge of my mattress, my fingers digging along the carpet, trying to find it in the dark. Then I nudged something, and as it shifted, the blue outline of its screen, which was face down on the carpet, gave it away easily.

I swiped it up and hit the button, finally.

"Yeah?"

I knew it was not going to be good news. The station didn't call you when you were off duty at six in the morning because they wanted to thank you for a job well done.

"What took you so long?" the voice on the other end greeted me.

"Why are you waking me up at this hour?" I asked.

"Some of us are always up at this hour," the dispatcher noted. It was Grace, who I'd worked with since I started on the force.

"Shut the fuck up."

"Not until I give you an assignment," she answered. "You're going to want to check this one out yourself."

"And why is that?"

"Well…it's someone you know."

My heart jumped. My first thought was of Renee. Had she gotten home and found her husband was suspicious…and then he got violent? I was still fuzzy, but I thought hard and remembered seeing her to the door to catch her Uber around twelve-forty. She should have been home at a reasonable time, given her usual shop hours.

But that wasn't it at all.

"We just got a call from Robert Trevail, at 145 Cedar Lane," Grace said. "Trevail says his wife has disappeared. He asked for you."

Her words sounded strange at first. "I know that you know her…." Who was she talking about? And then the last name came into focus and I opened my mouth to ask, but no sound came out. I could feel my throat closing.

"Ribaud, Eleanor Trevail is missing."

I wanted to scream, but instead, I managed to regain control of my voice and finally choked past the lump. "I'm on it. I'll be over there in fifteen minutes."

★　★　★

Eleanor lived out on the edge of town, where the streets grew narrow and rutted, and the bougainvillea bushes and the mandevilla vines hung with thick, fragrant flowers over wooden fences that buckled beneath the force of unbridled life. Here, the old sidewalks heaved and dipped in drunken paths and the houses were hidden behind the overgrowth of green.

There were no mansions out here, just small weathered cottages sprinkled along twisted, sometimes unmarked roads. I'd been here before, after Amanda disappeared. Eleanor had made me a special charm that was supposed to help me find my wife.

Obviously, it hadn't worked.

I hadn't met Eleanor's husband then.

So it felt doubly weird to be walking up the limestone slabs that led the way to her door to meet him now.

A thin dark-skinned man with short graying hair came to the old aluminum screen door before I could even knock.

"You Detective Ribaud?" he asked.

I nodded and the door creaked open.

"They told me you'd be comin'. You knew Eleanor."

"Yes. I saw her just yesterday morning."

"Follow me," he said, and turned away.

He led me past the sitting room. Instead of turning down the hall toward where I assumed the bedrooms were, he walked through a kitchen with linoleum floors and crooked brown cabinets and into a room beyond. The doorway was blocked, not with a door, but with a curtain of beads. Knowing Eleanor, each long thread had likely been hand assembled and all of the beads were no doubt carved from some special cypress wood or something. I could see that there were tiny lines and designs on them, but couldn't take the time to see what they were. Eleanor's husband pushed the threads aside and I followed him in.

The room beyond the kitchen was an add-on. If I had to guess, it probably had been hand built by the man in front of me out of wood from the swamps beyond his house. The wood was rough and ranged from tan to gray, where you could see it. Which wasn't a lot. There were totems and tapestries hung everywhere. An electric light on a tall stand stood lit in the corner, but there were shelves on all four walls with candles in various states of melt. I'd guess that the electricity was not on here much. The reason for the focus on candlelight was in front of me. A table against the far wall. It was covered in a black tablecloth which hid two small risers. On the very top level, hugging the wall, a statue of the Virgin Mary with hands folded and clad in blue and white stood next to an Infant Jesus statue, who wore a king's raiment. A golden halo crowned his head. One of his arms was chipped.

"I woke up this morning and realized she wasn't in bed, and so I came out here. She sometimes falls asleep in here, making her gris-gris bags and praying and all. But she wasn't here. I turned around to leave the room, but then my foot slipped. When I turned on the light, I saw why."

That's when I looked down.

I hadn't seen it when we walked in, because my eyes had been drawn to all the pictures and masks and totems and statues that covered the room. She even had strings of Christmas lights hung behind the statues on the makeshift altar.

But the floor.

Now that I looked, I saw that the unfinished wood planks were dark. Wet.

Covered with blood.

It had seeped into the wood so that in spots it only appeared as a dark stain. But when I really looked at the center, it was clear the circle was a dark but deep red. And a glob of something crimson and fist-sized sat in the middle. I knew without a doubt that it was a human heart.

Eleanor's heart.

My heart skipped and stalled and I wanted to yell something bitter and angry. But my emotions were nothing compared to the feelings of the man beside me. Decorum insisted that I remain stoic and calm.

And as I locked my feelings down and stared hard at the floor, well, that's when I realized that there were strange trails across the wood that suggested bloody wetness. As I looked at the edges of the bloodstain, I saw that tiny ripples of wet twisted and led away from the circle.

Instead of looking to the center, for the heart, I got down on my knees and looked to the edges of the room, following the trails.

"What are you doing?" he asked me. I put my hands flat down on the planks and began to move carefully toward one of the walls where a shelving unit housed jars and vials and boxes of what I assumed were ingredients for spells and rituals.

"Following the signs," I murmured.

When I reached the black-painted wall unit stacked with magic jars and potions, I heard the first telltale hiss.

It came from beneath the 'book' case.

"Do you have a stick or a thin pole?" I asked. Robert Trevail left the room, but returned a moment later. He handed me a yardstick. I took it and slid it along the splintered planks, following the dark stain that emanated from the center of the blood.

And when it disappeared beneath the shelving unit, I pushed it gently to the left.

A moment later, a thin black snake slithered out and into the light of the room.

When I pushed the yardstick in the other direction, another snake shot out and disappeared beneath the cloth that cloaked the altar.

So....

Snakes had been there, slithering in the midst of Eleanor's blood. And then they'd retreated to the far corners of the room, covered in her life.

What did it mean?

I moved the stick toward the first snake, which coiled angrily in the corner, not knowing where to go to escape. It opened a wide-hinged jaw with white, dangerous-looking fangs and hissed faintly at me.

"Did Eleanor keep snakes in here?" I asked quietly. I didn't want to enrage the thing with loud noises. Otherwise, I might have screamed. A little.

"No," he said. "She didn't believe in sacrificial rituals or using animals to work her spells...."

"That sounds like the Eleanor I know," I said. "Somebody brought these snakes in here, while you were sleeping."

Eleanor's husband nodded. "I want to know how someone got into my house and took my wife. She had us protected with all sorts of spells. She was not a child."

I shook my head. "No, she wasn't. And it wasn't a child who did this."

I reached out a hand to the corner, ever so slowly. When it was in position, I let it fall.

A moment later, I stood up, clasping a snake's neck in my hand.

"Do you have a plastic bag, by any chance?" I asked.

"I'm sure we do," he said, and disappeared through the door back into the kitchen. The snake writhed and protested in my grip. Its tail slapped again and again at my chest, but I didn't loosen my grip on its neck.

Robert returned with a ziplock freezer bag. It wasn't quite as big as I'd hoped, but the snake wasn't huge. It would fit.

"Hold the edges open and I'll put the tail in," I said.

He stretched the bag wide, and I lowered the snake tail first.

"On three, I'm going to let it drop," I said. "I need you to pull the lip tight so that it doesn't jump right back out at us."

He nodded. His face was impassive, but I knew he was not happy with the way this plan was going.

"One...two...three!"

I released the snake and he pulled the bag taut by its edges. Inside, the snake was throwing a fit, squirming and flashing its fangs.

"I'll take it," I said and relieved him of the bag. Carefully, keeping the top folded over, I put my fingers on the edge of the seal, and once the lip had slipped inside the track that would begin the 'zip' lock, I slid my thumb and forefinger across the seal until it snapped completely sealed on the other side. Then I poked a couple of airholes in it with my car key and set the bag to the side on the floor.

"That should keep him out of our way for a bit," I said. "Thanks."

I knew there was at least one more in the room, but I wasn't going to play snake catcher. I had the evidence I needed in the bag.

"What have they done with her?" he asked. "This is the same thing that happened to those people. In that case she was helping you with."

I shook my head. "It looks similar," I said. "But it's not the same. All of those people were taken from their beds on the night of the full moon. And there was no evidence that snakes were involved. Someone wants us to think this is the same, but it's not."

"Then why?" he asked. "Because she was helping you?"

That thought had already crossed my mind. "Maybe," I said. "It is definitely supposed to look like a voodoo connection."

The other man clenched his hands silently into fists. I had a feeling he wanted to use them on me. I couldn't deny that this could have been my fault for involving her in my case. But who knew she was involved? Who had she asked questions of, enough so that they thought she was a threat?

"Do you know who she has talked to over the past few days? Especially other people involved in voodoo?"

"Her business is her business," Robert said. "She don't share that kind of thing with me."

"Fair enough," I said. "Do you know where her phone is? And would you know the password so we can see who she's called?"

Eleanor's husband nodded, and disappeared into the kitchen again. He returned with an iPhone. Voodoo has come a long way.

He clicked it on, and then entered a code.

"Here it is," he said.

I looked at the recent calls section and the number at the top of the list caught my eye immediately. It was mine. The timestamp said she'd called me just before eleven-thirty last night. I hadn't heard my phone ring, but then again, I'd been a bit busy with Renee.

I pulled my phone out and thumbed it on. Sure enough, there was a one next to the calls icon. I'd apparently not heard it, and since a phone call had woken me up, I hadn't looked at my history on the way to Trevail's house.

I touched the voicemail button and held the phone to my ear. A familiar soft but firm voice spoke my name.

"Cork. This is Eleanor. I think I have the answer. Call me in the morning as soon as you can. I've found out exactly who is behind this curse, and I'm trying to create a counter-spell. I can't undo her curse, but I may be able to shield against it. I am working on it now. It's going to take a lot, though."

Goddamn it. I'd missed her call because I was making out with Renee. What if I'd picked up the phone? What if I'd gone to her house last night?

I stared at the blood on the floor. Apparently, I wasn't the only one who knew that she knew. Whoever was behind the mass killings knew that Eleanor was looking into them. Someone decided that she couldn't be allowed to live with that kind of knowledge.

Something scrabbled in the corner behind her altar. One of the snakes, no doubt. I looked at a small side table where there were shelves of small jars and vials.

There were several that had been used recently and not returned to a shelf. A white ceramic jar with a sickly green powder sat open on the flat surface, a tiny measuring spoon still inside.

Blackened leaves lay strewn about the space, and a small vial that had held something liquid had been overturned; the wood was black where it had run out. But what had she been making? Where was the protection spell she'd talked about?

Then I saw it.

There were shards of white broken pottery in the corner of the room, beyond her 'mixing station'. Behind and to the right of the altar.

It looked as if someone had taken the bowl she'd been mixing powders in, and thrown it against the wall. A shimmer of the green powder, mixed with other shades, dusted the lower half of the wooden paneling.

I assumed Eleanor hadn't upended the bowl herself.

Someone had come here to stop her.

They'd destroyed whatever spell she'd been mixing.

And then they'd destroyed her.

Goddamn it. This was my fault. I'd dragged her into this. And now she was dead. Oh sure, there was no body to prove that she was dead, just like the rest. She could be alive, tied up in the back room of a swamp shack somewhere. But I knew better. She was dead. I had no doubt.

I couldn't let her death be in vain.

But what had she left behind that would help?

I picked up a jar from the table and looked at the label. *Mugwort* was handwritten on the front. Didn't help me, though I had a vague knowledge that it was used in a lot of voodoo concoctions.

Looking at the labels of the other jars she had out didn't help either. I wasn't a houngan. Knowing what leaves and leavings she had put into the spell she was constructing wasn't going to do me a damn bit of good.

Then I realized that there was a nondescript book lying on the side of the table. I turned the cover over and saw Eleanor's handwritten script covering the pages within. This was her spell book.

Again, I didn't really know that it was going to help with anything, but it was a start.

I flipped to the last entry, and saw that she had listed some ingredients and amounts. Maybe the list related to the broken pot on the floor, or maybe not. It was impossible to tell because there was no preamble.

"Can I borrow this?" I asked Robert, who still stood at the entrance to the room. His face wrinkled for a moment. But then softened. He knew that I was a friend. He probably hated me for putting his wife in danger, but he also knew that I wanted to find her. Or find what had happened.

He nodded okay.

And then I remembered that I was still holding her phone.

I looked again at her call log. There wasn't a lot there. Eleanor wasn't a phone person. But there were a few from the past couple weeks.

I took a screenshot of the numbers and names, and texted it to myself. I didn't know if anything was going to pan out there, but I would look them up.

Then I handed the phone back to Robert.

"I'm really sorry," I said.

His face pinched. He wasn't going to say it was all right, and it wasn't. But he tipped his head. Just enough to say, yeah.

At least he didn't punch me out.

There wasn't much else I could do here. I'd have forensics run the blood type on the heart. I didn't know if they'd have an existing blood type documented for Eleanor. But if they did, we could at least rule on whether the heart lying in the middle of the floor was likely hers.

I was betting the answer was yes, though I hoped it was no.

"So what are you going to do about it?"

I jumped a bit at the question. It was valid, but he'd been so quiet the entire time.

"The best that I can, Mr. Trevail. The best I can."

"I hope that's good enough."

I didn't answer him, but in my head, I thought, *Yeah, me too.*

CHAPTER THIRTEEN

Friday, July 26

Feast of St. Anne

The morning was heavy and claustrophobically still. It was still early when I pulled up to a vacant parking space near my house. I nearly yelled out a victory cry. The more the area gentrified, the harder it was to park close to my place on the street. I had wished for years that this house had a garage, but no. No place to put one even if I could afford it. My house was just a four-room hovel jammed right against the next. Five if you counted the bath. No driveway. No parking.

I got out, took a breath and held it just to savor the early morning smell.

There were moments when it was better than anything I knew to live here. And a perfect morning like this...

...would have been great, if my phone hadn't buzzed before I reached my front door.

Fuck. I'd almost gotten to go back home for a little while. Wasn't to be.

I thumbed the call open, and Tarrington's cigarette-ruined voice suddenly filled the air.

"We need you out at Pernaud's Landing."

"What now?"

"We found something that I think you need to see."

"Not helpful."

"I couldn't begin to describe it."

"All right," I said. "Give me fifteen."

I picked up the bag with the snake and took it into the house. If I left the thing in the car for the morning, it would bake. So, I took it into the kitchen, and grabbed a knife. The thing coiled as I brought the steel tip near its head. I saw the jaws open and the flash of white teeth.

"Chill out," I said, and poked some more airholes around its head and across the bag. I wasn't going to let it out, but I didn't want to smother it while I was gone.

I left the bag sitting in the sink, and then headed back to the car.

★   ★   ★

Pernaud's Landing was a lost place. It had once been a popular nightlife spot in the Fifties, but over the years, it lost its way. Pernaud, the old swamp hugger the spot had been named after, had started renting boats to people in the Fifties to go out on the river. It turned out that the crescent current of the Crescent City was often just a little too powerful for a lot of the folks who tried to take a leisurely row out on the water, and eventually the Landing became more of a draw for food and drink than boat rentals. The place featured bands on weekends and people drove from around the city to watch the sunsets turn into the twinkling lights of the city at night. But eventually, the allure of the remote spot faded; it had never been on the beaten path to anywhere. Over time, the clientele soured from hipsters to thugs, and the bright party lights that hung from the aluminum roof and shone over the water at night dimmed from white to yellow. The place was right on the bank of the Mississippi with a short pier that extended into the water, a reminder of its early career. Katrina had nearly washed it away. But the old rotted wraparound balcony had somehow survived, and the dark, beer-stained planks inside had continued to draw feet inside, though less and less.

The last time I'd been out here – responding to a bar fight complaint – there had been two derelicts at the bar and a waitress who looked as if she drank right along with her patrons from dusk 'til dawn.

This morning, as I walked up the sagging wood steps from the broken stone walkway to the entryway, the place seemed diminished. The roof looked uneven and worn, and the walls, which once might have been brown cedar, were gray and cracked. It looked like a forgotten place, and it really, for the most part, was.

I pushed the old wooden door open and stepped into a dark room. The smell of stale beer hung thick in the air and I coughed when it hit my throat. I love beer, but there is something about the reek of wood that has been steeped in old hops for years that just turns my stomach.

"Ribaud," Tarrington called. His head poked around the corner a few yards away. He held out a hand and motioned for me to join him. "This way," he said and disappeared.

I walked across the empty, stale barroom and turned the corner. There was a long hall that appeared to stretch around the back side of the building. I followed the old planks until it opened onto another room. I could see the familiar plume of Marlboros.

That's where Tarrington stood smoking and waiting. Aubrey was bent over, staring at something on the floor just behind him.

That's also where three bodies hung from wires wound around hooks in the ceiling. They shivered and twisted faintly in the breeze.

As they did, the air filled with the buzz of flies.

A few of them shot past me, their wings touching my face with frantic flight.

I stepped forward slowly, toward the nearest one, and my gaze followed the pale skin of its heel up past its naked buttock and ribs and shoulder. There was a tattoo of Jake the dog from the cartoon *Adventure Time* on her left shoulder, and a triangle design that looked Aztec on her right. I could tell that this was the remains of a woman thanks to the space between her deflated thighs and the long ragged-cut blond hair that cascaded down her back.

She seemed unnaturally thin. Insubstantial.

Her arms were spread wide by the wires, and her feet were also tied apart, drawn by wires to hooks on the floor.

When I moved closer, I realized that her form not only seemed strangely flat, but distorted.

I took another step and understood why.

She wasn't totally there.

Or, to put it another way...her outside was hung out to dry; someone had taken her insides away.

It was an empty shell of taut skin that hung from the ceiling. There was nothing within.

The flies had flown from the slice in her chest. I walked slowly around the wires that tied the empty bags of her feet to the floor, and saw the perfect hideousness of what Tarrington had called me here for.

Somehow, someone had removed all of the bones and blood and guts from this girl, and left a costume of her skin to flap in the breeze of fly wings.

How do you steal the insides of somebody without any more than a small rip in the skin above where the heart should be?

It didn't surprise me that there was a hole there. Of course, her heart was taken. Probably the first thing. But how had they gotten the rest?

I whistled.

"They're all like that," Tarrington said. He dropped his cigarette butt to the floor and crushed it under one foot. "Like someone poked a straw into their chests and sucked all their insides out."

"How is that even possible?" I breathed.

"Maybe they pumped them full of bleach," Aubrey suggested.

"Do you smell bleach in here?" I asked. "All I smell is stale beer and old fish. And anyway, bleach would burn right through the skin."

"Good point."

"How did you end up here?" I asked.

"Call came in when the manager opened up for the morning," Tarrington said. "Supposedly the place was empty when they closed up last night. And, obviously, these weren't here then."

"Do we have a positive ID?"

He shook his head. "Just skin and no bones," Tarrington said. "The tattoo on the one might be an identifiable clue, but there are plenty of *Adventure Time* tats out there, I'm sure."

"Jewelry? Other remains?"

"Nope. Nothing left behind of these folks but their skin, Ribaud."

"Are we sure it's real skin and not some kind of fabrication?"

"See the flies? They're here because there are still little bits of meat stuck to the skin. Just a little. But enough."

Aubrey rose from the floor then. "I've been trying to find anything that might have bled or rolled from the bodies into the corners of the room," he said. "There's nothing here. Empty skins, a puddle of blood, and that's it. No clothes, no rings or jewelry."

"And the last person out last night?"

"Isn't answering the phone," Tarrington answered.

"Mildly suspicious," I suggested. "Or maybe she's still here." I gestured at the tattooed skin.

He nodded. "We sent a squad to her house. They should be checking in any minute."

"And the owner?"

"On vacation in New Hampshire."

"Convenient."

I paced around the...what could I call them? They weren't 'corpses' or 'bodies'. Skins, I guess. The one in the middle was male – somehow his dangling bits remained intact. The one on the far side of the room was another female. A heavy ponytail pulled the skin of her head backward at an impossible angle, distorting her face in an elongated grotesque.

I looked at the floor beneath the end of that ponytail. The stain of red was heavy beneath her, but I realized something right away.

There were swirls in the blood.

I followed them with my eyes and saw the faint tracks where they continued out past the circle of death. The faint tracks of red twined and continued to leave marks across the wood beyond the blood. The marks were faint, but I turned the flashlight app on my phone on, and got down on my knees near where one of the tracks exited. As I illuminated the dark wood I picked up the traces of where something had dragged along the planks. I crawled along to the wall and then turned. The telltale traces were fainter and farther apart now, but this particular line disappeared behind the bar. The floor there was stacked in liquor and beer boxes, along with some empty bottles that had apparently been discarded for pickup later.

I knew where this was going, and I wasn't going to start moving the boxes with my hands.

"Hey Tarrington," I called. "Is there a board or a broom or any kind of long-handle thing out there that you can give me?"

"Hang on," he said. "There's a closet over here."

I heard a door open, and a moment later he was pressing a steel pole into my hand. "How's this?"

"Perfect," I said. "Thanks."

"What've you got?" he asked.

"Something that slithers and bites if my guess is correct. Better back up."

He didn't need to be told twice.

I pushed the pole beyond a Jim Beam box and shoved it away from the bar and toward the back wall. There was no snake inside, I confirmed, as the box slid past me.

A NOLA Brewing box followed, and then a J&B Scotch box in telltale red letters over yellow.

A bottle clinked and rolled and I backed up a little more as I poked the pole beyond the last box. With a quick flick, I kicked it out of the corner where it had lain. As it passed me I saw something shift in the dark corner of the underside of the bar. I picked up my phone from where I'd set it on the floor and the light of the LED flashlight glinted back at me from two beady eyes.

A black snake was coiled where the box had been. The top of its head still held spatters of red. Its neck rose slowly, the snake blinded but attempting to show dominance over whatever creature had disturbed its dark hiding spot. As it did, I saw the flash of two more eyes shifting from beneath the coil of its tail. And then two more.

"Snakes again," I whispered with disgust. "Tarrington," I called again. When he sidled closer, I handed him the light, still keeping it trained on the creatures in the corner.

"Keep that in their eyes," I said.

"They?"

"Yep. Our little monster has friends."

I picked up the J&B box because it seemed sturdiest, and laid it on the floor, with the mouth facing the snake coils. If I pulled this one off, I should get a guest spot on a nature show.

"You are not going to try to catch it," Aubrey said from behind us.

"Evidence," I said simply.

I silently counted to three and shoved the box forward as fast as I could until it slammed into the inside wall of the bar.

Something thumped and slapped against the cardboard just beneath my hand.

"You're crazy," Aubrey said. "What if it's poisonous?"

"Then I'd better not get bit or you're going to suck it out for me."

"Over your dead body."

The thumping slowed, and I took a deep breath. With any luck, I'd trapped all three of the snakes inside. Part one was easy. Part two was where I might get bit.

I had all four flaps of the box folded out. I needed to flip the box upright and slap them closed over the opening. Before a snake shot out to bite my hand.

"No time like the present," I mumbled and made the flip.

I caught a glimpse of black coils moving inside, and slapped the left cardboard flap down. Then I reached and did the same with the short flap on the left. I was reaching around to pull the other long flap closed when I saw the glint of the light catch the top of a snake's head. It was in motion, propelling itself out of the box through the small remaining opening.

I didn't take a second to think, I simply swatted at it with my hand. There was a faint cool brush of something oily and solid beneath my hand and then it was gone back in the box. And I banged the other two cardboard flaps down to seal it.

The box exploded with sound as tails and heads whipped back and forth inside, trying to find an exit. They could still see light from the room getting in at the top where the flaps all met, and the sounds of thumping cardboard were strongest there.

"Anyone got some packing tape?" I called, holding the top down tight.

"Might be a tall order, Inspector," Aubrey said. "But try this. Found it in the closet."

He handed me a long board.

It would have to do. I laid it across the top of the box and it was heavy enough to hold the lids down and weight the box in place so that it wouldn't tip over thanks to the writhing of the inhabitants inside.

"Great," Tarrington said, handing me back my phone. "You've caught a couple snakes, Boy Scout. Now can we get back to the case at hand?"

"They're part of it," I said. "Look at the blood. Closely."

I stood up and traced the exit trail of one of the snakes from the blood beneath the tattooed woman with the light of the phone.

"There are snakes all over the swamplands," Aubrey said. "So what?"

"You really think it's an accident that these people are strung up here with no flesh and bones, and snakes evacuated from each puddle of blood?"

"Are you saying the people had snakes inside them?" Tarrington said. He frowned, and tapped a new smoke out of the pack from his chest pocket.

Aubrey one-upped him. "Are you saying the people *became* snakes?"

I shook my head. "No, I'm saying that someone used these snakes here in some kind of ritual. Now we just need to find out what kind of ritual and who might have done it."

Tarrington looked at me funny. "You wigging out on us, Ribaud? Am I hearing you say you think voodoo sucked out these people's bodies?"

"Nope. But whatever happened here, I'm betting there was some kind of voodoo ritual around it all. I found a snake at my first case this morning too."

"So now if there's a snake around, that means the cases are connected?"

I snorted. "Of course not. But it does seem a little suspicious in this instance, don't you think?"

The other cop shrugged. "I suppose we've got nothing else to go on."

"Just so."

"What now?"

"I'm going to take these monsters to someone who might know something about why they'd be writhing around in blood."

I reached down and carefully lifted the box, keeping the board pressing the lids closed.

"I'll let you know if I find anything out."

CHAPTER FOURTEEN

I had an old fish tank stashed in the back of a closet at home. Fish hadn't agreed with me. You'd think a quiet, no-fuss pet would be easy, but the damned things had gone belly-up on me more often than a drunk says 'I'll have another' at his favorite bar. I pulled it out from the closet, and a half hour later the tank had new, slithering occupants. Maybe I'd have better luck keeping snakes alive in it. I put a cardboard divider down in the middle to separate them, in case I needed to know which snake was from Eleanor's and which were from the Landing. I couldn't imagine why I would need to know such a thing, but...I'm a detective. We're trained to be detailed and precise.

Eleanor's snake had survived the day in the sink, though it didn't look very happy when I dumped it into its new cage. It slapped its tail against the sides of the glass and then pushed its face right up to the corner. I could see the anger in those yellow eyes.

The other three all squirmed and wound around each other before trying to slide up the glass to the top. Looking for a way out. I stood back once the top was on and stared at them for a while.

What did I need to give them to stay alive? What did snakes eat? I'd put a small bowl with water on each side, so that was covered at least. I remembered seeing a kid buying crickets once at the pet store and he'd said it was for a turtle or snake or something like that. Maybe that was the ticket, short term.

For the moment, I figured they'd survive with water. I pulled out my phone and took a couple pictures of them. I wasn't going to drag the tank around, but I had someone I wanted to show them to.

The lid was on, so I figured they'd keep awhile.

I locked up and headed back toward the Quarter.

★   ★   ★

Second Street was quiet when I pulled down the section where Mythologica was. I figured it would be. New Orleans – particularly the Quarter – comes alive at night. Nobody wants to walk these sweaty streets in the ninety-five-degree days when the air feels like you're walking through soup.

Still, there were a couple people inside the small occult bookstore when I opened the door. A bell rang as the door swung open and I took a deep breath of air twenty degrees cooler and substantially thinner. No soup in here. But definitely some incense. It smelled like I'd just entered a church in the midst of a High Mass.

I stepped into the first aisle of books, intending to take the place in a bit before I looked for my real aim. The shelf I'd chosen was devoted to Satanism. I saw Anton LaVey's name on several titles in a row: *The Satanic Bible*, *The Satanic Rituals*, *The Satanic Witch*, *The Devil's Notebook*, and *Satan Speaks!* I supposed any Satanic section was going to prominently feature the founder of the Church of Satan.

I picked up one with a black leather cover. While the name was on the spine, the front of the book featured only an upside-down cross.

Subtle. I'd become aware of LaVey when I watched an old horror movie focused on Satanism called *The Devil's Rain*. It figured that he'd show up in a film – I suspect that his 'religion' was more of a carnival showman at work than anything that actually conjured up the Devil. I probably believed more in the potential of voodoo to raise spirits than in the black masses of Satanism. But what did I know?

I put the book back on the shelf and wandered down the aisle to the back of the store. There were statues and a couple of small altars here. The walls were covered in figures that I recognized from multiple religious sects. From big-belly Buddhas to the four-armed Vishnu to a figure with a ram's head, there were all sorts of belief systems represented here.

After leaning in closer to stare at the detail of a nude woman with large breasts and menacing wings leaning over an equally nude but seemingly petrified man, I turned to walk the next aisle and found a real woman standing there. Silently watching me.

Désirée.

"Um, hi," I said. I'm sure my voice betrayed my startlement, because she grinned.

"Caught you looking."

I shrugged. "It's a nice piece of work."

"It's demon porn. Be real."

I wasn't sure how to respond to that. But she didn't make me. Instead, she put me on the spot.

"So how did you find me here?"

She remembered me from Turtle Bay. So maybe I had made an impression after all.

"I asked Maria," I admitted.

She didn't seem to have a problem with that. Instead, she critiqued my promptness.

"Took you long enough to come by."

"It's been a busy month," I said. "Ritual killings, disappearances and dredging swamps."

She pointed at the shelf I'd been browsing. "So you're a Satanist?"

I jumped. "No. What makes you think that?"

"I saw you holding the LaVey book."

"Just looking. I'm a police detective. I don't make the crimes, or sacrifice the goats. I try to find who did."

She nodded. "So this isn't a social call, I take it."

"I'd like it to be," I said. "But no, this time it really isn't."

She raised an eyebrow, but said nothing.

"I remembered that you had a connection to snakes," I said.

Désirée held up the hand with the snake ring I'd noticed the first night I met her. "Because of this? You have a good memory."

"You talked about them too," I reminded her. "Ceremonies and loa and all that."

"You buy a girl a drink and what you remember is that she liked snakes." The way she said it, it sounded like a condemnation.

"I remembered that I wanted to see you again and learn more," I offered.

"Apparently you didn't want that very bad. It's been a month."

"You didn't even give me your name."

"But you figured it out." She shook her head. "Look, I've got a store to run. What do you need?"

I pulled out my phone and showed her the picture of four black snakes in a fish tank.

"Very nice," she said. "I suggest you talk to the pet store about them."

I shook my head. "I caught all of these today at two different murder scenes. I think they were part of a voodoo ritual of some kind. I was hoping you might be able to tell me more about that."

She thought for a minute. Then she turned toward the front of the store. "Come with me."

I followed her to the front desk. A dowdy-looking older white woman with curled, frosted brown hair was standing in line at the counter, looking around anxiously. She had a book about herbal spells in her hand. A black couple were behind her. He was holding a statue. It looked like Medusa.

Désirée rang them both up, and then pointed to a chair behind the counter. "Sit," she said.

I didn't argue.

"Tell me about how you found them."

I related the events at Eleanor Trevail's house first. Her eyes rose when I said Eleanor's name. I figured she'd know her.

Then I told her about the skins at Pernaud's Landing.

"In both cases, the snakes were clearly dropped in the middle of the blood, and slithered away to find some place in the room to hide. But the trails started *in* the blood in the middle of the rooms."

"How do you know?" she asked. "They could have just been crossing the room."

I shook my head. "The marks *began* in the center of the blood. They didn't cross it."

She pursed her lips, and looked at her own snake ring.

"It's no secret that snakes have a connection with voodoo," she said. "Though I don't know what the use could be in these instances. Every priestess really has her own brand of magic, her connection to the loa is specific to her. The desires that they carry out for her come from her. So voodoo changes, depending on the executioner. There are some priestesses who eat the brains of snakes in order to obtain the wisdom of the serpent. And others will commune with snakes in order to show that they have no fear…thus they gain the trust and obedience of the snake."

"And what does that get you?" I asked.

She tilted her head. "Whatever the mambo wants," she said. "Snakes are powerful. They own the earth. They are the original creatures. There's even a conjure spell that takes the hairs of the intended victim and puts them in a jar of rain. The bottle is then covered and kept near the door. With the right calling, the hairs will begin to grow and eventually turn into snakes that can then be used to draw someone to your home."

"Snakes, the original Mickey Finn," I joked.

She didn't blink.

"Some say that snakes are of the Devil," I said.

"Some do. And maybe some are. Voodoo can call on all sorts of powers, from the pureness of perfect desire to the darkest vindictive power. All things are possible, all powers exist to be called. The vessel that calls and houses the loa determines the path of the magic."

"So, someone could be using snakes as part of a ritual to kill," I said.

"Sure. From what you described, though, I'd say killing is just a byproduct of the real goal."

"What do you mean?"

"Missing bodies, fleshless skins…these aren't simply the result of someone who wants someone else dead. This is not a simple revenge spell at work."

"Have you heard of a ritual where the skin is all that's left behind?" I asked and then thought of the larger case at hand. "Or just the heart?"

Désirée shook her head. "No," she said. "Though you could certainly look through our books here. I know a lot, but I don't know everything."

"Are you a priestess?" I asked.

At that moment the bell above the door jangled.

Désirée smiled and stood up. "Maybe you'll buy me a drink again sometime and we can talk more."

With that she slipped around me and went to help the new customer. The faint scent of lavender stayed behind in her wake. I breathed it in and wondered. Did she mean that I should ask her out? Or was she just thumbing me off?

I pulled out one of my cards and picked up a pen she'd left behind on the desk.

Call me, I wrote. *I hope your response time is better than mine.*

I left it on the keyboard of her computer.

Désirée was holding up a book and pointing to a particular chapter and nodding quickly.

I let myself out.

CHAPTER FIFTEEN

"We don't allow pets at the station," the chief pronounced. "Get that outta here."

I shook my head. Then I set the fish tank down on his desk.

"No can do. This is state's evidence," I said. "From two different murder scenes."

His face wrinkled up. "Evidence?" he growled. "What murders?"

"Eleanor Trevail to start," I said. "I found one of these in the room where she was murdered."

"Disappeared," he said. "There is no evidence that she was murdered."

I rolled my eyes. "Whatever. I don't have ID on the others. But you know the case where I found the rest of the snakes – the murders at Pernaud's Landing. There were three there."

"There were three *skins* at Pernaud's Landing," he answered. "I've told you before – nobody is to call these murders until we get some more evidence. I'm not saying that I believe they're not murders, but the best thing we can do to keep this from turning into a media bloodbath is to watch how we talk about them. For all we know, somebody robbed a cemetery and those were corpses that the skins were taken from. Grotesque, but less frightening to the public than a triple murder. We still don't know much of anything, even though I sent you out there to figure it out."

I caught the accusation at the end of that one. It didn't make me happy. "There were also three snakes there." I pointed at the coiled black things behind the glass. "What did you want me to do? There were a million fingerprints there – it's a bar. There were no eyewitnesses because whatever happened there happened after the place was closed for the night. There were no notes or other evidence left behind. We combed the place. And all I found were these snakes, which were apparently dropped in the middle of the blood as part of some kind of ritual."

"How do you know they were dropped in the blood?" the chief asked.

"Because the exit trails started in the middle of the pools. There was no trail leading in."

"Maybe the snakes fell out of the skins."

"Now you sound like Tarrington," I said. "Look, the snakes are the only evidence we have. Other than skins that we can't even trace. Has anything come back from DNA scans?"

He shook his head. "Nothing conclusive. The victims most likely did not have criminal records from the past five years, that much I can tell you."

I nodded. "So what we have are these snakes. Aren't you glad I caught them so that we have some kind of evidence to follow up on?"

"Get 'em out of my office," he said. "Take 'em home and name them if you want, but get them out of here."

"Who should take them?" I asked.

"You!" he yelled. Then he stood up behind his desk. "You should take them home. I hear snakes make nice pets. We don't need any pets here."

Inside the tank, one of the things was slowly raising itself aloft; its tongue zipped in and out, snapshot glimpses of pink as its head rose inch by inch up the vertical incline of the glass.

"Captain, I'm not taking these things back home. But if you want, I'll set them free here in your office."

I started to remove the lid of the fish tank. He reached out and slapped the lid back down. I swear he was breathing harder. And I don't think it was simply because he was annoyed with me. Something inside my chest warmed. The chief had an Achilles' heel. He was afraid of snakes.

"All right," he said. "Take them down to Bernard. Tag 'em for the cases. But I don't know what good they're going to be. We can't put them on the stand. And they're not going to play deep throat for us."

That comment led to an image in my mind which I'd rather not describe or revisit.

"No," I agreed. "They may not be called as material witnesses, but maybe we can find out where somebody bought them."

"What makes you think they were bought?" he said. "We have

hundreds of acres of swampland where you can catch any breed of snake you want. There is nothing here for us, Ribaud. Nothing."

"Got it," I said. "I'll have Bernard put them in lockup."

"I don't know what you think we're going to do with them," he said. "But I'd like you to get back out there and come back with some real leads in this case. We're not a zoo."

I picked up the tank and got out of the chief's office before he got really annoyed.

★   ★   ★

Eleanor's friends were not a talkative bunch. Over the next few days, I set up interviews with each of the people on the call list of her phone for the past two weeks. Each one of them turned out to have some link to voodoo. If they did not run shops or lead a group of followers in regular gatherings, they certainly were very knowledgeable. Enough so, that while they said they didn't lead any secret ceremonies, I concluded by the end of our interviews that they probably did. Connections aside, they didn't have much to offer me that would help the case. Eleanor had called them recently, they said. She'd asked about rituals that would require bleeding out the body, removing the heart, and then taking the empty shell of the body away for some other use.

None had been able to give her an answer.

"It sounded as if she was trying to trace down the origin of a very powerful Black Seduction," one of the contacts said. She was a voodoo priestess who practiced near the edge of the city. "I don't play with such things. They're dangerous in too many ways. When the Midnight Loa come, they show no mercy. I don't even want to know about the words that could bring those devils among us."

One by one, I went down Eleanor's list. And they all echoed the same thing. Their voices often dipped when they began to speak of the Midnight Loa. Hushed tones, as if they were afraid of being overheard by something or someone nearby.

The belief in the closeness of spirits was deep in all of them.

★   ★   ★

There was just one number that I couldn't seem to connect with. Every time I called, it simply rang and rang.

After a couple days of setting it aside, I finally got wise and decided to run a trace on it.

My contact at the precinct ran it down in a couple minutes and spit out an address for me. An old house in the Garden District, not far from St. Charles Ave. I knew right where it was. I turned off my computer and picked up my cellphone. Just as I turned toward the door, a voice came from behind.

"Hey Ribaud, you know you still need to bring me back some snake food. I'm not taking care of these damned things."

I shook my head and waved him off. "I know, I know," I said.

"They start eating each other, and there goes all your evidence."

The thought of a snake swallowing another snake for some reason made me laugh.

"You think it's funny? Those things start stinking and I'm throwing them in the trash."

I ducked around a desk and headed to the door before he could say any more. I had promised to find something for the things to eat, and hadn't delivered. Maybe on my way back from the Garden District.

★   ★   ★

The sky was overcast and angry gray when I hit the street. A storm was blowing in; despite the humidity, the back of my neck felt a chill as I opened the car. I hoped I'd get back before the rain hit. I slipped into traffic and drove for ten minutes. Once I turned into the old district of classic houses, it grew even darker. The whole neighborhood was sheltered in a canopy of old trees that hung over the old mansions, so with the gray skies, it felt like about eight at night.

A large wrought-iron gate across the street had a number 542 hung in the middle of it, which was the address I was looking for. I wondered if the gate was open, or if I was going to be shut out here as much as on the phone. I walked across the quiet street, and put my thumb on the latch.

It clicked open easily. I breathed a sigh of relief. One hurdle down. The door pushed open with a low squeal of infrequent use and I stepped inside. There were old cracked limestone steps leading to the gray wooden stairs at the front of the house. The place was surrounded by heavy bushes, and one of the windows near the front door was made from stained glass. A black cross hung in the center. As I looked around the yard, I saw several statues that suggested that this was a house where voodoo was in practice. One of them depicted a priestess, nude except for her necklaces, dancing over a bed of snakes.

Another was really a mini outdoor altar, with an array of talismans strewn around the feet of a gaudily depicted Virgin Mary statue.

I walked past them and stepped up to the door in the middle of the long veranda. A small couple's swing sat just a few feet away. It moved slightly in the breeze.

The front door was painted a dark blue. Unlike many on the street, it was windowless. So I wouldn't be able to tell from peeking in if anyone was coming to the door or not.

I shrugged and took a deep breath. And knocked.

Then I listened carefully, to see if I could hear any movement inside. The street around me was almost completely silent. A dog barked somewhere a couple blocks away. I could vaguely hear the traffic out on St. Charles, but it was just the slightest hum.

After a couple minutes, I shifted my feet on the deck, and knocked again. There was no doorbell to ring.

It was starting to look as if nobody was home…or at least nobody was going to answer. And then, without warning, the door creaked open.

A stern-looking woman with long black hair stood in the doorway. She wore a long loose black house robe. A surprising outfit for the end of an afternoon. Maybe I'd woken her?

"Can I help you?" she asked. She didn't sound at all interested in helping.

"I hope so," I said. "My name is Lawrence Ribaud. I'm a friend of Eleanor Trevail."

Was it my imagination, or did her brow tremor slightly when I said Eleanor's name?

"And your business here?"

"I was hoping that I could talk to you about the last time you spoke with Eleanor."

"I'm not sure what help I could be."

"Do you know she is missing?"

She shook her head slightly. "I had not heard that."

"I'm trying to talk to everyone who spoke to her before she disappeared. And your name was on her cellphone recent calls list."

She said nothing.

"Would you mind if I came in for a minute?"

This time she hesitated. Then I saw something change in her eyes. She pulled the door open wider and gestured for me to enter.

The inside of her home was dark. A candle burned in the room to our left. A sitting room, with an old piano, a long couch, and... an altar. That's where the candle was. The stained glass I'd seen from outside faced the room, and threw burgundy shadows across the walls in competition with the flickering shapes thrown by the candle.

She motioned for me to sit on the couch and took a spot across from me, on a hardback chair.

"I'm afraid I don't actually know your name," I said.

"Then how did you find me?" she said. Her eyes stared at mine, unblinking. It was a little unnerving to be at the center of that gaze.

"I found your number on the list of people Eleanor called before she disappeared, and I did a reverse lookup. The system just said M. Lackshire."

"Then you do know my name."

"Well, I assume you don't go by M."

That brought a faint smile. "No. My name is Madeline."

"So do you remember when you talked to Eleanor last?"

"Are you a cop?"

"I'm a detective," I admitted. "But I also am a friend of hers."

Madeline raised an eyebrow. "Indeed."

"I'm looking for anything that she might have said that would give me a clue to find her."

"I don't know what I can tell you," she said. "I was not a close friend of Eleanor. We run in similar circles, but I only see her once or twice a year."

"But she called you last week, didn't she?"

Madeline nodded.

"Why did she call?"

"I really don't recall," she said.

Utter bullshit, and I knew it.

"If you could try to remember, it would really help. Did she ask anything about particular voodoo spells or rituals?"

"Since when is the New Orleans Police Department investigating voodoo?" She shifted in her chair, leaning back to look dismissively comfortable. Her body language read, 'You're not getting a word out of me.'

"I'm not investigating voodoo," I said. "But voodoo was a large part of Eleanor's life, and the evidence we have in this case points to a ritual of some kind that was performed just prior to her disappearance."

"Maybe she conjured up the Devil and he took her home with him at the end of his visit."

"That seems unlikely."

"Only unlikely?" she said. "Not highly unlikely? Or impossible? Hmmm, maybe there is hope for you to become a convert yet."

"How do you know I'm not?"

"Because if you knew anything about the local voodoo scene, you'd know who I am and that Eleanor and I did not follow the same beliefs when it comes to practicing."

"Which makes it even more curious that she called you," I said. "Were you actual rivals? Did you try to steal each other's initiates?"

She snorted slightly. Then shook her head. "Nothing like that. We simply follow...different paths. There are many schools of voodoo, and let's just say that she and I do not agree on the curriculum."

It occurred to me that Eleanor had always been a kind person, eager to help, and eager to teach. I'd always associated her breed of voodoo with a positive 'spells to make your life better' kind of vibe. I'd never much believed that her herbal bags and tincture vials and dolls had any actual power at all. The demeanor of the woman across from me was 180 degrees from Eleanor, however. Somehow I suspected that her 'path' was perhaps not one I wanted to know more about. And for some reason, I feared that whatever voodoo she was involved in might not only work, but might bring a cloud over the house of those she chose to use it against.

Call it a hunch or intuition. But Madeline struck me as quietly dangerous. I suddenly got a chill, and wondered if I should have come into this house at all.

"What makes your path different than hers?"

"Mine achieves results," she said.

"But how is your magic any different than hers? You all call on the same spirits, do you not?"

Her chest shook with a silent laugh.

"I commune with the forces of earth. There are ancient and deep powers in this world that few are brave enough to call upon. I've spent my life understanding these things. Eleanor did not believe in courting the true powers that are waiting beneath our feet. She used herbal remedies and relics blessed by prayers to provide her charms and talismans. Surface things. I don't know if she ever truly danced with a loa or not."

"But you have."

Madeline's lips split into a grin that spread cheek to cheek. "Oh dear boy," she said. Her eyes suddenly glowed. "I have and I do. Every week I dance with things that you cannot and will not see. But they are there. And they can change the world as you know it."

"Can you offer proof of that?" I asked. "I'll be honest, all my life I've heard people talk about spells and charms and talismans and all that. And I've never seen any evidence that voodoo is anything more than a bunch of tea bags and half-naked dancing rituals around a firepit. Show me an actual, measurable change brought about by your rituals and spells, and I'd be happy to believe. But I have yet to see any provable evidence that voodoo is anything more than yet another false religion."

"You're investigating a series of missing persons and bloody beds, aren't you, Detective?"

"How do you know that?"

"As you've pointed out, I did talk with Eleanor recently."

"So, you do remember the conversation."

She raised an eyebrow, but said nothing more.

"She told you about me then?"

Madeline shrugged. "She told me that she was helping a friend try to figure out who might be involved in the cases you are investigating. She told me about the hearts and the blood."

At that point, Madeline rose from her chair.

"I am afraid I couldn't help her any more than I can help you. I trust that you will eventually find the answers you are looking for."

The interview was over, as far as my host was concerned. And while I would have loved to have pressed her, it was clear that she was not going to offer any additional information right now. Best to leave things on a 'friendly' level rather than force her to throw me out. I stood up, and followed her to the door. Which she had opened before I even stepped into the foyer.

I held out my business card from the precinct. Meanwhile, my phone started vibrating in my pants pocket. I ignored it for the moment.

"If you think of anything that might help us find Eleanor, or if you have ideas on what kind of ritual could have been performed with the blood and missing persons…please give me a call?"

She took the card after a moment. "I'm sure I won't," she said and slipped it into a pocket in her house robe.

I stepped past her onto the sagging wooden porch outside. She said one more thing.

"But I'm also pretty sure that none of us will be seeing Eleanor again."

"What do you mean by—?" I began to ask. But the door shut before I'd finished my question.

I didn't think she'd be inviting me in again any time soon.

CHAPTER SIXTEEN

Wednesday, July 31

Night of Hekate Suppers

The call I missed at Madeline's was about a liquor store robbery in Uptown, and since I was nearby, my plans for the afternoon were instantly scrapped. I headed there next.

It was a mess. Two twentysomething punks had come in and nosed around for a bit, casing the store. One tall thin black guy with shoulder-length dreads in a faded Tulane T-shirt and a bulldog of a white dude with a shaved head, a Tool black T-shirt and about a hundred extra pounds, all hanging right above the belt, apparently walked every aisle (and there were only three) for at least fifteen minutes. Then, when the last customer left, the two had converged on the cashier. Ordinarily, that would have been an easy 'empty-the-cash-register' moment and they would have walked away with a couple hundred bucks each. But this afternoon, the owner had been minding the store.

Henry Pontain was actually a retired New Orleans cop. He'd worked in the back alleys of our seedy city for something like thirty years before taking an early retirement and opening this place to stay busy and keep some extra dollars and cents rolling in. So Henry wasn't afraid of a couple punks. He'd quietly armed himself when he realized the store was being cased. And when the two approached the cash register and the black guy pulled a gun and began to say "Open the register," Henry didn't miss a beat. He pulled the gun out from beneath the counter and fired.

The bullet caught the guy right in the shoulder, just as he'd intended. But as the bullet hit, the guy squeezed off a shot that got Henry in the chest. The white guy apparently started screaming,

"Oh my god, oh my god," as he ran for the door, and Henry hit the floor behind the counter. Still, Henry managed to hold the gun up and shot three times in rapid succession right through the barrier. Even with a counter in front of him, he knew exactly where the door was.

One wailing scream told him what he needed to know, and Henry passed out behind the counter with a smile on his face as blood pumped quickly out on the tile beneath him. When he came to twenty minutes later, he was on a stretcher being loaded into an ambulance. The body of the white guy lay still on another stretcher. A trail of blood led out of the store and down the sidewalk outside.

The first response officers rode with Henry in the ambulance and were able to get a description of the incident, which was passed on to me when I arrived.

The trail of blood, unfortunately, disappeared after a couple blocks, and though I scoured the area I couldn't find any other trace. He'd clearly gotten into a car and taken off.

So…back to running down the history on his dead accomplice. Turned out all that padding hadn't helped stop a bullet to the heart through the back. Henry was a crack shot even when he couldn't see what he was shooting at.

It wasn't hard to track down next of kin. I just hated being the one to deliver the message. But if I was going to find a fast trail to his accomplice, I needed to do it. Martin Robbins turned out to be a twenty-six-year-old restaurant server at Luigi's Cafe on Fifteenth Street. He lived with his divorced mother in a two-bedroom, one-bath shack at the lost end of a dead-end street. She came to the door with a towel around her head and an annoyed look on her face. That look didn't get any friendlier when I tried to get her to tell me the name of her son's tall black friend. It really didn't get friendlier when I told her that her son's friend's trigger finger had gotten her son killed.

After that, it was a lot easier to find out the identity of the wounded perp. We found him lying on a beat-up couch in his apartment, holding a hand and a bloody rag over the bullet hole.

Case closed.

★   ★   ★

By the time I got home, it was after dark. The hum of cicadas filled the summer air, and I walked slowly to my side door, partly because I was enjoying the night air, which was finally cooling from the swelter of the day, and partly because I liked to hear the slowly oscillating buzz of the insects. Once I went inside, I'd just be getting ready to go to bed...and that meant getting up again in a few hours to do it all again. I wasn't really ready to start that cycle again, so I moved slow. But the end was inevitable.

I picked up the credit card bill and junk mail from my mailbox and finally walked up the three side steps to the door and let myself in. I flipped on the hall light, and dropped the envelopes on a side table. I'd look at them tomorrow. Maybe.

There were three NOLA IPAs in the refrigerator. I popped the caps on two of them and poured them both into a tall, heavy stein I kept in the freezer. This was a night for a double. Then I walked down the short hallway toward my bedroom. I was going to drink in bed. Probably with the TV on.

Something moved in the shadows at the edge of my bedroom.

I stopped. Took a breath.

Was it my imagination? I was sure I had seen something.

Slowly, I moved backward until my shoulder blades touched the wall. I bent down and set the oversize beer mug on the floor. Then I edged toward my room.

My eyes hung on the edge of the shadow. Waiting for one more shift in the light.

Had I imagined it?

I replayed the moment in my head. I couldn't tell what I had seen. But I was sure that I'd seen something shift suddenly at the doorway to my room.

Another step forward. I was holding my breath. My chest burned, reminding me to inhale.

Something moved in my bedroom; I heard a soft thump.

There was somebody here.

I pulled my service revolver and eased my back along the wall, staying out of sight. When I was alongside the door, I dropped down to a crouch. Idea time. If I could slip into the room and surprise the intruder with the lights, I'd have the jump. He wouldn't expect to suddenly be blinded, while I'd be ready.

The doorjamb melded with my spine as I shifted around the old wood frame. I tried to move slowly, silently, but once I was fully inside, with the faint blue light of the night beaming across the floor from the window near my bed, I had to act.

I reached my hand up and found the switch. And flicked it up. The overhead dome light threw the room into a sudden bright yellow glow.

I jumped up with my gun pointed, two-handed, in front of me.

And saw no one.

My eyes scanned from my dresser to the wall where my *Ex Machina* movie poster hung. I was looking for someone standing up, moving around the room. But then I saw the bed.

I gasped.

In the center of my comforter, there was a writhing mass of black coils. Snakes.

There were at least a dozen thick black snakes moving around where I slept. Probably more. They seethed and spun and wound around a small figure in the center.

A one-foot-tall doll.

A doll I recognized, even though I'd never seen it before. Because the face on the doll was a cutout picture of me.

My face.

The doll was dressed in navy blue pants and jacket, which wasn't me at all, but the photo taped to the face was unmistakable.

It was the same embarrassingly stiff photo that graced my driver's license and the police force website officer roster.

For a moment, I relaxed. There wasn't someone in my bedroom waiting to kill me. The place was empty, except for the things on my bed.

Then something pressed against my ankle, and I jumped.

Two eyes stared up at me from the floor, a thin pink tongue spitting out and back again.

"Goddamn it," I whispered. Why couldn't this have been the chief?

Maybe there was nobody in my room, but somebody had dropped a bucketful of snakes onto my bed. That was a message. I wasn't sure yet what it was supposed to tell me. But it also meant that somebody still could be here. I stiffened and turned back toward the hallway. If someone else was still in my house, I definitely was going to nail them before they did me.

I went into a routine that had been drilled into me for years. Back to the wall, careful steps forward, gun at the ready.

My house was small. There were not many places to hide. I slipped into the bathroom, flipped on the light, stared at the shower curtain and then swiped it aside with one hand.

I almost screamed.

I had expected nothing. It should have been a perfunctory check.

But in the bottom of my shower there were seven snakes. Their heads shifted to stare at me as I opened the curtain and the bathroom lights shone down on them.

"Goddamn it," I said again.

Softly.

Who was fucking in my house? And how had they gotten in? I thought for a moment and confirmed that the front door had been locked when I'd gotten home. They'd have needed a key to throw the bolt. And I didn't exactly hand those out.

I stepped back from the tub, trying to think of who held a key to my place. My wife, of course. But...she was dead, right?

I hadn't given anyone else keys. I hadn't had a strong relationship since the days when I'd dated Amanda. I'd given her a key and never expected that I'd need it back.

My back shifted along the walls as I moved from room to room. It didn't take long to cover them all.

There was nobody here.

After going over the place a second time, I returned to my bedroom. There was still a mass of snakes on the bed. And now that I was looking, a couple moving slowly about on the floor.

That was what had caused the shadow movement I'd seen when I first walked in. A snake on the threshold.

I pulled a hanger from my closet and used it to prod the things aside so that I could get to the doll that they congregated around. The wire of the hanger pressed against them and they squirmed and slithered and moved to get away from the pressure. I watched the heads. I did not want to get bit.

But they seemed largely sedate, tongues slipping in and out silently as they moved away from the wire of my hanger.

I picked up the doll. It had no real hands, just rough-edged sticks for arms that pressed through the sleeves of the small shirt.

It was made of wax. The blue 'policeman' clothes mostly hid how amateurishly it was carved. And the face was a blank flat surface. My picture had been cut out and taped all the way around the blob of wax at the top to make it stay in place.

But what did it mean?

As I asked the question in my head, I saw the white of paper beneath the black scales of my new bedfellows.

"I am not sleeping here," I whispered to the room. And then I used the clothes hanger again to prod the snakes aside. When the center was clear enough to make me feel like I wouldn't get two fangs stuck in my wrist, I reached down and quickly retrieved the paper.

There were three words on the paper, handwritten with a black Sharpie.

Beware the Bite, they said.

When I turned the paper over, there was something else on the other side.

A hastily drawn sketch of a human skull.

Lovely.

My chest felt suddenly tight.

This was a message. And I certainly understood the intent. I wasn't easily threatened. But if I could find out who sent it...I'd have a big leap forward in solving my case.

Of course, the message was absolutely intended to say, 'Leave it alone or die.'

The practical side of me kicked in at that point. I needed to get the snakes off my bed so that I could go to sleep. Because there was nothing I wanted more than to lie down in my bed with the beer I'd left in the hallway and slip off to a fuzzy-brained sleep.

I went out to the hall closet, found my heavy rubber gloves and then reached down and returned to the room with a tall plastic bucket.

"Okay," I said to the writhing black mass of coils interwound on the bed. "Who wants to take a little trip?"

CHAPTER SEVENTEEN

Thursday, August 1

New Moon

Who do you go to when you trust no one? Somebody I had quizzed had clearly not liked my line of questioning and decided to send me a message. But…who? Madeline Lackshire? One of the workers at Eleanor's store? Someone else who I'd interviewed? I'd talked to a dozen or more people who I'd found in the call list on Eleanor's phone. Or, had one of them told someone else and the warning wasn't even from anyone I'd met?

I decided it was time to talk to Renee again. She'd know something about the meaning of the doll that had been left on my bed if nothing else. Plus I needed someone who understood voodoo culture to talk to about all the interviews I'd done.

After work I headed into the Quarter to Eleanor's Arcana. The place was crowded, as usual, and I eased my way around people holding up satchels that boasted various powers, from protection to love potions to good luck. They were all designed to improve someone's life versus ripping someone else's down. Eleanor didn't believe in using voodoo for harm. Though it could certainly be turned that way. That was part of what Madeline had critiqued her over. Clearly, Madeline believed in the power of voodoo for personal gain, regardless of who stood in its way.

And there were many voodoo priestesses – and, I supposed, the male version, houngans – who practiced their religion with a much darker intent than Eleanor ever had.

I picked up a couple of small canvas-wrapped dolls. Their insides were stuffed with moss, and two round black seeds were glued onto the material to serve as eyes. *Let the Tree Children see your path*, a small piece of paper read. It was tied by a thread around the midsection of each doll. These were dolls designed to help when you became mired in self-doubt. They were intended to help 'show you the way' to success, love, career, whatever.

I set them back down, though I would certainly have welcomed some help in finding my way right now. Because I really didn't know where to turn. I was fishing in the dark without bait. I had nothing but a threat.

That thought reminded me of why I was here, and I again looked around the shop. Renee was nowhere to be found.

I went to the front counter and waited until an excited young couple checked out with their new wall hanging. The guy helping them looked high. His hair hung in half-hearted braids held back with a black leather strap. His eyes were droopy, and his voice sounded like he hadn't slept in days.

"How's it going?" I asked.

He looked up and raised an eyebrow. "It would be a lot better if we knew what happened to Eleanor."

I had no good answer for that. Though I had to agree.

"Is Renee working tonight?"

He shook his head. "No man," he said. "That's why I'm stuck here tonight. This day is going to last forever."

"Where is she?" I asked.

"Called in sick," he said. "But she's probably out at a party. It *is* Friday night."

I thanked him and drifted back to the front of the store. It wasn't like Renee to call in; I hoped her husband hadn't beat her up again. Part of me wondered if I should make the drive out to her house, but what was I going to say if he answered the door? 'Hi, I came to see Renee.' That would not help the jealousy factor one bit. There was no excuse that was going to allow another guy to stop at the house and ask for her without her getting in trouble after I was gone.

I walked back out onto the street, which was mobbed with the Friday night tourist trade. I wandered until the street got empty and dark. This stretch usually stopped the less informed tourist from going any further, but I knew better. After a few blocks, you found Lafitte's Blacksmith Bar, which looked like a shack, but was one of the oldest drinking holes in the Quarter. Sometimes, thanks to Yelp, it was jam-packed, but as I reached the end of the block, I saw that for now, at least, it had remained fairly quiet for a Friday. I was able to get a seat at the bar, which didn't happen often. The bartender brought me an Abita Turbodog and a shot of bourbon, and then another round.

And another.

Finally, I paid the tab and got up to walk back to my car. I really didn't want to go home tonight. What if there was another load of snakes waiting for me when I did?

Or something worse.

Plus, my questions hadn't been answered. But Renee wasn't the only one I knew who could answer them. Suddenly my feet changed direction and I headed away from Bourbon toward the water. I thought the store would still be open since it was before eleven.

It was.

The orange glow of Mythologica was strong as I approached. Someone walked out just before I reached the door. I caught it before it completely closed and stepped in. There was still another person browsing inside, but Désirée was behind the register.

"You again," she said. I couldn't tell if she was angry or pleased to see me. Or indifferent.

"I need to talk to you about something," I said. Even as I said it, wasn't sure if this was the right thing. She could have been the very one who sent me the warning. She wore a snake ring, after all. But probably half the voodoo priestesses in New Orleans wore one of those, so that really didn't signify much. She was probably a safe bet.

"What's that?" she said. "We close in fifteen minutes, and I've got someplace I need to be tonight so...."

The hourglass was already low on sand.

"I wanted to ask you about this."

I pulled the doll out of my pocket, and held it out to her. Did her eyes widen slightly when she took it?

Désirée turned it around in her hands, and then looked closely at the head. Then she looked up and stared at my head. Not at my eyes or face, but my hair.

"Is this yours?" she asked. She pointed to the thin strands of black hair that were coiled around the mouth of the doll.

"It could be," I said. "I don't know. It's the right color."

"So, you didn't make this?"

"Me?" I laughed. "No. I came home last night and this was lying on my bed. Surrounded by a dozen black snakes."

This time her eyes did widen. Very carefully, she set the doll down on the counter between us.

"Have you made enemies lately?"

"Why do you ask? What does it mean?"

She pointed at the chest of the doll. "Do you see this spot?"

There was a dark circle on the brown wax of the figure. I nodded.

"That is probably the blood of the priestess who made this doll. It gives the effigy power. The hair is most likely yours. It does look the same color, and if she was in your house, she could easily have found it in your bathroom. She is using it to still your tongue from speaking something. May I remove the photo?"

"Sure."

She carefully slipped it from behind the hair that held it in place. There were crude gouges behind the picture to represent eyeholes and a mouth. Another strand of hair was wound around the eyes there.

"That's what I thought. She has also bound your inner eyes. There is something she wants to hide from your sight and thought and speech. And she is using your own power to keep it from you."

She pointed at the roughly carved legs. "Do you see how the ankles are bound?" There was hair wound there as well. "She hobbles your legs as well as your eyes and mind and heart. All with your own strength...or weakness. I don't know what her spell is calling, only that she is using you to stop you."

"So, what should I do," I asked. "Burn it?"

"Absolutely not." Désirée shook her head vehemently. "We don't know what hex is on this or what she may have hidden inside the figure. It could hold an inner secret curse. Burning it could trigger something that harms you more than hobbles you. However, we can certainly remove the bonds and cleanse it of her outer curse, without worry."

She reached under the counter and came back with a small bowie knife. She pressed it softly to the hair around the legs, sawing gently until it fell to the counter. Then she did the same to the hair around the figure's eyes. When it was all off, she carefully scooped the severed hairs off the counter and dropped them into a small oval bowl. The image of a snake wound all the way around the bowl.

Désirée then picked up a lighter, and used it to ignite a handful of pine needles that she pulled from a jar on a nearby shelf. When their edges flamed up, she dropped them in the bowl with the hair and there was a brief flare of fire. The store filled with the scent of pine and smoke.

"The pine cleanses. The fire neutralizes. The ash that remains is pure."

"That's good, right?"

She gave me a thin smile. "Her block on your senses is removed. Whatever it is she was trying to hold."

Désirée took the photo next, and with the lighter, lit the edges on fire. When the tongues of flame grew, she dropped it, too, in the bowl.

She walked out from behind the counter and disappeared down an aisle. When she came back, she held two vials in her hand. She pulled a small glass stopper from one, and slowly poured the contents over the chest of the wax figure, allowing the runoff to fall on the wood floor of the shop. After a few drops she stopped and rubbed the center of the doll with her finger, loosening the dried blood there. Then she poured more water over it and repeated the action.

"Holy water," she said. "Blessed during a special ceremony in the cathedral."

"They allow voodoo inside St. Louis Cathedral?" I asked.

"I did not say *which* cathedral," she said. And did not elaborate.

Finally, the water slowed, and she laid the doll down. She dabbed it dry with a small towel. Then she uncorked the other vial, and poured two viscous drops of something clear but yellowed onto the chest of the doll. With her finger, she massaged it all across the surface of the figure. "The oil of catechumens," she explained. "In this your effigy is reborn, freed of all evil holds that may be upon it."

She then wrapped it in a paper towel and handed it back to me.

"Keep this safe," she said. "It is now under your power, not hers. Keep it close to you, and it cannot be reclaimed."

"Thank you," I said. "Can I ask one more question?"

She raised an eyebrow, as if to say, 'Make it fast.'

"Can you tell me anything about the Black Seduction or the Midnight Loa?"

Désirée looked as if she'd been slapped. Her eyes went wide and her whole body stiffened.

"Why do you ask about those things?"

"A friend of mine has disappeared and someone said she might have been trying to find out about them."

Désirée shook her head vehemently. "Bad juju there. Anyone who calls the Midnight Loa is asking for trouble. Like, more than just death kind of trouble. Horrible pain and torture kind of trouble. The Midnight Loa are the spirits who are most powerful in the dark. The ones who help create the worst curses. They delight in watching people suffer. It's rare, but there still are those who do call upon them, but they risk everything every time they do."

"What is the Dark Seduction?"

"Not anything you want to try," she said. "Just imagine what giving your body over to the Midnight Loa would be like – creatures who relish the ultimate in defilement. Think of what it would be like if razors and hot coals were beneath you as someone pulled your fingernails off with pliers – all at the same time. But the kicker is, all of this would be while you were having an orgasm. The Dark Seduction is a specialty of the Midnight Loa. It supposedly leads to the ultimate in human sensation, combining both pleasure and pain in an explosion of feeling that most people do not survive. Typically, a Black Queen has used the Dark Seduction to punish a lover who has wronged them in some way. The horrible part of it is that the victim has to willingly submit...the lure that is part of the Dark Seduction spell is enough to make the victim ignore the hellish pain that they are agreeing to. There are stories of people trying to stop someone in the lure of a Dark Seduction from walking into torture chambers where the Midnight Loa await with hooks and knives and glass and flames... and the victim will fight viciously to be allowed to walk forward to their certain death. It's not the kind of voodoo you want to play with. In fact, just looking into it can be dangerous. It's not something you should ever speak of out loud. It's just best not to."

The woman who had been browsing when I walked in finally approached the counter at that point with a small book.

"That all for you tonight, Rowan?" Désirée asked.

"Yes," the woman said. She was small, but her hair was big. Wild and red with curls and kinks that seemed untamable. Her eyes looked dark and intense. "I want to travel light." She leaned in closer to the counter and whispered, but I could still make out the words.

"Are you going to the circle tonight?"

Désirée's eyes flashed. She shook her head, just slightly. Then she looked over the woman's shoulder, directly at me. She wasn't saying that she wasn't going to whatever the 'circle' was, she was telling the woman to shut the hell up. Which certainly piqued my curiosity.

I waited until the woman paid and began to walk away.

"What about the snakes that were on my bed with the doll?" I asked.

Désirée shrugged, and began to put things away around the counter. "Snakes and voodoo, voodoo and snakes," she said. "They go hand in hand."

She took the small bowl with the burned hair and pine and walked to the front of the store. When she opened the door, Désirée emptied the bowl on the street, and then returned.

"I need to close up now," she said. "I've done what I know for you. I'd suggest you ask fewer questions and watch your back. Because someone else certainly is."

"I was really hoping that you might—" I began to say, but she cut me off.

"Look, I'm sorry, but I can't be late tonight. Maybe another time?"

She gave me a thin 'we're done now' smile, and I got the hint. This conversation was over.

"Thanks for your help," I said.

Désirée nodded and turned her back to me, picking things up from the floor behind the counter, and then shut down a laptop. I turned away and left the store. The bells jangled behind me as the door shut.

I walked to the end of the block, and turned, but stopped at the edge of the bar on the corner. I leaned against the wall and stared down the street back the way I'd come. Curiosity had me stopped. Locked. Ready.

I wanted to know where Désirée was going after this.

A couple minutes later she exited the store, turned a key in the lock and began to walk down the sidewalk away from me. After she had a decent head start, I began to follow.

If she got into a car, I was screwed.

Luckily, she didn't.

Désirée walked about six blocks and turned right. I could still hear the sound of voices in the distance, but they were growing increasingly far away. I slowed my step again, letting another couple houses come between us. I didn't want her to turn around and see me following her. There was nobody else on the street. If she didn't run, she might mace me.

Her path wound away from the tourist zone and deep into an old neighborhood. She was clearly in a hurry; her pace increased the longer we walked, and I was pretty sure it wasn't because she noticed me. She looked at her phone a couple of times, and each time she began to move a little faster.

Finally, she reached the entrance to a small park. I waited at the gate as she walked past the children's playground and then took a path between two thick stands of trees and disappeared into the shadows.

I slipped around the edges of the park in case she looked behind her. Then I followed her path. The brief copse disappeared quickly, and I found myself standing across the street from a cemetery.

There were houses on either side of the park, but across the street was a long black iron fence. Désirée moved between the tombs inside the fence not too far away. The gate was directly across the street.

Always nice to build a kids' playground adjoining a cemetery, I thought. From birth to death in fifty easy steps.

The whole area was thick with tree cover, and it looked as if the cemetery went on for blocks. I couldn't see houses beyond it, just the dark shadows of trees. They surrounded the cemetery and blotted out the sky with thick branches that also supported long strands of Spanish moss hanging like human hair from nearly every long branch.

Désirée picked her way back and forth between the rows of stone burial places, but then she walked behind a particularly large mausoleum and I didn't see her reappear. It was time to cross the street and head into the cemetery. The gate was open, despite the fact that visiting hours were long over. I moved as fast as I could without running. It was dark, and I didn't want to trip over something and fall face-first on one of the many outcroppings of granite. But I didn't want to lose Désirée either.

In less than a minute, I was standing behind the mausoleum. I peered out along the left side and still didn't see her. Cautiously hugging the wall, I moved along the side of the stone house of the dead. When I reached the back wall, I peered into the dark rows of tombs beyond, searching for any hint of movement. Désirée had been wearing black, which didn't help, but the sky was clear and the light of the moon lent the whole cemetery an eerie pale blue-white glow. I could see the shadows of the trees on the far end where they touched the grass along the wrought-iron fence.

There was no movement there beyond the gentle shaking of the branches in the low breeze.

Where had she gone?

I looked around the back of the mausoleum but nobody was there. There were a couple other granite 'houses' nearby, but I should have been able to see her walking to them from across the street if she had.

What the hell. I looked around again and again, half expecting her to bolt out of the shadows from behind me and hit me over the head for following her.

Then I began to walk across the grass behind the mausoleum. I stopped after four steps.

The ground dropped off midway across the back of the structure.

There were granite steps leading down into the earth behind the house. A rare thing in New Orleans, let alone in a graveyard. Even though we were on higher ground, who would build a below-ground room in a cemetery? I crouched down next to the first step and saw two metal trapdoors had been opened, unveiling the stairs. My guess was this was not the normal state of this place.

Désirée must have descended these stairs. I decided to follow. But before I did, I looked back toward the cemetery gate, making sure that nobody was immediately behind me. If the stairs were open for people to enter for some kind of secret gathering, there could still be people coming after Désirée.

The cemetery and street beyond appeared empty.

I put my foot on the first step, and gingerly made my way down.

There were five steps in one direction, and then five more at a ninety-degree angle. And then three more at another right angle beyond those. As I made the last turn I could finally see the glow of light from within. It was hidden from the opening above by the corkscrewing staircase and a corridor that stretched several yards in another direction just beyond that.

I heard voices coming from the end of the narrow hallway. Just a murmur, but there were people somewhere near. And no place for me to hide if anyone came through here.

Did I bull forward, or go back outside and wait awhile to make sure nobody else was coming? I was torn.

Curiosity won out.

I pressed my back to the cold stone wall and inched my way down the corridor. The ceiling was just inches above my head, and there wasn't enough room for another person to pass by without their chest touching mine. This was a tight hole beneath the crypt above. But why was it here at all?

The light increased with every step.

So did the beat of my heart.

I had a growing sense of unease. Should someone catch me here, I might become the subject, not the observer, of a ritual.

Given the things I had seen of late, I was quite sure that I did not want that fate. I'd seen way too many bloody sheets and disembodied hearts. Not to mention empty skins.

I could hear my breathing, even though I was trying to hold it in. I swear if someone was nearby, they could have heard my heart.

At last, the edge of the short hallway was just inches away. The passageway was probably only about ten feet long, but I swear it took me five minutes to reach the end, I was moving so slowly. I could see now that it opened onto another room. It was a space that seemed much larger than it should have been. It clearly was bigger than the mausoleum above it, which begged the question....

I considered the path I'd taken to get here and realized that this space wasn't even *under* the crypt. The way the stairs and hallway aligned, this was in the clearing to the right of the mausoleum. The two were probably not truly structurally connected at all, I realized. The back of the mausoleum just provided a cover. The entryway was constructed to look like a storage area for the mausoleum, but was, in fact, a standalone underground chapel beneath the cemetery.

Yes. Chapel. I could see the altar at the far end, a low structure covered with a black sheet in front of a black cross that stood floor to low ceiling.

There were eight people inside. All of them had their backs to me. Their hands were joined, and they appeared to be praying, their voices rising and falling in unison in a singsong but serious cadence.

Their attention to the cross in front of them allowed me to peer closer into the space. There was another altar at my end of the underground room. It was stacked with candles and dolls and talismans. But most importantly, it was draped by another black cloth. That could provide my cover. I took a breath, and moved into the back of the room and darted in three steps to crouch behind the back altar.

I held my breath and listened. The chanting continued, uninterrupted. There were no cries of, 'Intruder!' or, 'Get him!' I knew I was safe for the moment. But what if someone came in from the hall? They'd see me hiding back here.

Unless.

I crawled *under* the table, and leaned my back against the side facing the corridor. That should hide me from people walking in. However, now my view of the proceedings ahead of me was blocked by the tablecloth. I reached out and carefully tugged it to the left. When a crack of light was finally exposed, I put my shoe on the bottom of the cloth to hold it in place. I'd exposed just enough of a slit that I could see through it, but should be safe from being seen unless someone was really standing there staring at the crack.

Fingers crossed that didn't happen.

"Hello, my heathens," a male voice suddenly called from behind me.

I'd gotten in place just in time.

Someone new had entered the room. A moment later his legs strolled into view as he crossed the room toward the rest. He was dressed in black from head to toe: black boots, black pants, a black button-down shirt. His hair matched his attire: long, shoulder-length greasy black locks that framed a long thin chin.

The group turned toward him and I could finally see them all now. There was Désirée in the middle, a blond older woman next to her, and a thin black man next to her. Rowan, the fiery redhead from the bookstore, was there too, and a stout bald white guy who looked like he could have just left a biker gang. They shared one thing in common: all were dressed predominantly in black. The biker in a leather jacket, the others in T-shirts or blouses. In a moment, I would learn, that wouldn't matter.

An African-American woman with wide, deep brown eyes, long dreads and a dozen silver and black leather necklaces raised her hands, and the individual conversations that had broken out upon the man's entrance stopped immediately.

"It is time to call the circle together," she said. "The week has passed and now is the time for us to come together and give praise to he who allows us to move and dance without suspicion among those who would cast us out if they knew our true purpose and pledge."

She turned and gestured to the white-haired woman. "Rosalie, have you brought the offering requested tonight?"

"I have," the older woman said. "It is ready on the offering altar."

"Artur, will you light the flame?"

The leather-clad man nodded and bent to the ground.

I saw now that there was a circle of stones near their feet. Inside, a small pile of sticks and brush had been piled. He knelt and held a lighter out to something inside on the floor. Kindling of some kind. Probably paper, because it caught fast. A small flame spiked up and grew larger as it made its way up to the center of the pile. The room filled in seconds with the smell of burning…and in that smell was a heavy scent of some kind of incense. They were not simply burning wood. This was a ceremonial fire.

"Make yourselves ready," she said. "You can't face Antimons in costume. Show yourselves. Your true selves beneath the dark veils. Let us begin."

The group separated, walking to different sides of the room. And then I almost gasped when I realized what they were doing.

Rowan had walked over near my altar. She kicked off her shoes and stood barefoot on the stone ground. Her ankles were delicate and her toes looked creamy and pure as a child's. She was facing toward me, away from the fire. I could see her hands moving near her neck, and then lower. She was unbuttoning her blouse!

She dropped her top on the floor, just a few feet from where I hid. I could see that her shoulder and sides were inked in a thorny tapestry of sinuous scales that bound Frazetta-esque women torn by thorns and facing a leering skull. Rowan was a dark fantasy girl, for sure.

Then she slid the black pants off and stepped out of them. I could see that the creamy complexion of her ankles and feet extended to her legs and midriff. Her tummy was perfect, nearly flat, with just the faintest rounded curves near her thin belly button cleft, where her muscles clenched as she moved. Her skin *glowed*. Unlike a lot of redheads, she had no freckles; her skin was flawless. She stood before me wearing only a tiny black silk brief and matching black bra that didn't appear to be designed to hide much or offer much support, though it did have some kind of lacy edging. With one quick movement she reached behind, unclipped the sheer bra and shrugged it off. Then her fingers slid between the threads that connected the front and back triangles of her panties and slipped the silk across her thighs and knees.

The contrast of the black on her creamy white skin was startling, but not as electric as the look of her hair hanging first across her thighs, and then as she stood, cascading in unruly curls across her breasts. It didn't hide the pale pink areolae. She wasn't 'stacked' but she definitely had enough to want to hold. And the thin vibrant landing strip of hair in the delta between her thighs confirmed that she was a real redhead.

I felt something stirring as I lay there secretly admiring her body and forced myself to look away. Not that it really mattered. Once completely naked, she turned away from me to face the fire. That's when I saw that all around the room, the other eight had done the same. Each had stripped and now, as the last one kicked off underwear, they began to move as one to reunite around the fire.

"Brothers and sisters, we are together again. Join hands and let the circle unite. In our union there is power. In each other, there is power. In our calling of the loa, there is power. In our sacrifices to the elders, there is power. Let us give thanks."

As one, the circle raised their arms in the air, hands clasped in each other's hands. I couldn't help but look for Désirée. She held the hand of the heavyset guy who looked like he'd fit in with a motorcycle gang. Naked, his gut was more obvious, but also obvious was the fact that he could clearly satisfy a woman if he chose to. At the moment, he wasn't trying, but looking at Désirée, I don't know how he restrained himself. She was even better than I'd imagined. Perfectly round rear, large, well-sculpted breasts, and a dark thatch between her thighs that even across the room looked lustrous.

I forced my gaze away from her and realized they all looked pretty good naked. Even the older woman. And the dreadlocked leader...her skin gleamed like dark fire in the light of the flames from the pit. As my attention turned to her, she released the hands of those beside her. She addressed a thin, young-looking black man standing beside her.

"Play for us, Raphael. Bring us to rapture."

He nodded and sat down near the circle next to a small hand drum. With his fingers and palms he began to sketch out a rhythm. As he did, the older woman lifted a golden chalice. She dipped her fingers inside, and spread some kind of liquid across the chest of the biker man. She rubbed it in, moving her hips as she did with the beat. He moved with her, and then when she was done, he took the chalice and returned her attention, smearing something wet across her breasts. They glinted in the firelight as the two of them moved together in the sinuous rhythm of the hand drum.

The chalice then passed to Désirée, who slowly rubbed the liquid — was it oil? — across the biker dude's hairy chest. She didn't confine herself to his chest, however. When his nipples and hair glinted with wetness, she reached down and stroked the heavy head of his manhood. It was no surface pat either; she gyrated her hips in a low circle as her fingers kneaded his balls and the long tube of flesh that was growing even longer above them.

When she was done, he wet both of his hands in the chalice and passed it on, allowing him to place both of his palms on her breasts. He wasn't shy about feeling her up at all. In seconds she gleamed from thighs to neck. The drum beat heavier now, and as all of the assemblage were anointed, they each began to circle another, moving with seductive grinds and swirls. The men and women were not evenly matched; there were only three men. But they were all visibly aroused by the women who danced around them, draping black fingernails across their chests and groins.

The dancing began to grow more frenzied as the drumbeat took a heavier cadence. And slowly the circle began to rotate, both men and women swaying and teasing, touching each other and pulling back as the group circled the flames. Sometimes they reached dangerously close into the fire, and then raked fingernails heated by the flames across whoever danced next to them. The dancing grew wilder and more frenzied and the group began to chant words that sounded foreign. Guttural and strange. The drumbeat rose in pitch and speed until suddenly it stopped with one thunderous crash. There was silence.

"Who will be ridden tonight?" the dreadlocked woman called. The frenzy had been meant to reach this climax apparently.

The cries of, "Me!" were instant and unanimous.

"Who will bend to the heavy prick of Antimons?" she said. This time, the group did not instantly cry out.

"I served him last," the older woman said.

"And I did before her," the motorcycle man announced.

The circle was silent for a minute. I didn't know what was going on, but I could feel there was tension in the air the longer the silence grew.

And then Rowan stepped forward to volunteer. "I will be his mount," she said. Her voice was soft. Maybe it trembled slightly. What the hell were they talking about?

"So be it," the priestess agreed. "Bring the offering."

There was almost an audible exhalation from the rest of the gathering.

The white-haired woman walked toward me. I noticed as her legs drew close, she did not have 'old woman skin'. There were age spots and freckles but…her calves were surprisingly toned and smooth. And as I looked up at her thighs, I realized that she was shaven clean. She was like an ancient child. An old woman-girl. She suddenly seemed strangely exotic.

She removed something from the altar above me, and I held my breath as her knees swiveled slightly, inches from my face. What if she could hear my breath? What if she could hear my heart? I could hear it pounding right now in my ears louder than the drumbeat.

Then her knees turned away and she began to walk back to the group. She held a basket in her hands.

"Place it on the altar of our communal heart," the priestess demanded.

The woman did, and the priestess held her hands in the air. "Now we show our commitment. Our devotion. We call upon the spirits around us. We call upon the dead to lie with the living. Together, we can cross worlds. Together, we can change worlds. Together, we can create a new reality. A place where the power to love and kill is ours to direct."

She turned and walked to the altar and lifted the lid on the basket. Then she reached in with one hand, and pulled out a chicken by the neck. It was alive – fat and covered in white feathers. But it barely struggled in her grasp as she held it aloft so the gathering could all see. The creature had to be drugged...or nearly dead. I could see a foot twitch and a wing flutter a little, but mainly it just hung in her grasp. And it hadn't made a sound previously when it was in the basket apparently right above my head.

"Tonight we accept this offering from Rosalie. It shows our dedication. It shows our affection. It will bring Antimons into our circle once again. And with him on our side, we can do anything."

She held out her free hand in the air and after a moment, the old woman – Rosalie, I guess – stepped forward and handed her a long silver knife.

"Let the mount take her position for our master," she said.

The biker dude and the thin black guy moved to either side of Rowan and took her hands in theirs. Then they led her to the edge of the front altar, and helped lift her to the dais. She leaned back then, with her thin white feet pointing to the ceiling on one end, and her firecracker hair exploding over the white marble like a burst on the other. Her skin glistened and shone in the flickering light of the room. The pale points of her breasts were engorged. She was alert and excited by what was to come. I had to wonder exactly what that was. Where was this ceremony going?

The priestess took a place behind the altar with the chicken and held the knife to its neck. "It is time," she said.

The drum began to beat again and the room echoed with energy. The priestess swayed to the slowly swelling rhythm, and began to speak in a language I did not understand. Twisted phrases and strange syllables.

The rest of the group gathered on either side of her, and reached out to place their hands around the altar. They formed a semicircle, the only open end facing me because there were not enough of them to completely close the circle.

The priestess continued to call out in a singsong chant. It sounded something like, "*Aben dou, nopen touley serenado ische two. Ine maistros baey.*"

The group answered her as one with a single word. "*Bonete!*"

There was more; strange phrases and gestures with the knife, and each time the room echoed at the end with, "*Bonete!*"

It was clear that this was not a one-off thing; they had all participated in this ceremony before. After several rounds, the priestess held the knife against the chicken's throat. The creature seemed to sense the danger finally, and a single wing tried to flap in her grasp. But its fate was decided hours ago, clearly. The priestess dragged the knife hard against its throat and with a spray of red, the poor bird was cut.

But that wasn't the end of it.

The priestess held the still-trembling body of the creature above the woman on the altar as blood spurted and sprayed and rained down on her glistening chest.

There were foreign words and the dramatic wave of a dying chicken that suddenly thrashed in the air seconds after it was completely too late, and Rowan's face and chest and belly were soon dotted and spattered with red blood.

The group all cried out a ceremonial word that sounded like something from a Satanic mass or a druid chant. And then the priestess called out in a loud voice, "Antimons."

And the assemblage echoed her.

The call and response happened several times, and I was beginning to wonder what the point of this all was when Rowan's body suddenly convulsed on the altar.

That's when it really got strange.

Rowan's toes began to shift right and left, as if she was dancing. And then her legs suddenly pulled up; her knees rose in the air and her legs spread as her arms lifted.

"Take me, my lord," she cried out.

It would have been slightly comical, except that her knees appeared to be swept to each side, as if a vast weight had suddenly lain down on top of her. At the same time, I could see her stomach and chest flatten, and her face turn from a welcoming to a fearful visage. Her arms stretched out from the altar, no longer in a 'take me' position, but rather, in a 'you're crushing me' position.

The spray of her hair spontaneously lifted from the side of the altar, as if someone had reached behind her head and gathered all of her hair in one hand to pull. It rose in the air like a rope, and Rowan's mouth pulled apart. I could see her teeth snap open, and the room was filled with a horrible scream.

That's when I noticed her hips start to buck.

Her buttocks smashed hard to the marble and then rebounded, again and again. It was clear what was happening, as her breasts and body flattened and rose, and her screams came in an increasingly rhythmic cadence.

Something invisible, and apparently cruel, was fucking the shit out of her.

The crowd around the altar were not sympathetic. A low chant of, "Antimons," began. The group began to pair off, women on women and women on men, each touching and teasing the person next to them, as they repeatedly called the name of their loa.

It apparently responded, because their 'mount' only cried out louder and louder.

I wasn't sure where this was going, but it occurred to me suddenly that I didn't want to be here when it ended.

Because at a certain point, I would have no hope of getting back out of here unseen.

Or, I could stay behind and likely be locked into this underground chapel until next week; because I'm sure they didn't leave it wide open for just anyone to wander in.

I decided to leave.

The group were all reasonably occupied, kissing and touching each other as the woman on the altar screamed in the middle of them. I rose in a crouch and readied myself at one end of the altar. Finally, I took a breath and chose one moment. They were all occupied and there wasn't going to be a better time.

I bolted for the corridor.

When I rounded the corner, I stopped and pressed my back to the wall as I listened.

The cries and moans and chants of, "Antimons," continued unabated.

They hadn't seen me.

I glanced back to confirm that they all remained occupied and then began to move toward the stairs.

When I got there, I needed to use my phone's flashlight to see where I was going. It was pitch black at the stairwell. I fumbled with the light, but once it came on, I froze.

What was I going to do?

The door to the outside at the top of the stairs was closed. The loud-mouthed last guy down must have pulled it. I climbed all the way up and pressed my hands to the steel doors that lay flat over my head.

They didn't budge.

Fuck. How did I get out of this one?

I have to admit I panicked. I pushed against the door, and then began to pound both hands against it. The only thing that stopped me was when I realized that the people down the hall might hear the sounds and come running.

I held my hands back and forced myself to think. How was the door triggered? What would that last guy probably have to do to open them again? Obviously, they could be opened from within... that's where we all were.

That's when I noticed the steel rod. It crossed the two doors on one side in a small channel.

It was a simple 'last one in' kind of lock mechanism.

I pulled it back and when the rod cleared the hook on one of the doors, I pushed against it with one hand. The door lifted easily.

So. There was no way out without letting the people below know that someone else had been in here. Because...there was no way for me to fasten it after I left.

At the moment, I frankly didn't care.

I pushed the one door open and left the rod half in place. Let them wonder.

I climbed out and set the steel door back down gently until it was closed and I could no longer hear the word 'Antimons' screamed in ecstasy from the corridors below.

"What the fuck were they doing down there?" I whispered as I stood on the edge of the secret door.

After one look around the cemetery, my feet began to move of their own accord. Whatever the hell that was, I wasn't sticking around any longer to find out.

CHAPTER EIGHTEEN

What had I just witnessed?

Was it really voodoo, or just a bunch of kinky degenerates?

Had the redhead really been possessed and 'ridden' by some invisible spirit?

I found it difficult to believe in any of that, and yet...they sure hadn't looked like they were playacting.

Either way, my gut said they weren't the group behind the disappearances. Chicken blood and simulated sex in an underground chamber – however unusual that chamber may have been – didn't seem to have much to do with disembodied human skins and blood-soaked beds. Different level of game entirely.

I couldn't shake the image of the redhead, Rowan, spreading her legs on the altar and looking both afraid and excited at the idea of an invisible thing pressing down upon her. Real or not, the whole thing had been bizarre.

And who had built the underground locked chamber? And for what?

Those questions would remain unanswered for the night. I threaded my way out of the cemetery and back through the park to my car. Now that it was done, the intensity of the last hour caught up with me. My legs felt rubbery. I don't know what I would have done if they'd chased me. I could barely walk, let alone run.

When I finally arrived home, I was yawning every thirty seconds. Still, as I approached my front door and pulled out the key, I hesitated. What if something bad was lying in wait on the other side? Something worse than a few snakes and a wax doll?

I tried to shake the feeling off, and pushed the door open.

It smelled like home. Mildew and old socks.

I closed the door and flipped on the hall light. Nothing jumped out at me. I stared at the floor and the tile floor of the kitchen. There were no snakes or rats or spiders waiting to pounce. I took a breath and walked into the bedroom and clicked on the light.

No snakes.

I walked into the bathroom.

And jumped a foot in the air when something touched my shoulder.

I stepped backward and saw the shadow of two arms and a torso just in front of me.

"Oh my god," I choked. My fingers fumbled and flipped on the wall switch. I knew there was going to be a human skin hung in my bathroom, ghoulishly awaiting my return.

Then I saw that the arms were blue.

It was a shirt I had hung from the shower rod to get the wrinkles out.

I shook my head at the patheticness of it all. Brushed my teeth. And went to bed.

It took a long time for my heart to slow down.

CHAPTER NINETEEN

I didn't go back to the hidden chapel over the next week or two. I wanted to, but the pace of insanity in New Orleans took an upswing, and every day was like a marathon. We'd stopped dragging the swamps looking for bodies, but no other clues surfaced. Day by day, the last full moon receded into memory as the next full moon ticked closer. People put the events that had happened during the last one out of their minds.

Time moves on. Top of mind is what happened today. Or yesterday. Last week is ancient history.

I did make a stop at the county clerk's office, however. I was curious about how and why a cemetery had a large underground room.

"You'll need to come upstairs to the special records room," an old woman with gray, tightly curled hair told me when I asked about how to look up the records on Francesca Cemetery. "Those plans and permits are all still only on paper."

She hobbled out from behind the granite counter and led me past the broad white steps leading up to an elevator at the end of a short hallway instead. My guess was she couldn't easily navigate the steps. She was frustratingly slow just walking on flat ground.

"The more recent records are on the digital reader, right there," she said, and pointed to a computer terminal. "But the original building materials, those are on the shelf." She waddled over to a tall steel bookcase that had hundreds of oblong bound books, and after pointing at three or four, finally nodded and pulled one out.

"Here you are," she said. "Please treat it carefully."

I thanked her and leafed through pages of old yellowed and flaking legal documents before I found what I was looking for.

A letter dated June 23, 1923. It detailed a special construction project funded by the Rivera family.

In memory of Veronica Rivera, the family has requested a special permit to construct a chapel adjoining the Rivera Family Mausoleum. Plans are attached.

I looked at the drawing and shook my head. The plans showed the small stairwell that I'd climbed down the other night, but the underground room only measured twelve by eighteen feet in length. It was the size of a large bedroom underground. The room I had been in had been at least twice that size. In fact...there was a small room at the bottom of the stairs, but then a hallway had opened onto a much larger space.

I leafed through the rest of the documents, but outside of an inspection letter noting that the construction had passed, there was nothing about any changes to the plan. At the back of the sheaf of papers, however, was a handwritten note. *Additional cemetery variance documentation available post 1950 electronically.*

Nothing like keeping it all in one place. I closed the book and went to the digital records station. Calling up Francesca Cemetery brought up five references. The most recent was from three years ago, and again, centered on the Rivera Family Mausoleum.

There wasn't much to go on. A simple line drawing of a much longer space than the original chapel had been. And a simple note: *Underground chapel renovation variance requested by Walter Trask. Existing chapel water-damaged and unsafe. Construction firm will rebuild supports and add an additional space for storage. APPROVED.*

The last sentence made me snort. Storage? What did Trask plan to store underground in a forty-foot room next to a mausoleum? There was nothing else about the secret room. But it wasn't exactly secret, I supposed. It was fully documented in the house of records. Still, something about it seemed strange to me.

★ ★ ★

I had moved to a new barstool at Turtle Bay when I saw her walk in.

There was no mistaking the electric wild hair.

It was Rowan.

I half wondered if she'd recognize me, but while I'd seen plenty of her – in fact, *all* of her – I had to remind myself that she'd walked past me as a customer at an occult bookshop. We'd never spoken. As far as she was concerned, I had no reason to even know her name.

She took a barstool two empty seats down from me, and ordered a Jack and Coke.

I wondered if I should try to talk to her. And knew that there was no way I could not. I had to try.

"Hey," I said after she had taken a couple sips of her drink.

She turned and nodded at me with no recognition. I'm not sure if that was good or bad. I introduced myself and asked if she ever went into Mythologica.

Her lips split into a faint grin, though she also looked faintly puzzled at the same time. "Yes," she said. "It's one of my favorite places."

I met her grin with one of my own. "I thought so," I said. "I was there a couple weeks ago and I swear I saw you."

She shrugged. "Not too surprising. Do you know Désirée?"

"Not well," I said. "But we've talked a couple times. I had an issue I needed her advice on."

Her interest piqued at that.

"What kind of issue?" she asked.

I told her about the snakes and the voodoo doll. And about how Désirée had 'cleansed' my doll of curses.

"She's right," Rowan said. "You just need to be careful that there's not some bomb hidden in that doll. You can't know what its heart holds. Désirée did good to purify the outside, but you never can tell what things lie within."

"That's kind of what she said." I gave her my best clueless look. "I wanted to burn the thing but she said absolutely not."

Her eyes widened and she nodded quickly. "No," she said. "Désirée knows this stuff. You have no idea what could be buried there. Best to leave it alone."

I agreed with her and made other small talk before buying her another drink.

And another.

Turns out, Rowan was a huge fan of *Firefly* and *Farscape*, two of my favorite classic science fiction TV series. Don't ask me how we got on the *F*s. After debating the necessity of wholesomeness in the character of Kaylee from *Firefly* (played by the ultimate 'girl next door' Jewel Staite) we agreed that this was a connection we needed to continue. Rowan texted me so that I'd have her number.

I bought us another round.

We didn't really talk about voodoo that much, in the end. She told

me about her job as a sales associate at a shipping firm near the docks.
I talked about police work. Anyone listening would have been bored
stiff. But I couldn't stop looking at the way twists of her hair ducked
along her shoulder blades and shifted as she laughed. And that faint
crease next to her right eye that dimpled every time I said something
that made her smile.

At some point after 1 a.m., we agreed that it was probably time to
call it a night. There was only one other person left in the joint, and
he was talking to himself at the end of the bar.

"Want me to walk you home?" I asked.

She took a look at the mumbling man at the bar and nodded 'yes.'

They had kept the door and front windows open all night at the
front of the bar, but you could still feel the humidity increase when
we stepped out onto the broken sidewalk outside. It had cooled down
though since I'd arrived, so it actually felt good. Night air always had
a different complexion somehow. I took a deep breath and asked her
which way.

Rowan pointed left and I slipped my arm around her waist. The
two of us may have stumbled a bit, but whenever that happened, one
managed to steady the other. It was a nice feeling, holding each other
up in the middle of the night.

I walked her several blocks until we were into the quiet, dark
shadows of her neighborhood. Small, older brick homes. Lots of trees
and bushes and the hum of late-night locusts. No rats, which is always
a welcome relief after leaving the heart of the Quarter.

When she pointed at a place a couple houses down, and announced
it as her own, I asked her if she wanted me to come in.

"Yeah, I do," she said. Her lower lip puffed out then. "But...no,
you can't."

I frowned. "Why not?" I asked. While her participation in bizarre
voodoo rituals made me a little nervous about getting close to her, I
couldn't deny how attracted I was to her at the same time. Part of me
really wanted to spend the night with her. And honestly, I also really
didn't want to have to consider the idea of walking all the way back to
wherever I'd left my car.

"My husband is home," she said. "I don't think he'd like it too
much if you came upstairs."

That was logic I could understand.

"Gotcha," I said. "But I can't say I'm not disappointed."

She put her hands on my chest and turned her body to face me. Right in front of me.

"I know," she said. "I am too. This was a great night. Would you give me a rain check? Maybe…Wednesday? He's going to be out of town that night, and we could have all the time we want to… talk more."

"If you're sure you want to," I said. I didn't want to pressure her. Lord knows tomorrow morning, she might have a completely different take on this evening. And the paranoid part of me suggested that maybe I'd be better off if she said no.

She nodded quickly, and then bent her head to press her lips to mine. They were warm, and the tongue that slipped past them was even warmer. We stayed locked together like that for minutes, leaning on an old iron fence just down the block from where she apparently lived. I discovered that her hair was surprisingly soft despite its wild kinks and color. And that her body was as curvy as it had seemed on the altar.

I hated it when she finally pulled away.

"I'll text you," she promised. And then turned and slipped away from me to walk two doors down, through a fence and into a heavy dark wooden door.

CHAPTER TWENTY

Wednesday, August 7

First Moon

"What do you make of this?" Aubrey asked me. I'd just walked into the back of a shop near Decatur. The kind that sells T-shirts and gris-gris bags indeterminately. One of the cashiers had instantly ushered me to a doorway in the back. Inside, there was a long narrow dark room. Brick wall on one side, wood on the other. Old stained-wood floor. Odds and ends stacked all around.

But in the center of it all….

A man's body. Or pieces of it anyway.

I'd gotten the call during lunch; it was the kind of call that you wish you had let go to voicemail.

"Who is it?" I asked.

"They called him Flip Frenzie," Aubrey answered. He shrugged and nodded at Tarrington, who was leaning over something in the back of the small room. "He got the call."

I walked over to the other detective and looked over his shoulder. He was gently prodding a human leg with a ballpoint pen. The leg moved. Just a little. Unfortunately, not because it was alive.

"What's the story?" I asked.

Tarrington looked up at me. I couldn't tell if he was a little green, or if that was just the bad lighting in this creepy little back room. Either way, he didn't speak fast.

"Call came in when they opened up this morning," he said. "The staff found the owner back here when they needed some Scotch tape and came looking for a roll. You just don't expect to trip over your boss's left arm when you want a piece of tape."

I got his point. The bloody shoulder stump of Frenzie's arm

lay just in front of a small desk that hugged the long wall of the room.

"I would guess the arm was the least of their concerns," I said.

Tarrington nodded. "Yeah, when they saw the guy's eyes were open and staring at them, they bolted out of this room. One of them left the premises completely and won't come back. Can't say that I blame her."

I shook my head. "No. Can't say that I do either."

I crossed the room and knelt down in front of Flip Frenzie's wide-eyed gaze. Someone had mounted the man's head on a steel spike. It was part of a small palisade made up of a half dozen spikes. It probably had served as a demonstration piece at some point. But now it served as the place where the owner's head was impaled.

The man's mouth hung open. Something dark glinted from within. I reached out with my thumb and forefinger and gently extracted what someone had pushed into his mouth.

It looked like nothing more than a smooth black rock.

"What do you think of this?" I asked, holding the stone up for Tarrington.

The other man looked up from the disembodied leg and shook his head. "They get weirder every damn time," he said.

"Find anything to suggest what the hell this is about?" I asked.

Aubrey piped up then.

"Just this," he said. "It was in the middle of the floor, but I don't think it belonged to the store."

I looked to where he pointed and shook my head almost immediately.

Aubrey's find was a black snake. But this one wasn't alive. It was pinned to a piece of wood, with spikes going through its back every couple inches.

It occurred to me that that was basically what they had done with Frenzie's body as well.

"Who did he piss off?" I whispered.

"Voodoo mafia?" Tarrington asked. He pulled out a cigarette and lit up as he explained. "They sawed him up and stuck the parts on little spikes all around this room."

"Well, I see the leg and arm and head," I said. "But what the hell did they do with the rest of him?"

Tarrington shook his head. "Look up, Detective."

I did, and regretted it instantly.

Spread across the dark wood ceiling was the rest of the body of our man in question. It was stretched tight by metal rods. Or nails. Spikes. I didn't know what to call them. I just knew that right above my head, a man had been nailed to the ceiling, either just before or after the leg and arm on the floor had been chopped off.

This was not the call you want to receive right after lunch.

"Where did they do it?" I asked. The room was not awash in blood spray, so it seemed clear to me that Frenzie had not actually been killed in this room.

Tarrington shrugged and blew a cloud of smoke in my face. "Dunno. Staff says he stayed here late last night. That's all they know."

"Naturally."

I turned over the black rock that had been in the man's mouth. And saw that it was not simply a blank stone. There was an emblem carved into the bottom of the stone. It was faint, but to me, it looked like a snake, coiled in the shape of a nine.

I stared at the thing for a minute and then pocketed it. I didn't know what it meant, but it surely meant something.

And snakes seemed to have been a theme lately.

I walked around the room, but saw nothing of note, other than the lack of blood spray. This was not the murder scene. The fingerprint guys would see if there were any suspicious prints around the body or the room. Until they did their thing there was nothing that I could do.

I walked the perimeter around the leg and arm one more time. And then I gave Tarrington a ten-four.

"Let me know what you find," I said. And left.

There were only so many clues you could find at the scene of the crime. At a certain point, you crafted a theory based on the evidence left behind. And I wasn't one of the guys who were going to discover what was in the room that was traceable. I'd need to wait for their report.

I had the one find in my pocket that could be a clue. And I was going to take that to someone who might know what it was.

CHAPTER TWENTY-ONE

Thursday, August 15

Corn Moon

"Any idea what this could be?" I asked.

I held out the 'snake stone' in my hand over the counter so Désirée could see it.

"Hi," she said. "It's nice to see you again too."

She took the stone from my hand and rolled it around in her palm. When it came to rest with the snake facing upward, her fingers stopped moving it. Instead she brought it closer to her face and stared closer, studying the stone.

Finally, she looked up from her hand with an unreadable expression. "Where did you get this?"

"So you know what it means?"

"Maybe. Where did you find it?"

"In a dead man's mouth," I said.

She nodded.

"Does it mean something?"

She shrugged and handed the stone back to me. Then she stepped out from behind the counter and went down an aisle. She reached up with a key to a locked cabinet in the shelf above her head and brought down a book. She took it back to the register counter and leafed carefully through it, looking for something.

I edged closer to see myself, but she shifted her hips and blocked my view. I could only see glimpses of words and diagrams through the wisps of her hair. After a minute, she turned around with the book in hand, this time letting me see the page she was reading. I could see an illustration of the symbol on the back of the black stone.

"It's a death stone," Désirée said. "So, I would guess a dead man's mouth is one of the most likely places to find one."

Then she quoted something from the book. "The voodoo priestess must soak the stone in the blood of the person she wishes to pass sentence on. Only after the stone has been cured in blood can she use it to provide any otherworldly intervention for her purpose. When the blood of the lamb and the blood of the wolf have been commingled with the sign of the snake, the priestess's intention will be written upon the stone. Placing the stone in the mouth will make the doomed swallow the curse and its potency."

"What book is that from?" I asked.

"Reference guide," she said. "Limited edition."

"Can I take a look?"

She moved it away from me. "These are almost impossible to come by. Nobody touches this but me."

I couldn't read the title on the spine, but I did see a number of symbols embossed on the dark leather binding. The book did look old. Désirée closed the book suddenly and locked it back in the cabinet.

"Okay, then," I said. "Where would someone get one of these 'death stones'?"

She shook her head. "I don't know. I've never actually seen one before."

At that moment, the bells rang at the front door. Someone had just walked in.

I looked and saw a familiar tousle of very red hair. It was Rowan. She wore an emerald-green shirt with a drastically low V, and a black, short skirt. She could have just been working at either a very liberal bank or a very stodgy gentleman's club.

There were neither of those things within the surrounding few blocks.

"Hello, Red," I said as she walked toward us. She looked surprised and then her lips spread into a cautious smile.

"You two know each other?" Désirée said.

"We met at a bar a couple days ago," Rowan said. "And we seemed to hit it off okay."

"Well, you did like *Firefly* and *Farscape*," I said. "Based on that, I think we have a ninety-nine per cent chance of becoming best friends."

"Very possibly," she said. "Except that you were supposed to call or text me by tonight."

I shook my head. "Just the reverse. If you recall, you were trying to limit the incoming messages on your phone?"

Rowan had told me that night that her husband was the jealous type, so…she'd be in touch. And so, I'd waited.

Her eyes widened with remembrance. "I did tell you that. Damnit. Here I've been writing you off."

"When I was just waiting for you," I said.

"I'm so sorry!" She laughed. "Can I make it up to you?"

"If you're still free tonight, sure."

"Just let me get a few things here," she said. "And we can decide what to do. I've got all night."

I couldn't think of more provocative words.

Rowan walked up to the front counter and said something in a low voice to Désirée.

The two of them disappeared around a shelving unit. I waited, pacing back and forth in front of the Satanic shelf yet again. This time I refrained from pulling out any Anton LaVey tomes. I was just reaching for something labeled *Necromonicon Explained*, when a hand brushed my shoulder.

"Are you done here?" Rowan asked.

"Yeah, I think so."

"Wanna buy a girl a drink?"

"Are you thirsty?"

She smiled. "Always."

★   ★   ★

We went to a tiny bar around the corner, The Green Night. It was a long thin bar, darkly lit, with small green lights like fireflies strung all around the back mirror behind the bar itself. They specialized in absinthe, but while Rowan sampled a pour of the green fairy, I went for a bourbon on the rocks. This was definitely not a beer bar.

We sat at the far end of the bar, deep in the shadows. There were only two others there, one of whom was talking quietly but animatedly with the bartender.

"I was hoping we could do this again," I said, after clinking my glass to hers.

"I was too," she agreed. "It's lucky that we happened to be in the same place at the same time again. What brought you to the bookstore tonight?"

"Research," I said. I pulled out the stone and held it out to her.

"Interesting," she said, turning it over. "What did Désirée say about it?"

I told her about the book. She only nodded.

"I wouldn't put that in your mouth if I was you."

I had to laugh. "No, I suppose not."

"Do you believe in voodoo?" she asked.

"I believe that people try to call on spirits for help and power using voodoo rituals," I said.

"That doesn't answer the question." She took a sip of her absinthe, but her eyes never left me.

"I will believe in it when I see it in action," I said.

"Be careful what you wish for."

★　★　★

After three more drinks, I walked her home. She leaned against me now and then and laughed more easily than my quiet jokes deserved. I suppose I leaned on her a time or two as well. We were both feeling no pain.

This time, she led me all the way up the sidewalk, through the wrought-iron gate and up old stone flagstones to a porch wreathed in bougainvillea. Then she fumbled in the shadows with the key to her front door. She dropped it, and I leaned down to pick it up from the stone stoop. When I straightened up, I found her leaning crookedly against the doorframe, watching me with an amused look in her eye.

I turned the key in the lock and the door eased open.

"Will you help me across the threshold?" she said softly.

I put both of my arms around her waist and drew close enough to breathe her breath. "I would love to," I whispered. Then I drew her into a tight hug and lifted her in the air. The twists of her hair tickled my cheeks as I stepped across her doorway and gently kicked the old wooden door closed behind us after I set her down.

"You're a gentleman," she said. She laughed softly, as if that was funny.

"And you're a lady."

Rowan snorted. "Hardly."

She grabbed my arm and pulled me into a sitting room. Then she turned on a table lamp, throwing a dull yellow light across a long velour settee, an old couch with deep red cushions and ornate wooden edging and an equally dark wood bureau. She moved immediately toward that and lifted a panel. I saw that it was, in fact, an old bar. The kind that had doors and lids that folded and closed to hide the fact that it was a bar when the owner didn't want its secrets known. But Rowan showed them to me, gesturing to a row of blue, green and brown bottles.

"What's your pleasure?" she asked. "We have more, if you don't see something here you like."

"Bourbon on the rocks," I said. "I like to stick with a theme."

She nodded. "As do I," she said, pouring something green into a glass. Rowan joined me on the couch and once again, clinked glasses. In moments, the drinks were set aside, and she was in my arms.

"I don't like to be in this place at night alone," she said. "Thanks for coming in with me."

"Happy to," I said. "But your husband..."

"...is gone for a week. Don't worry about him."

"What should I worry about?" I asked.

She raised an eyebrow. "Snakes and voodoo. They'll get you every time."

I kissed her, and her lips were thick and warm. And presently very moist. They parted easily at my touch and we toyed with each other for what seemed like hours, shifting and groping on the couch. Sometimes one of us would take a break to sip from our glass, and then another button would be popped on her shirt, or mine.

At one point, when our glasses were empty and our shirts were on the floor, she suddenly pulled away from me and stood up. Then she grabbed my hand and pulled me after her.

"Stay with me tonight," she said.

Rowan took me up the stairs to the second floor. Down the hall to her bedroom. Like the sitting room, the furniture looked old, ornate.

Dark wooden edges with curved ornate designs. It was an old classic New Orleans home with furnishings that hearkened back to a much earlier period.

There was a mirror behind the bed and another behind the long dresser. If you stood between the bed and the dresser where her gilded hairbrush lay, you could see yourself arcing in an endless chain of reflections.

That effect was exciting when she reached behind and unfastened her bra. It was less so when she helped undo the belt of my pants and those joined her bra.

It didn't matter in a moment, as she pulled me down to her bed and rekindled the deep, desperate kiss we'd begun downstairs. We were both hungry for each other in a way I'd not experienced in a long time. My fingers grasped and kneaded her flesh as I hugged her tight; she responded, digging fingernails into my shoulders and pulling me even closer. I could feel the heat of our bodies building in the place where she ended and I began. Her skin entranced me. Milky-white and perfect in parts, and then wreathed in sensual and occult-themed tattoos around her shoulders and back. I'm not brown-skinned, or even tan, but she made my arms look like coffee when she wrapped hers around me. The curls of her hair looked like flames flickering, as she moved and shifted against me. It was a perfect visual effect because it felt like we were on fire.

Her hands slipped down my waist and gripped my thighs as we kissed on her bed. And then her hands began to move up, until they brushed against the soft skin that I rarely let anyone touch but me. She palmed my penis, drawing her hand up and then around. And then she broke our kiss and bent down to taste me.

I moaned so loud it made her chuckle in the back of her throat, just a little. But that only seemed to give her more energy to deep-throat me. It felt amazing, but I didn't want to be brought to the edge that way. Not the first time.

I pulled her back to my lips and shifted until our hips were touching. She knew what I wanted and didn't hesitate. Her warmth engulfed me again, but different this time. I was inside her with barely a thrust, and she held her body just over mine, her hair cascading down to tickle my face, her breasts hanging low enough that her nipples grazed mine when she shook. When she moved, my entire body felt electrified. She opened her lips at one point to gasp and then dropped her entire weight on me, fastening her lips to mine as she moved her middle faster and closer to me. I could feel her orgasm approaching; her mouth opened and began making fast, tiny cries with every slap of her hips against mine. I couldn't hold back myself any longer.

If there had been anyone in the adjoining rooms, it would have been embarrassing. We both cried out without restraint in the ecstasy of the moment.

When our motions finally slowed and she collapsed to lie against my chest, I felt complete, sated. It was a strange but wonderful feeling. At the end, I'd known Amanda was unhappy, and possibly unfaithful. And that had only made me withdraw from her even more. Tonight, I had just given myself more to Rowan than I had to my wife for months before her disappearance. And I barely knew this girl.

Of course, like Renee, she also wasn't available. This was quite possibly a one-time thing. That thought made my heart contract as if it had been stabbed. Why was life so cruel?

After a while, she rolled off me to lie back with her head on a pillow.

"That was pretty good," she said with feigned nonchalance.

"Pretty good?" I asked. "I think we just won the award for best debut performance."

She raised an eyebrow. "We'll have to do better next time, then. I hate it when the first time is the best and things just go downhill from there."

I took a breath. "I'm not sure I can top that, but I promise to try."

"I did most of the work this time," she said. "Next time you can drive."

"Deal," I said.

She nuzzled my neck. "So, there will be a next time?"

I nodded. "If you'll have me."

"When I find something I like, I don't let it go easily," she said. "So yeah, I'll have you. We'll find a way to make it work."

She was quiet for a couple minutes and both of us just breathed, and gently touched each other. Then she said something I wasn't expecting.

"I might have an idea about where that stone came from," she said.

My whole body tensed. She felt it, I know. She ran two fingers across my forehead and down to my lips. "I didn't really want to tell you before," she said. "And I want to tell you even less now. It could be dangerous."

"It's important that I know," I said. "People are dying, and I need to find a way to stop it."

"Promise me you'll be extra careful if I tell you."

"I have no personal death wish, if that's what you mean," I said. "Of course, I'll be careful."

She brushed a wisp of hair off her eye and pressed her forehead to mine. "There is one group that I know about that practices dark voodoo," she said. "They dance in a secret circle with loa who are cruel and powerful. Not the usual spirits at all. If anyone would know about and use ancient death stones, I'd think it would be them."

"Désirée didn't mention anyone like that when I showed her the stone," I said.

She shifted, pressing her chest against me as she gave my chin a playful kiss.

"Désirée didn't sleep with you."

"Good point."

"There's really a code of silence among mambos," she added. "What you see in the little tourist shops is just the surface of what is going on in bedroom chapels and outdoor rituals in the depths of the swamps. Every priestess has her followers and her own rituals. Do you know about the Seven Sisters?"

I shook my head.

"Eleanor Trevail was one of them," she said. "And yet, she never told you. You see what I mean about the code of silence? There are good reasons to keep things close to the vest. If some of the ceremonies were discovered, well...."

"So, what are the Seven Sisters?"

She rolled off of me to lie on her back. "It goes back a long time," she said. "After Marie Laveau, a lot of people tried to take the title of Voodoo Queen of New Orleans. But none of them could ever achieve the kind of power that Marie held over so many people. In the end, a group who called themselves the Seven Sisters ended up dividing the city between them. They each developed their own rituals and devotions, but they supported each other to the extent that if anyone tried to set up shop in one of their areas, the others would combine forces and force the newcomer to either swear fealty to the Sister who governed voodoo in that area, or leave. They kind of built up a secret society that existed all around New Orleans.

"In time, each grew more powerful and specialized in certain kinds of spells. The Ivory Priestess was the person to go to if you needed talismans for truth and devotion. The Lady of the Rose specialized in love charms. She also staged elaborate ceremonies for newlyweds to bind their souls together in a way that no Catholic ceremony would ever dare to suggest. She maintained that after a couple went through her Swamp Wedding, neither could ever find attraction in any other.

"There was also a Black Queen. She kept her chapel out in the swamplands, away from the city. And it is probably because of her that so many stories have been told about people dying from pins stuck in a doll. She specialized in using dolls to connect and manipulate people. If you had a grudge against someone and a lot of money, she was the one to go see. If you made it out of the swamp after paying her a visit, chances are, whoever you went there to hex wouldn't be so lucky."

"Correct me if I'm wrong, but Marie Laveau died over a hundred years ago," I said.

"Almost 140 years ago," she said. Her toes began stroking my calf, and presently, she shifted her leg over mine, pinning me.

"So how does the divvying up of the city by voodoo queens 140 years ago have anything to do with today?"

"Well, over time, the original Sisters grew old and died...but they always had someone groomed to take their place. So...the Seven Sisters continued to be a thing. The 'hold' they had over different areas has really pretty much disappeared these days, but there still are Seven Sisters. Eleanor, I'm sure it won't surprise you, was the Ivory Priestess."

"Do the seven have meetings? Is it like a voodoo council or something?"

She shook her head. "No, definitely more informal. Barely more than titles at this point, I think."

"Is there still a Black Queen?"

Rowan nodded. Slowly. "Yes."

"Is that who you think made the death stone?"

"Seems like a good bet. But...I don't know how you're going to do anything about it. You can't just walk into her chapel and say, 'Hey, did you stick this rock in a guy's mouth?'"

"I have more tact than that."

She rolled on top of me but this time it wasn't with a come-on look in her eyes. "I don't know how you can approach her and her group. If she knows why you're there, she'll put a curse on you. I know you don't believe much in all of this, but trust me, there are real consequences."

"How do I find her?"

She moved off me again. I could feel the hesitation in her.

"I wish I hadn't said anything."

"Rowan, please. I need to get a clue here. I've been trying to find some reason, some connection behind the disappearances and deaths for weeks."

"I know, and I want to help, I do. That's why I brought it up. But...I don't want you to get hurt. You don't know what you're dealing with here."

"I was friends with Eleanor for years. I have an idea. How do I find the Black Queen?"

"I don't know where her actual chapel is," Rowan said. "She's out in the swamps somewhere. I saw one of her ceremonies once, though. A friend took me because they were having a big ceremony and a lot of people from the city went."

"Do they hold things like that often?"

"Not like the one I went to, but I know that they have meetups. Really all of the priestesses hold them, I think. I go to one myself every week."

I bit my tongue before opening my mouth to say that I'd seen her at one.

"Do you remember where the Black Queen's group meets?"

She shook her head. "Not exactly. I was only there the one time, but it was somewhere in the swamps near a place called Pernaud's Landing."

My eyebrows shot up. That was where the 'skins' had been found.

"How near?"

She shrugged. "It's been a long time. I just remember passing the Landing on the way there."

"Maybe you could take me out there this week to try to find it again," I said.

She looked troubled. "I don't know if I could again; it's been a while. But if we try, we'd have to keep our distance if anyone is there...people don't just walk into these things uninvited."

Rowan rolled back on top of me. "We can talk more about that later. I would like to talk about something else right now, though."

She slipped a tongue into my mouth and cut off any answer I was going to give. Which was okay. I liked the silent conversation we were having. We could talk more about how and when to sneak into a secret voodoo ceremony in the morning.

I slipped my arms around her tiny waist and pulled her close.

We made the most of the nighttime.

CHAPTER TWENTY-TWO

Friday, August 16

Moon enters Pisces

The morning after swam into focus with a throbbing reminder of the night before. My eyes weren't even open yet and I could feel the 'too much bourbon' headache creasing the back half of my skull. My mouth was a desert. I blinked my eyes slowly open and the light of Rowan's window hit me like a spike in the forehead.

I rolled away from it to face her.

But she wasn't there.

The sheets were pulled down to the foot of the bed, as if she'd gotten up to go to the bathroom.

I knew right away that the bathroom was not where she had gone, however.

The pale blue sheets next to me were dark; sodden in crimson.

A heart lay in the middle of the blood.

Motherfucker!

I blinked away the headache and sat up.

"No, no, no!" I cried and punched the pillow in front of me. This couldn't happen to me again. Not twice. I couldn't get over the first one. And now I'd found a woman who really did something for me again and...*bam*. Gone.

Stolen in the darkest hours of night.

I wasn't sure whether to cry or scream. Then it occurred to me that *A*, I was naked at the scene of an unreported crime; and *B*, my phone would soon be going off with reports of more cases just like this. Last night had been the night of the full moon.

I needed a plan.

First, erase the evidence that I'd been here.

There were no security cameras in the house. I'd spent minimal time in any of the rooms of this place outside of this bed. So, I needed to erase any fingerprints or other organic clues. I knelt on my side of the bed and searched for body hair. One by one, I picked up any that I could see. I pulled the covers back and made sure that no others were down near where my feet had been. Then I went to the other side of the bed and did the same. I prayed there were no hairs obscured by the blood, but I damn well wasn't going to stick my fingers in it to find out.

After dropping the hairy evidence in the toilet, I took some toilet paper and wiped down the sink handles and the toilet handle where I may have touched. Then I did the same to the rim of the commode, watching for any errant pubic hairs. I wadded up some more toilet paper and used it to flush the toilet before I dropped the paper into the whirlpool. I performed a similar wipe-down to the nightstand near the bed before leaving the room.

There was a vacuum sitting in an alcove next to her washer and dryer at the end of the hall, which gave me an idea. I pulled the thing back to the bedroom, plugged it in and used the hose to suck any remaining skin or hair particles off the sheets. I had thought about removing the sheets entirely, but then I'd have to dispose of them, which only would make me appear more guilty if they were ever discovered. Plus I'd have to walk out of the house with them in broad daylight. No…a good vacuum seemed like the best bet. Leave it as it was, just hopefully with any residue of my visit removed. After all of the bloody beds they'd found the past three or four months, I doubted if forensics was going to dig too hard into this case evidence anyway. They had a stack of these that were all proving clueless.

Once I put the vacuum back, I went back out to the family room.

I'd sat here on the couch last night. And drank from a glass, which was still sitting where I'd left it, not far from hers. I wiped down the coffee table near where I'd been sitting and then took both of our glasses to the kitchen sink. I washed them both, dried them and found the cabinet of glasses where they belonged to put them away. No reason to leave evidence in the sink that she might have had company. Which sparked a thought.

I'd left my side of the bed looking slept in. Why?

I went back to the bedroom and rearranged the pillows and pulled the sheet and comforter on my side of the bed to cover the area where I'd been, hopefully succeeding in leaving the bed appearing to have been half slept in. Then I walked the place one more time to make sure there were no clues I'd missed.

Once I was satisfied that I'd removed any evidence that I'd been there, I had to figure out how the hell I was going to get out without any neighbors seeing me. The front door seemed like a bad choice, so I looked at the options for walking out the back of the house. There was a door to a patio through the kitchen. I wouldn't be able to throw the deadbolt after myself, but the key lock would allow me to pull the door shut and have it be locked. Before I left, I took one last look at the bedroom. My phone buzzed in my pocket but I ignored it.

How had a night of ecstasy turned into me cleaning off fingerprints and ducking out the back of a house as if I was somehow guilty?

I shook my head. The image of that lump of red muscle lying on the bed committed itself to indelible memory.

That heart had beat so hard against mine just a few hours before. Everything I touched died.

"I'm sorry, Rowan," I whispered. "I'm going to find the Black Queen. And if she's responsible for this, I'm going to make sure she dies."

I peered out the back door and scoped the neighborhood. The small backyard was bordered by high hedges, which played in my favor. I didn't see anyone out in the neighboring yards or note any faces in the surrounding windows. It was still early, and I decided I could take the risk of slipping out the back door, pulling it shut, and finding my way around the edge of the house and away without being seen.

That was the hope anyway.

As soon as I stepped out of the back and pulled the door shut with a faint click, a dog started barking just a yard away.

"Jesus Christ," I whispered. The dog was in the yard to the east of the house, behind a hedge covered in scarlet bougainvillea flowers. I couldn't see it, but it knew exactly where I was. Which meant I needed to get as far away as possible, as fast as possible.

I slipped around the corner of the house and pushed open a wooden gate. Nobody appeared to be out to answer the dog yet. I moved quickly along the edge of the house and then across the neighbor's front yard. I walked down their driveway to the sidewalk and then kept going, moving at a steady, but not frantic pace.

Just a guy out walking. I didn't look back.

After a couple minutes, I took out my phone. There were two voicemails and three texts. I looked at the texts first.

Ribaud — are you awake yet? Check in! We've got bloody beds.

Before that, it was, *Paging my favorite…okay, only…early morning detective.*

And before that, *Rise and shine sleepyhead, time to make the bloody bed. Five of them, so far, to be exact.*

I shook my head. They were all from Grace, the morning dispatcher. My phone said it was only 6:47, and she'd been trying to reach me for the past half hour. So I had no doubt, given the past couple months, that the cases had increased since her first call.

I hit the 'redial' link and put it to my ear. She answered almost immediately.

"There you are! Where have you been?"

"Sleeping," I said. "It's hard to believe, but I like to do that overnight."

I could hear her cluck. "Ain't no rest for the wicked, baby. We've got calls coming in whether it's 4 p.m. or 4 a.m. And this is one busy morning."

"How bad is it?" I asked.

"Bad enough. Two reports before 6 a.m. and three more since. How soon can you be somewhere? I need to get the last couple covered by someone. I'm out of bodies."

"So are these cases," I said.

"Not funny."

"No, I suppose not."

I turned the corner and saw my familiar license plate just ahead. Small favors: I'd parked near the bar last night, and not near her house. That played me well this morning as I didn't want to be seen driving away from her block. I pushed my key into the door of my car as Grace cleared her throat.

"You ready for an address?" she asked. "Because the phone is gonna keep ringin'."

I slid into the driver's seat and picked up the notepad I always kept near me in the car.

"Shoot."

She gave me an address that was probably only five to ten minutes from here, and we hung up.

"Okay," I said. "Time for a day from hell."

I started the engine and eased out onto the empty street. Nobody was moving in the neighborhood yet, and that was all right by me. Hopefully nobody had looked out and noticed the man walking down the block.

★   ★   ★

My first stop for the day was at the kind of house that I'd typically call a mansion. Manicured front landscaping, a big white wooden door with a dramatic overhang, and an honest-to-god brass doorknocker.

A tall, thin Spanish woman answered the door barely ten seconds after I knocked. She was visibly distraught and kept brushing twisted black curls of hair away from her face as she led me into the foyer and down a hall toward the sleeping area.

I had to force myself to pay attention to what she was telling me; this all seemed achingly familiar, and it was easy to let it slip by unheard.

They'd gone to bed early at ten-thirty because he was tired. And she had been annoyed that he didn't want to talk at all about their day or cuddle before drifting off to sleep. He'd rolled over and said good night without even a kiss and she'd been so angry she hadn't slept for an hour. But eventually, she had finally fallen into a sleep full of dark dreams. She'd dreamed inexplicably that her husband was beaten up by a heavyset, dark-skinned man in the back of her church.

"He came out of the shadows while Charles was kneeling and just started beating on him. Over and over again. He didn't have a chance. I mean, he tried. He punched at the guy a few times but I don't think he really hurt the guy at all and after a while, he just tried to shield his head with his hands. The guy didn't stop though, he kept punching and kicking at Charles until in the end, he just fell down right there by the altar. His hands actually fell back on the carpeted step right by where the statue of Christ was. It was as if he was reaching out to God for help in his final moments."

There were tears running down her face as she finished this dream story and motioned for me to step inside a bedroom.

"And then I woke up to see this," she said.

She motioned toward the bed, which, shock, was covered in blood. I made a cursory effort to check it out, walking around the sides, poking at the sheets and noting the organ that sat in the middle of the blood.

I'd seen it all before. I'd lived it myself half an hour ago.

I pulled out my notebook to take her story, but I already knew the drill. She'd woken and found her husband gone. She hadn't heard anything unusual during the night. He had no enemies that she knew of.

I documented all of it, but there was nothing new here. Maybe the lab boys would find something interesting when they sampled the bits left behind on the bed, but I doubted it. After a half hour, I apologized for her loss, answered my phone to take a call sending me to the next crime scene, and headed out.

That was the way the whole day went, really. One sobbing spouse after another.

Every now and then I thought of Rowan. Every case really reminded me of what I had woken up to this morning. Would my presence there somehow get discovered? I knew her husband wouldn't be back for another day, so I had a short reprieve. With any luck, it would simply be added on as an addendum to today's 'massacre/disappearance'. And any traces of me would remain unfound.

I didn't need to be part of this case, any more than I already was.

★　　★　　★

When I finally got home, I logged into my computer and pulled up my internet browser to search for 'New Orleans Black Queen'. Google didn't fail me. Though most of the returns were clearly historical and not likely to point me in a direction that was useful today, I did find one article from three years ago in the *Times Picayune* that referenced the Black Queen.

Picayune Arts Center Celebrates 150 Years of Voodoo

There may not be any zombies, but there will be plenty of voodoo dolls, spell books, love charms and other gris-gris on display this weekend at the Picayune Arts Center. The '150 Years of Voodoo' event will run from 10 a.m. to 5 p.m. on Nov. 15–18.

"The practice of voodoo of course goes back much further than a hundred and fifty years," said Arts Center Curator Millicent Verbow. "But the formal New Orleans tradition really began with the popular ascension of Marie Laveau in the mid to late 1800s. She really was the lightning rod. People of all beliefs went to her for love potions and protections. Before her, voodoo was spoken of in whispers, a backwoods tradition that seemed, to most, unsavory. But with everyone from politicians to housewives seeking Marie's help, the reputation of voodoo slowly changed to become an acceptable option for use in civilized life."

Verbow noted that without Laveau, voodoo might have remained in the swamps. But she drew people from all over New Orleans. After Laveau's death, several of her acolytes fought over the 'business' of voodoo, trying to carve out reputations for themselves. The result was the segmentation of the city into seven quadrants, each with a distinct voodoo 'queen'. Some came from well-known families of the aristocracy, such as Penelope Lemmel, who was known as the Ivory Priestess for her 'white magic'. Griselda Rivera, who was descended from a French duke, held court for many years in the French Quarter as the Lady of the Rose, and people still visit her mausoleum and leave offerings.

I smiled as I read that and recognized the surname of the Lady of the Rose. So...the mausoleum I'd been in belonged to the family of a voodoo queen. That's why the secret room had been built. Those 'secret underground meetings' must stretch all the way back to the 1920s. I wondered if the recent expansion project was funded by a relative. Something else to research. But for the moment, I returned to the article at hand.

None were as charismatic as their teacher and thus, the reign of voodoo went from a single queen to several. That history will be part of the weekend's focus, and at least three of the current reigning queens, descended from the students of Laveau, will be on hand to answer questions.

The current Black Queen, Madeline Lackshire, will provide a demonstration on the use of the voodoo doll....

I stopped and reread the beginning of that sentence.

Madeline Lackshire. I knew that name. It took a minute, but then I remembered why. The chilly woman I'd visited in the Garden District after tracing her address from the contacts on Eleanor Trevail's phone.

So, she was the priestess currently representing the 'dark arts' of voodoo? No wonder she'd been so cool to me. She probably would not welcome the police digging deeply into her spells and rituals. Or...maybe, as Rowan had suggested, she had something to do with all the bloodshed of late.

I thought about that for a minute. I had to go back to her house. Only this time, I might actually leave there with a suspect in handcuffs. But I had to play this right. She'd sent me packing before without telling me a thing that was of use.

A smile crossed my face.

I had an idea.

PART THREE
BLACK QUEEN

CHAPTER TWENTY-THREE

I made a stop at the station before heading to Lackshire's house. I went in the side door, because I really didn't want to be stopped right now. The place was quiet; end of the working day and yesterday there had been a lot of overtime.

The back storage area was always quiet, because hardly anyone ever was in here other than Bernard. Right now, he was leaning way back in a chair behind the tiny metal desk in an alcove surrounded by steel rack shelving units. There was a stack of cardboard boxes behind him that stretched from floor to ceiling. The contents were described in black markers with dates and other tracking numbers. But given that some of them were apparently twenty years old, they probably were never going to be opened again for casework. The boxes on the bottom read 7/98 and 10/01. The cardboard on those had accordioned, smashed down by the boxes on top.

Bernard looked up from the hot rod magazine he was reading and almost fell out of the chair. The magazine landed on the desk in a flurry of pages and he pointed an angry finger at me.

"You!"

He stepped toward me menacingly.

"You were supposed to bring me back food a week ago!"

I put both hands out, palms up. "Whoa, Bernie," I said.

That only made him angrier. "Do *not* call me Bernie," he complained. "Bernie is some dead guy who gets carted around by morons for an hour and a half of time that you will never get back if you choose to suffer through that movie."

"Sorry."

"Do you know what snakes eat? Do you?"

I shook my head.

"They eat each other, Ribaud," he yelled. "Snakes eat bugs and rats and frogs and other snakes. If you had done what you promised and brought back food for them, I wouldn't have had to figure that out on my own."

"I'm sorry, Bernard, I really meant to go to the pet store and—"

"Spare me, man. You didn't do it. You didn't give a shit. And now one of the snakes you left me here as 'evidence' is dead and gone. I've done what I could to keep the others alive."

I put on my best 'I really appreciate it' face, but I've never been well-known for my visible empathy. He probably didn't get it.

"I really appreciate it, Bernard," I said. "And I came to take one off your hands today."

"One? You're going to take one?"

"I guess I could take two?"

"Maybe I won't let you take any," he said. Bernard moved to stand in front of the tank that held the black snakes that I'd rescued from Eleanor's and removed from my house. "How about that? I've been taking care of them all this time. It was me that kept them alive and I don't believe you are ever going to need any of them to turn state's evidence. How about that?"

Clearly, Bernard had some anger issues about the snakes. And perhaps, a touch of something like Stockholm Syndrome.

"What if I took one of them with me, and you take the rest home so that they get the care they need?"

"You're patronizing me."

"No, I'm serious. We're probably not going to need them as evidence. But I do need at least one of them today."

Bernard mulled it over. Then nodded. "Can I keep the tank?"

"Sure."

He reached in and pulled out one black snake which, to me, looked identical to all the rest.

"Here, take Kuma. He's really standoffish and doesn't get along with the rest very well."

"You named them?"

"I had to be able to tell them apart. They each have personalities, you know."

I could feel my eyebrows rising, but I said nothing. Instead, I opened my backpack and let him drop the snake into the open pocket. Then I zipped it closed.

"Thanks," I said. "Any tips on picking him up without getting bit?"

Bernard shrugged. "Be fast and grab him just behind the neck."

"Thanks."

I turned to leave and he stopped me.

"Ribaud," he said.

"Yeah?"

"Kuma likes really small mice. The gray ones."

"Got it."

★   ★   ★

I pulled up in front of Madeline Lackshire's house just after sunset. I had not called ahead, so I didn't know if she was home. I was ready, no matter what. After I reached her doorstep, I opened the backpack and located the head of the black-coiled thing within. I took a breath, counted to three, and went for it.

A second later I was holding a snake by the neck. Its tail slashed back and forth, trying to find purchase. I didn't let it find one. Once I was sure I had it safely trapped, I rang her doorbell with my free hand.

She didn't make me wait long.

I heard her footsteps within, and then the click of the lock turning.

"You again," she said before she'd even finished opening the door.

"Yes," I said. "I brought back something I think you lost."

I held up the snake.

She didn't flinch.

"I don't think I did," she said.

"I've found a lot of these lately," I said. "In a lot of interesting places. I really think you should be more careful of where you leave your pets."

"Again, the snake is not mine," she said. "But please step inside. I'd rather the neighbors not see you waving a serpent at me."

"Thanks," I said, and stepped into the foyer.

"Put that away," she demanded.

"I was hoping you might have a use for him," I said. "He's not terribly friendly."

"Neither am I," she said, looking at me pointedly.

Got it. I dropped the snake into the backpack and zipped up.

"I didn't do my homework enough last time we met," I said. "I didn't realize that you were the Black Queen. Hell, at that point, I didn't even know there *was* a Black Queen."

Her face changed from annoyed to amused.

"You didn't do your homework enough this time, either," she said. "I'm not the Black Queen any longer. I stepped down last year."

I felt something in my chest deflate. I was sure I'd found her out. And actually, I had. But...somehow I still had missed the right connection.

"But you *were* the Black Queen," I said.

Her head moved, almost imperceptibly.

"Why did you step down?"

"There was someone who needed it more than I did," she said. "I had my time. Sometimes you need to know when to walk away."

"Who needed it more than you?" I asked.

"Is that an idle question, or something posed in your official capacity?"

"Well, it's not idle," I said.

"Why are you here, Detective?"

"There have been a lot of murders and disappearances lately, and all the evidence points to someone who has a connection with voodoo. The dark side of voodoo. As the Black Queen, or former Black Queen, I thought you might be able to shed some light on the situation."

I could see she was thinking about it. Conflicted.

"Please," I said. "Somebody left a bunch of snakes in my house. And a voodoo doll on the bed. Someone left snakes at Eleanor Trevail's house the night she disappeared. Just tell me where to go. I need to find the Black Queen...or whoever is responsible for what's going on. It seems like she'd be a pretty good place to start if you really aren't involved."

"I am not involved," she said. Her voice was tight.

"Then help me find who is," I said. "A lot of people have disappeared over the past few months and all we know is that their beds are bloody and a human heart was left behind. The people sleeping next to them never wake up and hear or see anything. Does that sound normal to you?"

"No," she admitted. "But why should I care?"

She had me there. How did you make someone care about other people if their career focus had been death and revenge spells?

At that moment, something chimed from the room beyond. The kitchen, I thought. It sounded like a church organ melded to a cry of orgiastic pain.

"Excuse me," she said and disappeared down the hall. A moment later, I heard the murmur of her voice, talking in a one-sided conversation. I took the opportunity to explore the altar in the living room. I'd sat near it the last time I was here but hadn't really gotten to look close.

It was different from other voodoo altars I'd seen. Usually they were garish, full of beads and tiny dolls and crosses and candles. This one… had bones. Small bones that looked like fingers, and larger ones that looked like the size of a child's arm. There was an S-curved thing that was clearly the spine of some creature. The interlocking vertebrae somehow remained interlocked, though all of the flesh was removed.

Each of these things was tied to something else; beads and string connected the bones to tiny dolls' heads and mummified lizard jaws. There were candles on this altar, but they were strangely shaped. Blobs of red wax that were maybe supposed to be human hearts, and flesh-colored ones that were clearly human sex organs.

There were bits of metal on the table as well…curved steel barbs connected to black leather strings and ragged shards of glass. There were also organic things…mummified bits of flesh that I couldn't identify. I'm not sure I wanted to. I could guess at the origin of a couple of the wrinkled things, and I hoped I was wrong.

At the top of all of this was a statue of the Christ Child. Only, unlike the pure face that such a statue normally radiated, this one appeared to be almost demonic. His gentle smile had been altered to a sneer. And the white drape of his traditional flowing garments was stained and spotted with red. In his hands, someone had attached a bloody head. The neck was ragged and gory, which explained some of the stains on the Savior's robes.

That wasn't the Christ figure you expected to see on an altar.

I walked past the altar to an adjoining room. In most houses, it would be a dining room, but here, it was a dark art gallery. The long walls on either side were completely covered in three-by-five and eight-by-ten photos in frames. There were many with people standing arm-in-arm, but I ignored those. My eye was drawn to the ones where a fire burned in the background. I walked up to one and could clearly see the naked genitals of both the men and the women as they danced around a bonfire.

But it wasn't the nudity that was shocking.

It was the figure on the cross behind the fire.

A naked woman painted in blood hung there, seemingly the center of the circle of dancers.

I looked at another photo, with a similar setup, and realized that the woman on the cross in this image was missing pieces.

Her face looked ragged, as if she'd been dragged down a gravel road.

And her left arm ended in a bloody stump, not a hand.

Above her, the carcass of a goat had been fastened. Its legs were stretched and bound to each of the arms of the cross, with the head of the wood holding the core of the animal in place above her head. But someone had sliced open its middle, and the guts hung loose to drip on the ruined woman's body.

"Jesus," I whispered.

"We don't talk about him much in the Dark Circle," a voice said quietly from behind me. I whirled around. Madeline stood behind me, a black silk robe over her shoulders. She'd worn a simple gray T-shirt and shorts before. Now she looked dramatic instead of comfortable. "There are others that we pray to for help."

"Where does the Black Queen hold her ceremonies now?" I asked.

"Do you really think that I would give you the keys to forbidden knowledge just like that?" she asked.

"I need your help. How can I get it?"

She looked at me for a moment, as if sizing me up.

"Are you saying you'd be willing to do something for my benefit to earn this knowledge?"

I thought for a second. "Sure," I said.

"Come with me," she said. "I just had one of my helpers cancel for today. So you can take his place."

I followed her out of the dining room and into a doorway to the kitchen. She opened a door there that looked like a pantry, but was, in fact, a door to a stairway that led down into the bowels of the house. This place had apparently been dug out below ground level, unlike most homes here. You could feel the dankness as soon as you took three steps down.

At the bottom of the stairs was a cement floor. She kept walking and I followed, until we stepped into a room carved out of the rest of the basement. This room was paneled in pale wood and lit with Christmas lights…only, someone had replaced all of the yellow lights with lights painted black. Kind of against the idea of light, I thought, but I said nothing.

"Take off your clothes," she commanded.

"Wait," I said. "What are we doing here exactly?"

"You said that you would do something for me," she said. "I need someone to take the whip for a time so that my offering will be accepted."

"You're going to whip me so a demon will come?"

"Not a demon," she said. "But something like that."

"I'm not into pain," I said.

"Are you into knowing where the Black Queen meets with her followers?"

I nodded.

"Then take your clothes off and take the lash. I promise I won't leave any *permanent* scars." She grinned, and I wasn't sure from the glint in her eye that I believed the promise.

I thought about it for a long time. She said nothing, just stood there, and watched me. Finally, she tilted her head and said, "Well? This shouldn't take long. I have to get something from you if you're going to get something from me."

"I don't think so," I said.

"Then please see yourself out." She pointed at the stairs.

*   *   *

There are a lot of things I'm not proud of doing, but one at the top of the list is the night that I took my clothes off in front of a demoted voodoo queen and let her whip my back and shoulders with a black leather crop.

Of course I relented.

I needed to get a break in this case. Not just because I was a detective. But because it was personal. I remembered a flash of Rowan's open mouth on the pillow beneath me, and suddenly my mind was made up. If this was the only way…I set the backpack with the snake on the floor to one side and began to strip.

When I was finished, she came to lock my hands into two cuffs that hung from the low ceiling and I declined.

"You're not tying me up," I said.

"If you do not keep still, this entire exercise will be for nothing. It's best if I tie you up."

"I'll be still," I promised. "Take it or leave it."

She shrugged and readied herself with the whip.

That bit of bravado was probably a mistake. Staying still under the flogging of a voodoo queen is one of the hardest things I've ever done. She brought the leather down hard and fast.

Across my shoulders.

Centered on my back. Tickling my ass with an unexpected slap and pain.

I had not come here for this.

But I stood still for it. I wanted the information. Needed it.

Madeline dropped her black robe and I realized that she was naked beneath it. She walked around me, whispering words that sounded foreign, alien. Eventually I tuned out and stopped listening to her. Periodically the small whip in her hand cracked...against my skin. I jumped every time, but I stood still. I would allow myself to be used to a point...if I could get just one clue to help me break into the dark side of this case.

When her hand slipped between my legs, I balked.

She didn't stop mumbling her incantations, but gripped my manhood like a vise instead, to keep me from moving. When I stopped trying to move away, she loosened her grip, and began to use it to her...or my... advantage. Who she was really helping out here was questionable at the moment, because after the whipping and seeing her near-naked...I had certainly been primed.

Her voice rose...as did I. Soon her words were echoing through the basement room. It sounded as if we were in some dark church, with a high priestess saying the Latin Mass. And I suppose, in a way, that's a little bit what was happening. I am embarrassed to admit it, but I closed my eyes and let it happen. There was no point in pulling back now.

I don't think I could have at that point if I'd wanted to.

It had been a hard week and finding some respite of pleasure was not a hard sell, even if it had started with a whipping.

I let go and moaned as I did.

Her voice let out a shriek that complemented my own sounds of orgasm. I opened my eyes then and realized that she was masturbating herself with her free hand. I couldn't tell at first with what. But her hand was wrapped around something and she plunged it hard inside her as she held herself in a half crouch, still milking my final release.

Even as she cranked one hand on me, and rhythmically shoved something inside herself with the other, she kept talking. Her voice was singsong and loud, rising and falling with the crests of our own personal waves. I don't know what language it was, though it sounded both island-accented and yet strangely French.

When her hand finally relaxed its grip on me, she screamed something that sounded almost like, "*La Familiglia Dos!*" and then pulled out the implement she'd been using on herself. My eyes widened as she did. She let go of me and collapsed to her knees, holding a long white thing in the air above her, as if in offering.

A bone.

She'd been masturbating herself with a bone.

Madeline turned toward me then and laid the bone at my feet.

That's when I saw what had been waiting to collect my own offering.

There was a bleached human skull lying on the ground. She must have placed it there after she'd gotten me in position and excited, because I swear it had not been there when I'd undressed.

It was now glistening with the evidence of my orgasm. Pearls speckled the cranium and hollows of the cheeks. There was even a spot on the skull's teeth.

Madeline took her bone and shoved it into the skull's mouth, and then raised the skull in the air.

She began a new chant, and I shook my head in disbelief.

New Orleans is a weird, wild place, but I never really considered that people might be jacking off in their basements with bones in some strange attempt to call to the Old Spirits. And now I was standing here naked participating in just that very thing. I assumed. Unless her real goal was simply to get off. But all the chanting seemed to support the spirit-calling theory.

I watched as she walked, still in a crouch, across the room to an altar. The altar was built around a small table; the center post had impaled a ribcage. On the table above were stacks of bones small and larger. The long ones were tied together with threads or leather straps to create a kind of leaning tower. The bone scaffold held other things. Shriveled bits of blackened flesh hung on tiny hooks screwed into the bones. Dolls' heads.

Necklaces and chains. A heart-shaped brooch with a woman's picture encased within.

Whatever this altar represented, I had a feeling it had not been positive for those who had bits of their lives hanging there still.

It occurred to me that I needed to leave Madeline's home without leaving a piece of myself behind.

But then she placed the skull and the bone on the altar before the eerie scaffold, and I realized that, for better or worse, a piece of me was on that altar. If there was any power in voodoo, I silently prayed that this did not give her some invisible hold over me now.

Madeline kept speaking, her voice a steady, quiet prayer. Suddenly, she tilted her head back and was silent.

Her eyes met mine. They were wide and unblinking. Her mouth opened in a silent scream. I couldn't believe she didn't fall backward the way her spine was arched. But somehow, her body was locked. The only thing about her that moved was her eyes. Just slightly. They didn't blink, but shifted to the left and right.

And then they locked onto mine, and I almost choked.

My throat simply locked shut.

No reason. I swallowed and then…those eyes caught my soul and I couldn't breathe. Actually…I couldn't move. My entire body seemed to go rigid with her gaze.

I tried to move my arm. I tried to lift my leg.

All I could do was stare into Madeline's dark, almost black eyes. After a minute, something like a faint smile colored the corners of her lips.

Was she laughing at me? Certainly, I was not amused by this. Not at all. I struggled to break free of whatever hold she had put on me and it was as if I was encased in lead. Han Solo stuck in the black cast thing to be transported to his torture and death.

Except I was naked and there was no black cast thing. I just couldn't freaking move a muscle. I suddenly, without question, believed very much in the power of voodoo.

Meanwhile, Madeline's head was still tilted dangerously backward. Still staring unblinking at me.

We stayed like that for what seemed like an hour, though it was probably only seconds. I tried to break free again and again, but nothing happened. Everything was still. Unmoving. Except for the faintest smile of a naked voodoo queen, silently laughing at me.

Something broke the silence. A squeal. Like an animal being strangled underwater. It came from Madeline's throat.

And then, just like that, the sound broke through the water and became a scream. As it did, Madeline's head snapped forward.

As it did, my legs suddenly crumpled, and I fell to my knees.

I gasped for breath, but before I caught it, I lifted one arm and then the other into the air, and then raised myself up from the floor and yelled.

"What the hell was that?"

Madeline twisted out of the awkward crouch she had been frozen in, and pulled herself upright. Then she picked up the translucent black silk robe from the floor and drew it back around her, mildly obscuring her nakedness.

I had no such convenience.

"That was a visit from a very good friend of mine," Madeline said.

"Glad I could help." My voice did not sound glad at all.

She grinned. The wrinkles that creased her cheeks and forehead, however, still looked strangely grim.

"So am I."

I stepped a couple feet to my left, picked up my underwear, and stepped into them. A moment later I pulled on my pants and picked up my shirt.

"What just happened?" I asked.

She smiled. And again it looked more wicked than whimsical.

"Nebante came to me. Came in me. He is drawn to the carnal. Like a moth to a flame."

"Is he a demon? A ghost?"

"He is a force."

"Why do you call him? What do you get out of it?"

She shrugged. "Strength. And more."

I buttoned my shirt. "You used me to bring him here. Tell me how to find the Black Queen. Tell me how to get the answers I need."

She nodded. "I will keep our bargain." She drew her silk close, wrapping it tighter around her, which only made the flesh of her breasts and hips protrude and show through more. "Come upstairs."

I followed her back up the steps and through the kitchen to a small alcove near the dining room where a laptop was set up. She sat down in a wooden chair, and launched a web browser. A moment later, Google Maps came to life, and I saw the wide expanse of the New Orleans metro area. She clicked the mouse and the map moved. There was now more green than street grids showing.

A wheel turned next to the computer. And then paper loaded. A spindle turned around and something mechanical shifted back and forth, printing out the map that she'd called up.

When it was done, she pulled it out and with a pen, circled a small green area, far to the right of the tangled roads of the city. I saw Pernaud's Landing noted in the lower right corner.

"Here," she said. "Before midnight on Thursday nights, you will find her and her followers here."

I already knew from Rowan that they met near Pernaud's Landing. But she hadn't known the when or exactly the 'where'.

"Who is she?" I asked. "How will I know her?"

She shook her head. "You'll know. I hope that she is not who you are looking for."

"You can't just introduce me?" I asked.

She laughed. It was the biggest smile I'd seen from her yet.

"Did I say my name was Judas?"

"I need your help," I begged.

"Get out of my house and don't ever come back," she said. "If you do, believe me, you will live, for a little while, to regret it."

I picked up the map and nodded. Then I walked to the front door.

She didn't follow.

I stood for a moment in the empty foyer and considered the events of the last couple hours. I realized I'd left the backpack downstairs and wondered if I should go try to retrieve the snake.

I hesitated, but only for a moment, before I let myself out.

CHAPTER TWENTY-FOUR

Look, there are only so many things you can do after a voodoo queen takes you to her basement and whip-rapes you into performing some bizarre dark magic ritual for her.

You can go out drinking to blackout-forget about it.

You can go find a girl to fuck-you-forget about it.

Or you can just go to bed.

There was a time that I would have hated to have admitted it, but I didn't want to find a girl or go to a bar.... Instead I went home, poured myself a shot of bourbon, and after downing it (and another in short order), I went to bed.

When I woke up, the sun was blazing through my bedroom window.

I felt strangely dirty. Used and sick.

But there was a map lying on the nightstand next to me. I picked it up and looked hard at the circle Madeline had drawn. I hadn't gotten a name, but I had gotten something from the night. Rowan had pointed me in the right direction, but Madeline had told me when to go and given me an exact address to go to. I prayed it really was the thing I needed it to be...because I'd given up too much to get it. Way more than I'd bargained for when I'd gone to that house with a snake.

Poor Kuma.

It took a lot for me to feel bad for a snake but who knows what she'd do with it. I wasn't sure I believed everything that Madeline had told me. But I couldn't deny that she'd made something happen. I suppose she could have drugged me to paralyze me for a few minutes, but...how? Why? And she had been in the same situation.

The more I thought about it, the less it made any sense.

All I knew was where I was going to be on Thursday night.

CHAPTER TWENTY-FIVE

Thursday, August 22

Moon in Taurus

The road out of town was bright with headlights at first. And then less so. After a bit, I realized that I was the only car on the increasingly dark road. There were no streetlights out here. The place that Madeline had marked on the map was a good half hour out of the city. I left downtown after dinner, because I wanted to be in place long before the Black Queen's entourage arrived. If there was an entourage. I had no idea what I was getting into.

The asphalt roads slowly grew narrower, more chewed up by potholes. The shoulders turned from paved asphalt to gravel...and then the roads themselves turned to beds of white rock.

The surroundings changed too; manicured lawns turned to just occasional structures set far back from the weedy ditches, and then the houses disappeared altogether, and I was driving into the swamp. The sides of the road turned to green: vines and trees and brush that threatened to overtake the road itself. I felt claustrophobic after a moment, as the road carved its way into the wild. The light grew dimmer, both from the tree cover, and the time. The night was slipping in.

I had put a pin in the center of Madeline's circle on my phone in Google Maps, so I had exact coordinates for the ritual site. The area around Pernaud's Landing was all overgrown swamp. You could get lost just from walking twenty yards into that mess, so if you didn't know exactly where you were going, you would probably never find it. As I followed the road and wound toward that pinpoint on the map, I saw that I probably wasn't going to be able to drive all the way into the midst of Madeline's circle. The road had already devolved into dirt tracks with rutted roots.

In the end, I probably didn't want to drive all the way to the destination; there was a good chance that I was not going to be welcomed here with open arms. It was probably best to find a pull-off to ditch the car and stay out of sight while the group assembled. Then I'd see how I was going to play it.

There was a small rutted path just ahead. The entry was overgrown with knee-high weeds, so I knew it had not been used in a while. Nothing like taking a chance. I cranked the wheel to the left and pulled off the crappy road to bounce and shake down a crappier one. According to Google Maps, my destination was about a quarter mile ahead and to the right. The path I was on did not show up as a road at all. Probably a long driveway for some abandoned shanty. The car shook and tilted as I bounced over roots and rocks and plowed down heavy stands of grass. Eventually it wound to a clearing.

The house that took up the center of the open but long-overgrown area did not appear to have been lived in for years. The roof was covered in green moss and vines hung from the rusted, collapsing gutters. It was framed in gray wood, and the black shutters near the front windows were sagging dangerously. A wooden porch listed toward the ground on the right side. As I crept closer, I saw that there was a blackened, rotted hole right about where you'd stand if you were going to knock on the front door. A bit of a dissuader for company. I pulled around the side of the place until my car was out of sight from anyone driving down the rutted path I'd just navigated. It didn't look like anyone was likely to be back this way; from the weed cover, this was not a traveled bit of property at all, but best to be safe.

The back of the house bordered a small river. While the brush had been cleared away from the immediate vicinity of the old shack, most of the river's edge was enclosed by a thick growth of twisted, heavy forest. It was impossible to tell at night, but I guessed that the sun barely filtered through the heavy green canopies behind and in front of me. Certainly, the glow of the stars and moon did not get through except for the small space around the house that remained clear of tree cover.

I turned the car off and got out. The air was heavy with humidity and the steady croon of night insects. And the faint gurgle of the nearby waterway. The house rose like a black sentinel against the deep dark blue sky behind me. I walked all the way around and verified that there were no lights coming from anywhere inside. Not that I expected any, but it seemed wise to be sure before I abandoned my car here.

The place that Madeline had sent me to was down the river a bit; according to Google, it was a seven-minute walk. However, I bet that it would take longer, because I doubted that there was a convenient walking path along the tree line. No, this would be a careful navigation through swampland where there were very likely snakes, wild boar, alligators. I didn't want to surprise any of them since that likely wouldn't end well for me.

My cellphone threw a harsh, narrow blue-white LED light on the heavy grass ahead of me, and I made my way along the edge of what had once been a backyard and into the dark shadows on the swamp forest. The grass died away as I wound around tangled roots and ragged bushes toward where Google Maps said I had to go. The walk wasn't as bad as I anticipated, though I kept seeing movement out of the corners of my eyes. I'm sure I was disturbing some critters; I flashed the phone to the right and left and made sure that any in the immediate vicinity knew that someone was coming this way. Fair warning. Leave and be left alone.

Step by step, I crossed the divide between the forgotten house and the circle of the Black Queen. It was a good thing that Madeline had blown up the map of the area as much as she had or I would never have known where to go.

It was after nine o'clock when I finally neared the place. I didn't feel like I was near; one black-trunked tree looks much the same as another in the garish light of a cellphone. But my phone said I was close. I started to move a little faster. Who knew what time they actually started arriving here? The ceremony would be held around midnight, I knew that. But when they began to gather? Impossible to say.

The ground was a maze of roots and soft spots between. I jumped from thick root to root, anxious to reach the clearing I knew had to be just ahead. There was a cluster of trees just a few yards ahead of me, and based on the map, that had to be it.

I didn't run, but I came close.

That's what got me into trouble.

My shoe skidded off a root and slipped into the soft earth. It was swamp. Pure and evil swamp. Instead of stopping on a bit of slimy earth, my foot plunged right through the area between two large roots and sunk about a foot into the peaty mess.

"Goddamn it to hell," I cried out as I lost my balance and fell sideways. My hands slapped the damp ground as a pain shot up around my calf and shin. I'd twisted my ankle as I lost my foot to the suction of the swamp.

"Goddamn it," I swore again, as I pushed myself into a hands-and-knees crouch and crawled forward to drag my foot out of the abyss.

It hurt like a bitch.

I could not afford for it to be broken. There was no way that I was navigating that long stretch of roots and brush back to the car with a broken ankle.

I pulled it forward and then slid around to sit. I ran my hands down my leg to touch my ankle, which was sending out hot spears of pain up my leg. I did not have time for this shit. Not now. Not tonight.

My pantleg was soaked up to the knee and covered in chunks of decayed bark and moss and scum. My hand slid over the material as if my leg had been coated in jelly. When I reached my ankle and squeezed, I let out a cry of pain. Yep, that hurt. I didn't let it end there though. Instead, I massaged the leg up above the ankle, and then moved my way down. It hurt, but a little less than when I'd just grabbed it.

I kept massaging and moving my hand over the end of my leg and little by little the pain faded.

By the time I finally dared to try to stand and put my weight on it, it was feeling a lot better. I grabbed onto a nearby tree trunk to help hold my weight, and carefully stepped down on the foot. A shaft of pain ached up my leg, but it wasn't debilitating. Maybe it was sprained. Maybe (hopefully) not even that.

My only concern was that it might be broken. And since I was able to stagger forward a couple steps on it without it giving way and me ending up back on the ground...I was banking on 'sprain'.

The next few yards went very slowly. I basically propelled myself from tree to tree, carefully grabbing trunk after trunk to support myself as I staggered down the hidden path through the swamp and toward the secret place where the Black Queen danced with her congregation on a Thursday night.

And then suddenly the trees ended. I had come to another clearing, again on the banks of whatever swamp-draining river this was. With the cessation of tree cover, the moonlight finally beamed in, and I could see that this was an obvious gathering point. Unlike the house I'd left, this clearing was kept clear; the grass was cut, and in the middle of it was some kind of stone structure. It looked like a firepit with an altar behind it. As I considered the import, I realized that there were many ways that it could be used in a voodoo ritual.

Speaking of which...there would be one here soon. Presumably. If I'd reached the right place on the right night.

I slid down to the ground in front of an old gnarled tree. I stretched the leg out in front of me, hidden in the long weeds, though I could still very easily feel the throbbing. I hoped that with an hour or so to rest, it would be ready to go once the need arose.

There was a small bush in front of the tree I'd chosen. I positioned myself so that I could sit largely behind the bush (at least from the perspective of anyone in the clearing) and yet see most of what was going on just down the slight hill.

I leaned back and got ready to wait. For all I knew, nobody was going to show up tonight at all. I had a map from a dominatrix/ former voodoo queen and the knowledge of her past experience that something was likely going to happen in this clearing tonight. It could be nothing but a joke at my expense. A part of me wondered if Madeline was going to come walking out of the woods to my right with a long stick and poke me as she laughed. "You think anyone would actually come out to this godforsaken spot with the spiders and snakes on a Thursday night? You're more stupid than I even thought you were the first time we met."

But Madeline did not show up.

The minutes ticked into an hour and then ninety minutes. I had brought mosquito repellant, but I still was swatting them off my arms and legs every couple minutes. I wanted something to happen in the clearing just so that I had a reason to get off the ground.

It was five minutes to eleven when I saw a light bobbing through the trees in the distance. That had to be them. I pulled myself to my feet, leaning hard against (and behind) a large tree trunk at the perimeter of the clearing. The light shifted and weaved, and then finally broke through the brush and I could see that it was held by an older woman. She wore dark clothing but her hair stood out in the night; it was gray and hung in long twists down her shoulders and back. She went straight to the firepit, and I saw then that she carried a bag strapped to her back. She shrugged it off and then emptied its contents into the pit. I saw her pick up and move some things in the pit and then she bent over the area for some time without visibly moving. After a few minutes, she nodded and stood up.

Now I could see what she'd been doing. A flicker of orange flame cut through a dark pile. In a few minutes, the flame spread, and the woman walked back and forth, gathering and adding fuel to the fire.

Soon, two more people joined her – a portly African-American man and a white girl half his size. Even in the minimal light, I could see from the growing blaze that her shoulder-length hair was highlighted in electric blue. They each shrugged backpacks off to the ground, and began pulling things out one after the other and setting them on the stone altar. I couldn't tell from this distance what exactly they were.

More people filed in, all coming from the same direction. There must have been some kind of road with parking space on the other side of that line of trees. By 11:15 there were nearly twenty people milling about the fire, which now had grown to a substantial blaze. Sparks shot out periodically as pockets in the wood opened to the hunger of the flames.

Most of the people gathered were women; from what I could tell, they were of all ages, ranging from twenty- to fifty-somethings. But there were a couple men. And the last one to arrive carried a hefty-looking black satchel that he showed the older woman before setting it in the center of the stone altar.

At eleven-thirty, the clearing was suddenly filled with the slow, rhythmic sound of a hand drum. And then another.

A Creole woman sat nearly naked on one side of the fire, with an ornate-looking drum between her bare legs. She wore a sash around her waist, and a necklace of long ivory shards around her neck. Teeth? Bones? I couldn't tell, but they draped and shivered at the top of her bare breasts as she slapped her hands gently on the drumskin in front of her.

A blond man wearing only a black sash hung with small skulls sat down on the opposite side of the flames from her and began to tap on a drumhead as well.

The older woman moved to stand behind the altar, as the rest of the group milled about. Slowly they began to form a loose circle around the flames.

"It is time to begin," the older woman announced. The murmur of voices ceased almost instantly, and the slow throbbing of the drums was all that could be heard above the buzz of night insects.

"The night is our time," she said. "The walls between worlds grow thin. Raise your voices and let the loa hear you. Tonight, we dance the serpent dance. We ask that Herodeus view our offering, and step through the gates at midnight to join with us in a coupling that will drive our cries through the veil. Call to him now."

"Herodeus, hear us," the group said as one.

"Again," their leader said.

"Herodeus, hear us," they repeated.

"And again," she demanded.

This continued, each repetition growing louder and more urgent.

"Show him that you are ready for the night to take over your heart," the old woman said. "Show him what he can have. What he can take tonight. All he has to do is slip between the worlds. Slip between your legs. Make your offering."

All around the circle, the people began to undress. There were two African-American women, an Indian girl and two white girls on my side of the fire, and each of them dropped their shirts to the ground behind them and flipped the clasps on their bras. But they didn't stop there. In moments their skin was completely bare and exposed, the flicker of the flames glinting off white and ebony flanks alike.

When they had all disrobed, they began to move around the altar. A woman with a tall, kinky afro took the lead with a small hand drum and began to gyrate and twirl. Slowly, the rest followed suit, dipping and throwing their hands in the air before bringing them down to touch their breasts and pubes before twirling and then throwing their heads back and calling out in some language I didn't understand. They cried out names and commands. Sometimes I heard the name of the spirit they petitioned, and sometimes they simply gave out erotic moans. Two of the dark-skinned girls turned toward each other on my side of the flames and began to shake their breasts in an almost frantic shiver. They stepped back from each other, and then forward, pressing their chests together as their hands intertwined and their hips slapped forward and back. It was a sexually charged dance, and I saw that around them, many of the others had followed suit. The clearing was soon alive with grunts and orgasmic screams.

"Take the god's offspring unto yourself and show him your intentions," the leader said, and a black girl stepped naked up to the altar, to where the older woman held the satchel that a man had deposited there earlier.

The girl reached into the bag, and when her hands emerged, she was holding a six-foot-long snake.

"Father Serpent, I serve you in all things, with all of my flesh," the girl called out. The voice sounded familiar. Then she held the snake up above her head and I saw her face. My mouth dropped.

The girl standing naked, holding the snake and proclaiming her servitude, was none other than Renee, from Eleanor's Arcana. I was shocked. What was she doing here, with the Black Queen? Eleanor would never have approved. She used voodoo strictly for white magic. She would never have supported snake dancing.

Renee lowered the snake and draped it around her shoulders, keeping her hands around the neck near its head. Then she began a sensuous dance around the circle, stopping and starting, turning and twirling, pressing the snake to her breasts and kissing its scales. At one point, she stopped and drew the snake between her legs. She held her thighs together and slowly pulled the snake through the cleft below the dark delta of hair. She was anointing the serpent with her vagina. You could see the thing glinting in the firelight as she drew it through and held it up again.

"Herodeus, hear me," she called. "As this snake, your child, touches me, so do I beg for you to touch me. Draw me into your will and let your seed fill me until I burst with your desire."

"Child, come," the old woman said, and Renee shimmied back to the altar. Then she stepped up two blocks of stone set next to the altar, and the old woman and one of the other women took her hand and helped her sit down and then lie back upon the stone.

"The union of the snake brings us to you," the old woman called. "The union of the snake is our union with you. We are open to you. Take us as your own. Inhabit our hearts. Taste our souls. Use our flesh as your own."

On the altar, Renee held the snake to her breasts. Its body twined along her tummy and disappeared between her thighs. The drumming began to grow in volume, and the rest of the assemblage danced with more and more fervor. They cried out words of a song that I did not know, and filed around the altar, each stopping for a moment to fondle both Renee and the serpent.

Soon she was moving her hips in a more than suggestive motion. The snake lay between her thighs, and she humped and ground herself against its sinuous body. The night began to fill with the sounds of her growing passion, small bleating calls of pleasure as the snake rubbed against her and she raised her hips up and down. The dancers began to press the snake against her crotch as they passed, helping her public masturbatory exercise before turning to whoever they were near and grappling with them.

It was obscene. I looked at my phone and nodded. It was 11:59. The energy had grown to a fever pitch just in time for the midnight hour.

As if on cue, the old woman called out above the drumming and chanting and moaning. "It is time," she said. "The hour is here. Call to the god and beg him to be among us this hour."

"Herodeus, see us," she cried out, and the crowd echoed her words.

"Herodeus, take us," she said, and again the response filled the clearing.

"Herodeus, use us now!" she cried.

"Your vessel awaits you," she said then, and held her hands in the air to the night sky. "Fill her body with your need."

Suddenly Renee cried out, a long, painful scream. And then she screamed one word.

"Yessss!"

Her hips began to shake violently, her ass slamming again and again to the stone altar so hard I could hear the slaps of her flesh above the drumming. She shook and gyrated so hard that three members of the entourage stopped their own dancing and took hold of her arms and a leg to keep her from throwing herself off the altar and into the fire.

"Yes," the older woman called out. "Use your vessel as you will. Fill your need in her, and grant us your presence for this hour. We live to serve you, and in serving, we fulfill ourselves."

The writhing on the altar came to a pinnacle at that moment, and Renee suddenly sat up, her eyes wide, and screamed, "The god is inside me! The world is on fire. My body burns...for him...for all of you."

And then she slid off the altar, leaving the snake behind. She stood before the flames, and one by one each of the group, still dancing to the tribal beat, moved toward her. She swept each of them into her embrace with eager arms, kissing and grabbing at them as if they were long-lost lovers just reunited.

One of the men picked her up, hugging her tight to his chest as he walked away from the fire and laid her down in the grass. He joined her, and the rest of the group came to them as well. I could see him on his hands and knees over her, and then the circle closed, and I could only get glimpses of Renee on the ground on her back. Every time I did see through the legs enough to spot her, a different body lay on top of hers.

A voice suddenly spoke. It was not in the clearing, but just a foot or two behind me.

"I don't think you belong here."

I turned to see the big burly black guy standing there, stark naked, with his hands on his hips.

He was far enough away that I had a chance still to escape his grasp. I turned to dart past him, but I barely made it two steps. As soon as I put my left foot down, it collapsed underneath me. For a moment I'd forgotten the sprain. My chance was gone.

Two hands grabbed me underneath my arms and hefted me off the ground. I kicked at him with my good foot, but one of those hands suddenly grabbed me around the neck. "Keep it up, and I'll strangle you before you even have a chance to explain what you're doing here."

I stopped struggling.

He marched me right into the clearing and into the heart of the ceremony.

CHAPTER TWENTY-SIX

"Charlaine Marie, I found this man over in the trees, spying on us." The burly naked man held me in front of the old woman at the altar. I don't think the rest of the group even noticed what was going on; they still moved in a moaning circle around Renee.

The voodoo queen's eyes flashed with irritation as she looked me over slowly. I felt as if she was spitting on me with her gaze. How dare I interrupt her ritual?

"Why are you here?" she asked finally. "This is a special ceremony night for us. I will not have anyone ruin it."

"I'm here to see you," I said. "You are the Black Queen, aren't you?"

She raised an eyebrow, but didn't answer me. Instead, she looked up at the big guy. "Tie him up for now. We'll deal with him later."

I don't know where the bonds came from, but a moment later he was wrapping my wrists in twine, pinned behind my back. When that was painfully tight, he bound my ankles. And then he laid me down next to the altar.

That was all right, I thought. While everyone else was out front, dancing around like a bunch of hippie sex maniacs, I could at least roll my way across the clearing and back to the trees. Then I'd be able to get myself upright, and hobble back to my car.

Before I was even finished with that thought, he slipped a piece of rope between my legs and pulled it back to a stone buttress beneath the altar. There was a gap between it and the stone above, and he used it to anchor the rope.

I was bound to the altar itself. I wasn't going anywhere.

Instead, I'd be forced to observe the perverted ceremony they were in the midst of. I kicked my feet against the altar, ignoring the jolt of pain that went up my left leg, and tried to angle myself to see Renee out on the grass, where she engaged in a ceremonial orgy of men and women.

And then the old woman took even that away.

"Blindfold him, Effram."

A minute later, my view of the proceedings ended, and for the next hour, I could only hear moans and screams and singsong prayers as the drumbeats grew in volume and speed.

Charlaine Marie talked about a sacred doll at one point, and how, with 'his' permission, they could keep a piece of the loa with them at all times. A piece to grant them power, and a piece that kept the loa hooked into them, so that he could always cross over to this world when he wanted. I guess that was supposed to be a win-win.

And then there was talk of giving someone to the god. I couldn't make out exactly what she was talking about, but the people in the clearing all drew close. I could hear their voices and breathing and feet on the ground nearby.

Charlaine Marie said a bunch of words in a foreign tongue; it sounded like, "*Masacresces!*" and then called out something else out to the crowd, who all screamed, "Yes!"

"Do you offer Mathias, then?" she asked.

Again, the crowd screamed yes.

There was some kind of a scuffling, people moving around near the altar, crowding close.

"Do you offer?" Charlaine Marie cried.

"Yes!" the crowd answered.

A man's frightened voice screamed, "No!"

"Then we give this blood to Herodeus!"

A second later, there was a horrible scream, and then a cheer from the crowd around me.

Charlaine Marie began to chant something guttural. I couldn't make out the words, but they were foul in any language. I could almost see her eyes wide and white as she spoke the evil syllables.

"It is done," she said at the end. They were the only three words I understood.

★   ★   ★

Eventually the drumbeats slowed, and the call-and-response between Charlaine Marie and her acolytes ended. The sounds of normal chatter began to grow. Someone grabbed me by the arm and yanked me to a sitting position. A moment later, the blindfold was pulled off my head, and hands grabbed both of my arms and hefted me up and onto my feet.

"Why are you here?" Charlaine Marie demanded. She stood next to me with her arms folded, a scowl on her face.

"I was looking for the Black Queen," I said.

"Who told you we would be here tonight?" she asked.

I wasn't going to finger Madeline. So, I really had no answer for this one.

"Lucky guess?"

Someone slapped me in the back of the head for that. I stumbled and fell against the altar. The stone was cold *and* wet. I looked at my arm, and it was smeared in something that looked red.

"Ribaud, is that you?"

Renee had finally noticed that I was here. I turned to see her walking around the fire still buttoning her shirt.

"What are you doing here?" she asked. "How much did you see?" Her face suddenly changed. "Oh my god, did you see me do the snake dance?"

I nodded, and I swear she blushed. Amusing considering we'd gone to bed together in the past, and she did that dance in front of lots of people.

"I needed to find the Black Queen, to find out about what might be a voodoo curse," I said, putting it all out there.

Charlaine Marie ignored that. She had a new target. "You know this man?" she asked Renee.

Renee nodded. "He used to come into the store all the time."

"Did you tell him that we would be here, tonight?"

"No!" she insisted. "I would never do that."

"Ever? Did you ever hint that you might not be able to see him because this night was locked out for rituals he could not be a part of?"

She shook her head. "I never did. You have to trust me," she said. "Would I have opened myself for the snake if I didn't give you my all?"

"True," the older woman said. "However, it is highly suspicious that on the night of your sacred dance with Herodeus, a friend of yours was in the trees watching."

She looked at me. "Did you follow her here? Is that how you found us?"

"No," I said. "I've been researching you for a while now. I staked out this clearing and hoped that tonight would be the night."

"Lies," she said. "Who are you?"

With Renee standing right there, I couldn't very well lie. "My name is Lawrence Ribaud," I said. "I'm a detective with the New Orleans police. I'm investigating a series of what I believe to be murders, only…we don't have actual bodies."

She made a face. "Then it sounds like you don't have much of a case."

"Look," I began, "I don't care what perverted things you do out here at midnight, I just need to talk to you about this case. There have been a lot of mysterious deaths and disappearances lately and whoever is behind them is making it look as if voodoo is to blame. Now, as the Black Queen, if anyone was going to be using voodoo for dark ends, you would know about it, wouldn't you?"

"I don't know everything," she said. Her mouth sounded as if it had gravel in it. "I only know that you are here without my permission."

"Last week, I woke up in bed and the woman I had gone to sleep with wasn't there anymore. Instead, there was just a bloody sheet and what looked like a human heart sitting in the middle of it all. Does this sound like there's nothing to investigate?"

She ignored me, and pointed to two people nearby. "Ben, Silvie…I want to take our new friend here back to the house. I think there are some friends there that he should meet."

Hands grabbed my arms on either side, and we began walking toward the tree line where I'd originally been hiding. Charlaine Marie followed; she said nothing, but simply walked alongside us.

Once inside the tree line, the two guided me back along the route I'd taken originally to get there. Sometimes I stumbled because of my foot, but it seemed to take much less time to reach the clearing of the old abandoned house than it had when I'd first come here.

I saw my car just a few yards away. If I could take them by surprise and make a break for it, I might be in the driver's seat before they could catch up.

They led me to a sagging porch and each of them took a step up, pulling me along. They pushed me forward to the next step, and as I set my injured leg down, I kicked backward with my good one and yanked my arms free at the same moment of surprise. One set of hands grabbed my arm tighter, but the man I kicked let go, as he lost his balance and fell backward.

I threw my weight against the man who held on, forcing him off balance so that he had to grab for the railing to keep from falling.

That was enough to lift his grip from my arm and I used the advantage, pushing off him to face away from the house. I stepped down the stair and my ankle twinged, but I refused to go down. Instead, I pushed away from the steps, put my good foot down on the leg of the man I'd sent falling backward, and staggered away from both of them toward my car.

What I didn't count on was the voodoo queen herself getting involved.

As I threw myself past her, she punched me in the gut. The wind went out of me instantly. I almost lost my balance, but somehow managed to remain standing. The moment lost trying to recover my breath cost me, however. I limped a few steps to my car, put one hand on the front hood to steady myself and shoved the other in my pants pocket to pull out my keys.

Just as my fingers closed on the cool metal, something slammed into my calves. I held onto the hood of the car, but then someone yanked my left elbow. Two hands fastened onto my ankles and I knew I was trapped. The guy below held on fast, and the guy holding my elbow used his free hand to punch me in the jaw.

There were extra stars in the sky for a second too long.

By the time I could consider fighting back, I'd been dragged right back to the stairs at the back of the old abandoned house.

But clearly, it wasn't really abandoned.

Charlaine Marie had a key.

She opened the back door and stepped inside. Her two henchmen dragged me toward the door. I tried to yank my arms out of their grip, but they weren't going to be fooled a second time. They held fast and dragged my feet across the threshold. Inside, the voodoo queen was lighting candles. They were spaced throughout the back sitting room on tables and wall sconces. She disappeared down a dark hall, and presently I saw a dull orange glow light the walls there as well.

"Come," Charlaine Marie called.

I did. Though it was against my will. The two dragged me across the dusty wood plank floor because I refused to move my feet. My resistance didn't matter. They were both taller guys and they hefted me up until my toes dragged. I couldn't stop them from taking me where they wanted if I tried. They led me down the hall and into an old kitchen. Charlaine Marie had already vanished, but I soon saw to where.

They pushed me through an old doorway down five steps into a sunken living room. There were candles already lit below. While the steps were dark, I could see where we were headed. Orange flickers moved against the wall at the base of the stairs. I couldn't concentrate too hard on them because now Charlaine Marie's two thugs were dragging me down the steps. When we reached the bottom, I understood why we were here.

The walls were all painted in a deep shade of crimson. A handful of candles had been lit around the room on the walls – they were housed in golden sconces. The place looked like a macabre museum. There were three human skeletons somehow held together and posed along the walls. One of them held its arms above its skull. Another was crouched, with its hands propped on its knees as the third stood immediately behind it, pelvis bone pushed out.

Death porn. I got the gist.

There was an altar on one side of the room. The statue of the Infant Jesus had been spray-painted black.

Around the statue was an assortment of bric-a-brac, from Barbie dolls to condoms. There were other things too, stones and pieces of what looked like wood, and maybe bones, and other strange things – bottlecaps, hairbrushes, and more. None of it made sense. There was a pair of discarded underwear lying next to what appeared to be a diploma.

I didn't get a chance to study any of it, as I was dragged across the room to where Charlaine Marie waited.

She held out a leather strap, attached to a chain on the red-painted wall. My left wrist was suddenly enclosed. And then a similar bond clasped my right.

The three of them stepped back.

"You were interested in keeping an eye on things," Charlaine Marie said. "Now you can. This house is not completely abandoned. Enjoy your night."

She began to walk away. But then she stopped and turned her head back to me with a smile.

"By the way, you should do your best to make friends. If you get bitten tonight, you'll be dead in fifteen minutes."

Then she blew out two of the candles that illuminated the room, lowering the light. The two men who'd dragged me here followed. She stopped on one side of the room and reached into a box. She pulled out something like a scoop and flung whatever she had drawn out of the box onto the floor. I couldn't see what it was, because a small table blocked my view. But I could see her smile. And I could hear her words. "That should whet the appetite," she said. I didn't know what she meant, and she didn't stop to explain. She and her henchmen headed to the stairs.

In a moment, I was alone in a silent room. I heard the door click shut above.

Part of me wanted to scream in the sudden quiet, but I knew better. That would only waste my energy, and my voice. Nobody who could hear was going to come back.

Instead, I leaned back against the wall and studied the room further. There were only three candles still lit in the empty room, and the flicker of those flames shivered steadily across the floor.

So did…other things.

I caught it first out of the corner of my eye. Something squirming on the floor. A shadow.

Something moved on the opposite side of the room as well.

Another shadow.

My eyes roved from one side to the other.

And then I understood what it was that Charlaine Marie wanted me to see.

Snakes.

As the light diminished and the people closed the door to the rest of the house, the snakes were squirming out from the corners. Apparently, they only came out at night.

And now was the night.

Charlaine Marie had left just enough light to see them as they came. None of them moved fast, but dozens of bodies were slowly slithering across the floor. Tails undulating in S shapes. Scales reflecting the orange glow of the candle flame. I watched one squirming across the floor toward my feet. I found myself praying that it would veer off before it reached me.

Would kicking one snake attract the interest of the rest? What if it bit me before I completed the kick?

The thing came near the tip of my shoe and stopped. I could see the pale pink of its tongue flicker. I'd heard that snakes use their tongue to sniff the air; was it considering what kind of creature had invaded its hideaway?

Would it bite at my ankles if it decided I was a threat?

I was holding my breath. The room suddenly seemed very warm.

And then the snake turned and began to move off to my right.

I began to breathe again.

But nervously. The floor slowly churned with glinting scales. They made almost no sound, but now and then you could hear the scrape of a tail as it slapped or dragged against something. Whatever Charlaine Marie had thrown on the floor had drawn them out.

With all the motion on the floor, the silence of the room was eerie. Now and then, a board creaked in the house. A scale dragged across the floor. A night bird let out a cry outside in the swamp.

But mostly, I could simply hear myself breathing. The sound was lulling after a while. As I stared at the dark shapes moving slowly around on the floor in front of me, eventually, my eyes began to grow heavy. My fear of fangs slowly diminished as the creatures moved away from my feet. They showed little interest in me, and as time slowly passed, the dark and the quiet and no doubt the stress of the day came down on me. I found myself beginning to doze. My head began to lean and then fall forward to my chest. It happened again and again, and each time I'd jerk awake and scan the room to see if a snake was nearby. That would jar me back fully awake for a couple minutes, but then my eyes would start to close again. It was late. I was exhausted. Soon, I didn't really care about the snakes anymore.

Something creaked beyond the door. Louder than any of the other house noises of the past hour or two. I jolted awake. Had Charlaine Marie come back?

I listened intently and followed the sound as it progressed across the floorboards. A small thump. A creak. And then the pained squeal of an unoiled door hinge opening.

A stair groaned with the weight of someone. Whoever it was moved slowly. They should have been in the room by now. But I could see the edge of the stairway door, and nobody had emerged.

"Ribaud?" a woman's voice called softly across the room.

"I'm here," I answered.

As soon as I did, a head poked past the stairwell door. For a second, I only saw long dark hair and the whites of her eyes. And then she stepped into the room.

"Renee," I called out. "What are you doing here?"

"Shhhh," she hissed and began to move quickly across the room, stepping around the snakes now and then.

"Be careful," I warned. "Don't get bit!"

She shook her head. "We use these snakes in our rituals every week. I know how to handle them. They're not dangerous. She just left you here to scare the shit out of you."

"She was successful," I said.

Renee laughed at that. "You look like you survived okay. Still, I couldn't let her leave you like this," she said. "But she'd wring my neck if she found me here. So we have to move quickly. I don't know if she's planning to come back tonight."

"I'm all for that," I said. "I can't feel my arms."

"That's what you get for spying on me."

"I wasn't spying on you," I said. "I didn't know you'd be here. What the hell *are* you doing here? Black magic isn't your style."

She reached above my shoulders to work on the cuffs on my wrists. Her chest brushed against mine as she did, and her lips were just inches from my face. She looked into my eyes with a gaze that was deadly serious. "You don't know what my style is," she said. "I loved Eleanor. She was one of my best teachers and I enjoyed helping her with her store. But do you think Eleanor's magic was ever strong enough to help me? You know the score. A drink of Tranquility Tea isn't going to fix my life."

"You were fucking a snake," I said. "I don't think that's going to fix anything either. You'll probably catch some disease. Or end up with baby serpents growing inside your belly."

Her hands stopped working on the latch and she stepped back.

"Do you want to get out of here or not?"

"I do."

"Then shut up."

I clamped my lips shut and nodded. The brown pools of her eyes had never looked so serious to me before, even after she'd been crying. I wondered what exactly she was thinking, but I knew she'd never tell. I only hoped she didn't change her mind about setting me free. After staring at me in silence for a few seconds, she reached up again over my shoulders and finished undoing the buckle on my left wrist. My arm dropped limp to my side as soon as she did. A few seconds later, my other arm flopped down as well.

"Thanks," I said, and stepped away from the wall. My bad leg instantly gave out and I collapsed to the ground.

"You're not going to get very far that way," she said. Her hands grabbed me under my armpits and pulled. The sensation was starting to return and her touch was something like a hot brand in the middle of a pincushion.

"Damnit," I swore, as I staggered back to my feet with her help.

"You're messed up," she observed.

"Twisted my ankle, or Charlaine Marie and her boy toys would never have caught me."

"Excuses, excuses."

She started to help me maneuver across the floor. We shifted to the right to avoid four large black snakes that had gathered together.

"What's with the snakes?" I asked.

She shrugged. "They're pets. She feeds them and keeps them here and they help us in the fire circle. They're conduits to those we wish to reach."

"Charlaine Marie left these in Eleanor Trevail's house when she killed her, didn't she?" I asked.

Renee stopped. "Charlaine Marie didn't kill Eleanor," she said. Then she moved us faster toward the stairs.

"How do you know?"

She didn't answer.

"Did she leave some of these snakes in my house?"

"I'm sure that Charlaine Marie has never been to your house."

"You're not answering my questions."

"Maybe you're not asking the right ones."

She pulled me up the stairs. I could move my arms again, but they remained on fire with pins and needles. It was all I could do to keep one wrapped around her shoulders for support.

When we reached the landing, she grabbed me hard around the waist and pulled me up and around the corner. She kicked the basement door shut behind us with one foot.

"Can you drive?" she asked.

I nodded. "My leg's not that bad, I just can't keep my full weight on it. And the feeling in my arms is coming back. Which, by the way, hurts like a bitch."

"Serves you right," she said. "You don't spy on the Black Queen."

"I still want to know what you're doing with her," I said.

She shook her head. "Not now. Not here. We both need to get away from here. She'll notice if I'm gone...and she can never find out that I set you free." Renee turned and grabbed my chin. "Do you understand me? She cannot ever know it was me."

"Got it," I said. "Maybe we could have a drink tomorrow and talk about it?"

"After all the times you've stood me up, now you want to see me?" she said. Then she laughed. It was a bitter sound. "I'll think about it."

She grabbed me by the arm then and moved us to the back door.

"I need to get home," she said. "If he wakes up and I'm not there...I don't know which would be worse. Him or Charlaine Marie."

I stepped gingerly across the old wood porch and down the stairs. She stayed with me until we reached my car, and then dumped my arm from her shoulders. I grabbed on to the trunk to steady myself.

"Do you have your keys?" she asked.

I reached into my pocket and pulled them out.

"Good. Get out of here."

With that, she turned and ran around the side of the house. I heard an engine start up just as I eased myself into my own driver's seat. By the time I started the car, and backed up along the side yard to finally reach the driveway, Renee was gone.

I caught a glimpse of red taillights down the gravel path and through the trees.

I gunned the engine and hit the gas to follow.

She was right about one thing. I didn't need to be caught here again.

CHAPTER TWENTY-SEVEN

Friday, August 23

Last Moon in August

The Black Queen knew who I was.

Even after locking the door to my house, that thought made me seriously uneasy. After spending time in her abandoned basement, I had no doubt that she was responsible for putting snakes in my bed. And if she could get into my house before, she had even more reason to do so now.

I kept the bolt drawn on the door, but that didn't really make me feel safe. Could a simple door ever keep one safe from voodoo? I fingered the protection amulet that Eleanor had given me. A silver star with a circle in the middle. I'd worn it around my neck for weeks now, and had nearly forgotten about it. So, I supposedly had some protection from spells. But I doubted that it was enough. It certainly hadn't stopped me from being locked in a basement, though maybe it had protected me from dying there. Regardless, the Black Queen was powerful. And no doubt very angry with me. She would be particularly angry when she discovered I'd escaped from her den of voodoo snakes. Hopefully, I had a few more hours before that happened.

I had to get Renee to open up to me. I would never have guessed that she would be involved with a black voodoo sect. She had always seemed so earthy and wholesome. Not drawn to evil. That had made it even more painful to watch her trying to navigate an abusive marriage. She didn't deserve the shit that she had gone through for him.

And I suppose that explained exactly why she had gravitated to the Black Queen. She wanted to regain some kind of power in her life. Maybe she intended to use the power she gained there against her asshole of a husband. Regardless, the vision of her on a stone altar, fornicating with a snake, not to mention the people of Charlaine Marie's voodoo coven, was still a bitter pill in my throat. How could she, after all the 'good' that Eleanor had taught her?

*   *   *

Ultimately, I was able to sleep that first night, but it was the next that I was worried about. Charlaine Marie would no doubt go back to her basement prison and find that I'd escaped. And that's when she'd turn her voodoo eye on me.

I didn't want that eye to find me.

The one person who could help me the most was no doubt dead. But her husband wasn't.

I pulled up in front of his house at dinner time. The spice of creole cooking wafted through the yard. I couldn't tell if it was from Robert Trevail or the house next door. Either way, it made my stomach growl. I'd never gotten a chance to stop for lunch today.

I stepped up to his front door and rang the bell.

He came to the door in a stained white T-shirt with a rip in the seam under his left armpit. Barefoot in khaki shorts. Sweat beaded on his forehead, and the twisted black curls of his hair looked matted and greasy.

Eleanor's husband looked like hell.

But it was his eyes that drew my concern. They were bloodshot and heavy. There were circles under them, as if he hadn't slept in days.

"You're that detective, aren't you?" he said. His voice sounded vaguely suspicious. "Have you found out something about my Eleanor?"

I shook my head. "Not yet," I said. "Can I come in and talk to you about something, though?"

He hesitated, and then shrugged, as if he had no energy left to fight... anything.

I followed him inside.

It was dark in the house, but he had not put any lights on besides the one next to the couch in the living room. He led me there, and gestured to the cushions for me to sit down. He sat in an old recliner near the couch with a low groan.

"What do you need?" he asked.

"I think I have found the woman who may be behind Eleanor's disappearance," I said.

He looked up at me with interest and attention then.

"Do you know of a woman named Charlaine Marie?"

He cocked one eyebrow. "The Black Queen?"

"So I'm told. I have been investigating a lot of different leads, and I think she might have a connection to this, and the other disappearances I've been investigating. Her focus is dark magic, after all."

He raised an eyebrow, as if to say 'duh', but said nothing, waiting for me to finish my explanation.

"I saw one of her ceremonies at a fire circle out in the swamps," I said. "And she caught me afterward and locked me up in a room full of snakes. I got out, but I know that when she discovers I've escaped, she's going to come after me. So, I was hoping that Eleanor might have left behind some spells of protection that I might use, while I try to figure out how to get at her again."

He nodded. "If you saw her practicing any secret rituals of night voodoo, she'll not be a friend of yours," he said. "She'll probably put some kind of a hex or dark curse on you."

"Do you think Eleanor might have some guarding spells that would help me protect my house from Charlaine Marie while I'm sleeping?"

"I don't know," he said. "But you can take a look for yourself."

He rose and led me back through the kitchen to her ritual room. It had changed since the last time I was there. The floor had been washed; the bloodstain that had taken up half the floor the last time I was there had vanished without a trace.

"You're welcome to read through her books," he said, pointing at the shelves on the wall which were lined with various texts, and then at her spell building desk, which had her handwritten journal on it. I'd looked at that briefly the last time I was here. "I can't let you take any with you, though."

"I understand," I said.

"Just let me know when you're done," he said. "I hope you find something that helps."

With that, he disappeared back through the beaded doorway.

I took a close look at Eleanor's altar before I began reading. It was densely layered with offerings and implements. I didn't know what all of the things were supposed to do or represent – there were tiny dolls and pieces of paper with handwritten notes and photographs and bits of clothing. And around the Infant Jesus' neck and arms were hung an array of necklaces with amulets. Inside each, I saw small photos of people.

My eye was drawn to them in particular because of the deep brown eyes I spotted in one. I put my hand beneath the locket and drew it closer to me. It was only an inch tall, but her face had caught my eye immediately.

Renee's gaze was captured in that locket.

I separated it from the rest of the chains, and slipped it into my pocket. I wouldn't take Eleanor's spell books, but I would confront Renee with this, the next time I saw her. Eleanor clearly had numbered her among her closest, and had tried to protect her by keeping her on this altar.

So much for the power of good.

Then I turned to the task at hand.

I didn't really know what I hoped to find, but I pulled down three books from her shelves that promised 'rituals' or 'spells' in their titles. Two of them looked to have been printed seventy-five or one hundred years ago. The paper was ragged and yellowed, and the leather binding creased and cracked. I scanned the table of contents of each for something that might help me. One boasted a chapter devoted to 'Protections and Guards' and I turned to that instantly. The opening sentence didn't give me a lot of hope, however.

There is no spell or potion that can truly protect one from the curse of a voodoo queen with strong friends among the loa. Certainly, there are wards that can deflect and diminish an attack. But every spell is a little different, possessing within it the unique spirit, will and intent of its caster. Likewise, a successful spell of protection must include elements to block the specific elements of the spell. Without knowing exactly who is crafting the attack spell and what elements it includes, it is impossible to completely guard against its power. Each 'shield' must possess the counter-elements of the spell it is designed to thwart. If you know the exact nature of the person and spell that they create to harm, then it is simple to guard against. If you do not (which would be typical), all that can be cast is a general warding spell. Such a spell can have value and defeat or at least diminish the power of an attack, but in all likelihood, it will not defeat a truly targeted attempt to cause illness or harm or even death.

Well, that was not exactly the news I wanted to read. It painted my case as hopeless. Still, I read on and at least got the basics of what I could potentially do.

Stop at the Door: The Sting

The most common warding spell is often referred to as 'The Sting' because of its black and yellow mix reminiscent of a bee or wasp. It is designed to repel evil intent and keep negative energy outside a house. There are two elements to the ward. The use of sulfur is a deterrent to spirits of the dark places. It reminds them of the pits from which they came and will deter them from entering a place that is bordered in it, as it tells the spirit that they are returning home, something most spirits set free in our realm are loath to do.

The other important element is black salt. The use of salt steeped in the ashes of the dead is an ancient practice that originated in the Santeria culture. Spirits find salt an element which saps their power in this realm and thus avoid crossing it at all costs. The spirits of the dead are also repelled by the remnants of the dead – which remind them of their loss of humanity. Thus, pure salt that has been washed in the ashes of the dead is particularly effective in warding off spirits, both of the idle wandering kind and those that have been commissioned by a voodoo ritual to seek out someone to do them harm. It either case, it takes great will and resolve to cross a black salt and sulfur barrier, if the material is mixed and put across the perimeter of a room or house. As long as the mixture is poured in an unbroken line around the area it is meant to guard, it is probably one of the most effective non-specific protection guards that there is.

The chapter went on to discuss carefully crafted personal wards, like the amulet that Eleanor had crafted for me, and spell bags, like the one Renee had gifted me from Eleanor's Arcana weeks ago. Those, naturally, were deemed the least useful in actually repelling determined evil intent.

After skimming that book and opening the next, I found another spell that also involved salt. This one intrigued me, as it suggested mixing the salt with the urine of the person to be protected, and then keeping the mixture in a bottle close to the intended recipient of the ward. I wrote down the ingredients of that, as there were also herbs and the addition of metal – pins or nails or something sharp to 'injure' any that sought to cross the barrier.

I set those aside and looked at Eleanor's personal diary. Unlike published books, her journal of spells did not, of course, have a glossary, so I couldn't leaf quickly to a section that I knew was of interest. Still, I enjoyed reading her delicately looped script, as she addressed all sorts of issues.

Today a girl came to me looking for a cure for her face. Not her complexion, but the actual structure of her face. Her cheekbones were flat and wide, and her eyes small and set far apart. Her chin was thick and square, and her nose almost flat. I understood what she wanted, but there is nothing that prayers and potions can do to change one's physical structure. She could have surgery, but even that can't really change the core structure that is behind what we are. I made her a spell bag tonight with lavender, cinnamon, pumpkin seeds and a peacock's feather. I can't change what she is, nobody can. There is beauty in everyone, if they can only find it. The only hope for her is to accept what she is…and to accentuate and celebrate that thing that makes her unique. I could think of nobody who could help her more than Oshun, the goddess of rivers, streams, beauty and sexuality. So I wrote her this calling to make while holding the spell bag each night:

Mother of Love
You understand the flow
The endless movement
The desire for change
The need for need
Help me to find my own tide
A flow that reaches completion
In a place of happiness
A flow that finds need
And sweeps it away
To end in pleasure and happiness
I pledge to you my energy
I give to you my worship
Help me in my hour of desperate longing
Free me from the traps of shallowness
Bring my sight to the secrets
That rise beneath the depths of
Currents dark and fast.
I beg you to whisper to me
To bring direction to my dreams
My soul is yours to use
My devotion is unending.

I flipped the page, but the entry was complete. There was no more about the incident. It left me wondering what the fate was of that poor, ugly girl. Had the prayers to a spirit of the ancient religion helped her come to terms with who and what she was? Or had Eleanor wasted her time and energy on a helpless case? Because in the end, could any acceptance really come from magic? The girl Eleanor had described had to come to terms with herself. No loa was going to impact that.

Or could they?

I realized that I kept assuming that spells and spirits were all powerless in our world, just rituals that some people went through to try to change the course of the unchangeable.

But maybe I was wrong.

And maybe I already knew it. I was here, after all, to find a spell that would stop evil spirits and spells from penetrating my home and stealing away my life as I slept. So…clearly at some level, I believed in the existence of the loa and that the work that Eleanor had dedicated her life to was, in some way, real and valuable. And I had been literally paralyzed in the lair of a voodoo queen. I had not been drugged that day; I could think of no other explanation than the touch of a loa.

I was at a crossroads with myself. I had always snidely (though silently) laughed at the idea of voodoo magic. I believed on some level that our spirits carry on, but I had never put much credence in actively calling upon spirits to do our bidding in the material world. In my weeks of investigating the 'bloody bed' cases, I had grown to believe that someone with a voodoo bent was behind them, but I hadn't truly believed that it was magic at work, but rather human hands. Despite the fact that bodies had consistently disappeared with partners sleeping soundly right next to them. I had assumed the survivors had been quietly chloroformed in their sleep to keep them under while the killer did his or her work.

Again, maybe I was wrong….

I flipped through her journal some more, marveling at the pages of spells and reflection. Frequently she had written for pages about thoughts she had had, and requests people made of her. Always, her solution was to try to use the powers of the voodoo world to bring acceptance and fulfillment to people. Not often to change their actual lives, but to change the way they thought about their lives, and themselves.

And really, what other magic does someone need?

I was about to close her journal and call it a night, when something on one of the latter pages caught my eye.

The words *Charlaine Marie.*

I slipped my finger in to stop the page from closing, and then reopened the journal completely and found the beginning of that entry.

I drove out to see Charlaine Marie today. It's been some time since we talked, and there are reasons for that. As the so-called Black Queen, her magic and mine have no connection. She practices everything that I'm pledged to prevent. But still, I remember the time that we both shared a ritual dance under Mother Mabemba, and we learned how to mix the herbs of the swamp with the intent of the soul. There was a time when that girl and I were friends. Before the woman she became chose the path of shadows.

There has to be some connection with the horrible things that are going on in New Orleans and Charlaine Marie. Even if she isn't causing them, she has the connections to uncover who is. Everything that Cork has told me about the murders and disappearances points to a ritual of the blackest kind. But to what purpose?

Charlaine Marie was cordial when she opened her door. "To what do I owe the pleasure?" she asked, and I responded that it had been a long while, and I had been thinking of her, wondering how she was.... She seemed to genuinely appreciate that and served me tea and cookies in her kitchen. It felt as if we were two housewives in a '50s television series. We spoke of foolish, pointless things and sipped our mugs and smiled. She spoke of how devoted her followers were, even in the age of disbelief, and I echoed her praise. The young men and women who worked in my store did it because of true reverence for the beliefs, not simply for a paycheck. They were believers in an age of skeptics.

When I could stand the small talk no longer, I finally just blurted it out and asked her why. Why the bloody beds and skins with no bodies. What did these things do for the loa, or for her? When would the killings on the night of the full moon end?

Her face changed from pleasant to stern at that, and she set down her tea.

"I knew that you had a hidden motive for coming here. You should know better."

Charlaine Marie stood up then, and pointed toward the front door. "Please get out."

I wasn't going to give up that easily, though. "Give me a hint," I begged her. "Is this a curse that is out of control? It seems to be growing every month. Or is it targeted, and soon will end? Tell me it is not going to continue unchecked."

Her face showed a war of emotions. Her lips parted twice, as if to answer, but then closed without speaking.

"Anyone who was harmed only harmed themselves," she said. "When the heart is deceitful, it will soon be broken. There can be no other end."

"So you do know what is going on," I said. "Is the curse yours? What are the conditions? What did these people do?"

"You assume too much," Charlaine Marie said. "Remember, those who get in the way of fate will be subject to its path."

"Are you threatening me?" I asked.

She shook her head. "You are threatening yourself. Don't concern yourself with things that do not concern you, and everything will be fine."

For some reason at that moment, I suddenly saw — really saw — all of the fixtures on the walls around me. The ram's skull with polished white horns. The tiny infant floating in a yellow-green liquid in a large bottle atop a bookshelf filled with tomes of mysticism and dark worship. I saw unfamiliar texts there as well as Santeria and spines embossed in foreign words or simply arcane symbols — stars and sickles and serpents and interlocking circles.

There were black candles — currently unlit — atop almost every surface, from bookcases to end tables. And on the wall behind the table we sat at, an oil painting. It depicted a naked tribal circle, women gyrating and dancing around the figure of a horned creature seemingly half-man, half-beast. His teeth were cruel, and his horns long and twisted. In his hands he brandished two knives, and in the foreground, a nude woman lay bleeding from multiple slashes on her torso on the top of a thin stone altar.

There were dozens of wooden figures carved in the traditional African style; maybe they were authentic. It looked much like my own collection of voodoo relics, only these portrayed figures doing violent and obscene acts. One in particular caught my eye: a dark man with thick braids knelt behind a woman on her hands and knees with exaggerated breasts that hung low enough to touch the ground. It would have been a standard 'doggy style' sex statue with one exception: his erection was the haft and blade of a long knife. Which had begun to bury itself within the woman.

I forced myself to look away from her disturbing walls and shelves to again see Charlaine Marie. Truly see her.

The lines around her eyes spoke of age and sadness. The rivers of fine lines around her mouth spoke of bitterness and cruelty. Her eyes were set deep, shadows hung around them like guards. You couldn't read her; she appeared ancient and inscrutable and yet still vital and powerful.

And, I suppose, she was all those things. She had made her life the study of the dark arts of voodoo. Who knew what spirits she had consorted with, what disgusting acts she had seen, and in fact, assisted in?

"What is the curse that leaves behind beds of blood?" I asked again, point-blank. "What have you done?"

"I have given you your last warning," she answered. Her face had grown smooth and mean. "Leave now or you may not leave at all."

She turned from me and began to systematically light the black candles set around the room. Under her breath I heard the syllables of calling, though I did not recognize the names of her benefactors. The tenor of the room changed, however, with every new guttering flame. Instead of warmth, each candle sent a new wave of chill through the air. I felt a presence. Or presences, swimming into power. The hairs on the back of my neck prickled, and I knew that it was time to go. Charlaine Marie was serious. If I stayed, she would loose her demons on me.

I walked quickly to the front door.

"Goodbye, Charlaine Marie," I called. As I stepped onto the porch an invisible push nearly sent me to my knees. The screen door sucked shut behind me with a crash.

A moment later, the wooden inside door closed as well.

I was no longer welcome.

I don't know what Charlaine Marie has loosed, but clearly it is something vicious. Maybe it is beyond her control at this point. No mambo parts with her 'secrets' easily, but I did not understand her refusal to talk about this at all, when her actions and responses clearly demonstrated that she did have knowledge, and more than likely, had something to do with it if she wasn't the architect.

She had given me one clue, however. She had spoken of deceptive hearts. Was this a love curse? Or, more specifically, a spurned love curse? If so, what were the parameters? And why were more and more people 'taken' by it every month?

The journal entry ended there, and the next day, did not revisit the subject. But I knew she had had an idea about Charlaine Marie's curse, and was, in fact, working on a protection spell against it on the night she had been taken.

Why hadn't she left some idea of what her idea was?

I looked around at her small workspace once more. But there were no other clues. If she had written anything else down, it had been taken by whoever had come here to take her.

I did see one thing that caught my interest, however.

A large jar sitting amid all her other ingredients. The label said, *Anna's Ashes*.

It occurred to me that I needed ashes for my protection spell. If I could truly cast such a thing myself without training.

I picked up the jar and walked out into the house to find Robert.

He was sitting in the front room in an easy chair. Legs spread apart. Gaze focused on the blank wall ahead of him. He looked lost.

"Do you know what might be in this?" I asked him and held out the jar for him to see.

He didn't answer right away. But he reached out a finger to touch the ceramic face of the jar.

"Eleanor's friend Anna," he said. "She passed on last year, but left Eleanor her body for whatever she might need."

"So these are her ashes?"

He nodded.

"May I use them?"

He looked confused for a moment, and then shrugged. "If they'll help you."

"I think they will," I told him and a moment later, armed with the ashes of a dead woman, I left Robert Trevail's home.

I placed the remains of Anna carefully on the floor of the back seat of my car and then headed toward the Piggly Wiggly.

I had to buy some salt.

CHAPTER TWENTY-EIGHT

Moon in Gemini

The urine and salt in a bottle was easy. I used an empty hot sauce bottle and once sealed, put it next to my wallet. I could keep that in my pocket when I wasn't home.

More difficult was mixing someone's ashes with salt. Not that the mixing was hard, but when I looked into that cannister and saw the chunks of black that represented the last remaining bits of a woman's life... well...I had a hard time lifting it out, dropping it into a bowl and stirring.

Maybe it's just me but I hope that when I die someone finds a better use for my body than a spirit equivalent of mosquito repellant.

Eleanor hadn't given a recipe per se, so I had no idea if it mattered how much body-to-salt ratio there was. I poured a cannister of salt into a bucket, and emptied an almost equal amount of ashes into it.... Then I used a large wooden spoon from my kitchen and mixed the two together until the salt all seemed to be blackened. There were other additives too – ground, dried powder of rosemary and pennyroyal to aid in warding. And I'd thrown in some burut powder, after seeing its properties when Eleanor had used it on the bloody bed.

When it was all mixed, I stared at the mess for a minute. What next? I was no houngan. How could I call upon any power to protect me when I barely believed?

I shook my head and steeled myself. If you were going to be in, you had to be all in. I closed my eyes and fashioned what was basically a prayer to any spirits who would deign to hear me – I called on them to give my powder the power needed to protect my home from harm and any unwanted intrusions. I fingered the charm around my neck as I did.

"Eleanor Trevail asked you to protect me from harm," I said. "I beg you now to help me spread this barrier to protect my home from evil. Keep the darkness outside and the light within."

When I had mixed and prayed and wondered if this was a ridiculous exercise or a lifesaver, I began to dispense the powder around the perimeter of the house. I started at the front door, and walked along the wall, letting a thin trickle of the black salt fall along the baseboards. As I emptied the bucket, I also said a prayer of protection out loud, begging the spirits to hear me...and save me.

Luckily, my house was small. I bordered every outer wall with the powder. In my bedroom, I lit a candle made of pure beeswax. I'd read somewhere that this was another way to purify a room and repel dark spirits.

At this point, I was willing to try virtually anything to make sure I could sleep without worrying about something evil and invisible slipping into bed next to me.

When I was finished, I still actually had some black salt left in my bucket. Not wanting to waste it, I walked around and dusted it across all the windowsills in the house.

If nothing else, I'd set myself up for a big mess for the first time I opened the windows and a breeze blew in.

After I cleaned up, I poured myself a Hopitoulas IPA and sat down in the living room. I didn't want to 'watch' anything...I just needed the background. I settled on a black-and-white episode of *The Twilight Zone* and turned the sound down.

At some point, I refilled my pint glass twice more. I drank and stared at the screen and I realized that the episode was about a girl visiting a witch.

How weirdly appropriate.

I shook my head and took another swig.

Eventually, the glass was empty. I turned the TV off and went to bed. I felt calmer. Maybe because I was a little buzzed.

When I lay down in the bed, I could almost hear the stillness of the air. That baseline 'buzz' kept me awake for a while, but eventually I rolled over and dozed off.

★ ★ ★

Someone pounded on the window.

My eyes shot open. My heart pounded like a machine gun. The alarm clock on the nightstand read 12:01.

I sat up in bed and listened. Something thudded against the window to my right. Again and again. Like a fist pounding to gain entrance.

The thing was, the noise didn't come from simply the bedroom.

All the windows in my house were rattling. It sounded as if I was in the middle of a hurricane, and the centrifugal force of the wind had all centered on my house.

Or like an angry mob had surrounded the place and they all were demanding to be let in.

Something howled outside. An angry, frustrated sound.

It sent a shiver down my back all the way to my toes. It sounded like the Devil himself. What the hell was out there? I sat there for a minute frozen, just listening to the pounding. I worried that any minute now, the glass would break.

I reached for my service revolver and then my phone. I knew that it wasn't possible, but I pulled up the weather.com app to see if a storm had descended on the area overnight.

Nope. It was supposedly 78 degrees and calm outside. No rain until the weekend.

Slowly, I slipped my feet out of the bed and stood up. Gun in hand, I walked the center of the house, just listening.

The pounding was everywhere. As if a hundred hands were all beating on the outside of my house, trying to get in.

I lifted a crucifix off the wall in the spare bedroom. I had a feeling that this was a far better weapon in this particular fight than my revolver. Then I walked slowly toward the front room windows. They were rattling worse than any of the rest, but they were also the largest windows in the house. With the cross in one hand, I reached out with my other and pulled the string to open the blinds.

It was pitch black outside. Black as midnight should be. I knelt on the couch and leaned toward the window, peering into the night. The shadows of the bushes just beyond the windows blotted out the view to my left and right. In the middle, I could see the faintest hint of sticks on the lawn, and the ribbon of the old sidewalk beyond.

I leaned closer, staring farther out, looking toward the streetlamp a block away.

A face suddenly stared back at my own.

Horrible eyes met mine and held them. I felt a connection. My body was frozen, my eyes compelled to stare into its endless orbs.

I pushed backward with my arms, breaking the gaze of the evil face and almost falling to the wooden floor. I held up the cross in front of me as I struggled to get back on my feet. I wasn't much of a believer, but in that moment, I prayed with as much devotion as I'd ever had.

And then it was gone.

But I'd seen it. Two deep-set eyes and wild hair. A heavy jaw and thick teeth as it grimaced through the glass at me.

It was there for a heartbeat, and then disappeared.

I realized then that when it had vanished, the pounding had ceased. The whole house suddenly seemed eerily still.

The Black Queen knew I had escaped. She'd sent her demons after me.

But Eleanor's warding spell had kept them at bay. This time.

I wanted to open the front door and peer outside, but I didn't dare to open any entry into the house now. Not in the dark.

I forced myself to go back to bed.

But when I tried to sleep, all I could see in the dark were those hellish, evil eyes.

I slept with the light on.

CHAPTER TWENTY-NINE

Friday, September 6

First Moon

There was a black rock the size of a fist on my porch in the morning. A rolled piece of red silk was wrapped around the stone; it held a white chicken feather in place. I untied the silk and laid the rock on the feather to hold it in place. Then I unraveled the silk. It was a square of plain red material, without design. However, in the middle of it, someone had written five words using a black marker.

You can't hide inside forever.

I didn't appreciate the threat.

Charlaine Marie had me at a disadvantage. She obviously knew where *I* lived, but I had not tracked her house down yet.

I knew now that Eleanor had not called the Black Queen on the phone that day she had contacted so many in the local voodoo community. She had gone to visit her instead. So I could not use the phone numbers as a way to look up Charlaine Marie's address. Worst-case scenario was that I waited, and drove out to the clearing where she held her rituals on Thursday night. Somebody had to know where she lived, though. I wanted to track her down before Thursday and bring the fight to her rather than waiting for her to catch me first. After last night, I knew that if this was a fight, I needed the element of surprise to have any hope of gaining the upper hand.

I could go through the phone book looking for people named Charlaine Marie without a last name…but I was sure there were a lot of them in New Orleans.

There were 157 of them, to be exact. The first thing I did when I reached the office was run a search. I saved the listing, but if I started working my way down the list, it would probably *be* Thursday before

I found Charlaine Marie. If she was even on there. She could be listed solely under her husband's name if she was married.

I set that aside for the moment. I had other questions that might take less time to answer with the help of Google. I was researching voodoo rituals on the internet when I suddenly caught a whiff of stale tobacco. A second later a white button-down shirt bellied up against the lip of my desk.

"You've been really quiet lately," Tarrington said. "Gotten any leads? We're supposed to be working on this case together."

I looked up and shook my head. "Not so far," I said. "How about you guys? I could say the same. You never seem to be in the station."

"We've been out dragging the swamps and talking to people on the street. You know, *detective* work. While you're sitting in here playing on the computer, I guess."

I snorted. "I haven't been in the station much myself either, to be honest," I said.

He nodded. "Yeah, I heard you checked out some evidence the other day."

I frowned at him. What was he after?

"What did you want a snake for?" he asked.

"I thought if I took one to a voodoo expert, she might be able to tell me something about it or why snakes were used."

"And?"

"No dice."

He grunted. "Somebody is responsible for all this. Chief's getting irritated that we're not finding anything."

"I hear you. Trust me, I want to crack this case as badly as you do. Probably more so."

He pointed at my screen. "So you think it's real voodoo behind all of it?"

"I don't know what to think," I said.

"I don't know why, but I feel like you *do* know what to think, and you're just not telling me."

"Whatever," I said, and slapped his broad belly with the back of my hand. I didn't appreciate him crowding my desk and accusing me of being a holdout. I wasn't going to tell him about my windows rattling or the silk note from Charlaine Marie. That aspect of the investigation was officially beyond the scope of the New Orleans Police Department. That was personal.

Until I had actual evidence on her, I wasn't talking about spooks and spells with anyone.

"I'll let you know if I find a hot lead," I said. "You do the same."

I looked away from him and leaned toward my screen, signaling that our talk was over.

"You do that," he said. After a few seconds of silence, the white shirt finally backed away and he disappeared across the room.

★   ★   ★

I took a drive to Mythologica. It was time to try to pull in any help that I could from the sources I had.

As soon as I walked in the door, Désirée was on me.

"Where's Rowan?" she asked. "She hasn't answered any of my texts since the night she went out with you."

My stomach clenched. I hadn't thought about Désirée's connection to Rowan. Or the fact that Rowan's disappearance might not be common knowledge yet. I didn't know if her husband had come back from his trip yet or not. And I certainly did not want to admit any personal knowledge to anyone. But Désirée could easily connect me to Rowan, if anyone thought to ask her.

"She didn't go home with me," I said. And that wasn't a lie.

"You're the last one I know who saw her," Désirée said.

"I haven't heard from her since that night either," I said. Again, not a lie.

She looked at me with some suspicion, but did not come right out and call me a liar.

"Why are you here?"

"I need to find the Black Queen," I said.

She took a step back. I held up the piece of silk so that she could read the message. "I need to find her before she finds me."

"I don't understand," she said.

I briefly told her the story of the past couple of nights.

Désirée frowned. "I wouldn't tell you if I knew," she said. "But I don't know. You know where her group meets, and I'm guessing that's probably all anybody really knows about her. Please get out of my store and don't come back again."

"I need help," I said. "There are very few people who I can turn to for something like this."

"I can't help you. And if the Black Queen finds out you've been here, she'll turn her gaze on me," Désirée said. "I'm sorry, but you have to leave. I can't help you, and you being here can only hurt me. Do you want to see me get hurt?"

I shook my head. Of course not.

"Please," she said. Her eyes looked truly frightened.

I could see I wasn't going to get anywhere with her. "I'm sorry I bothered you," I said. She didn't move as I started toward the exit.

I could still see her panicked look as I walked away from the store.

So much for the inside track there.

★　　★　　★

I headed toward my next stop. Madeline's house. If anyone knew where Charlaine Marie lived, it was her. She had been the Black Queen and knew where the ritual circle was. However, this time, I was not going to be lured into her basement.

She answered the door after I rang twice, wearing a black robe.

"You're back," she said. "I didn't expect you to come back after the warning I gave you the last time. Maybe you enjoyed it too much?" She motioned for me to step past her. "Come in."

I didn't move. "I can't stay this time," I said. "But I do need one more bit of help."

"I won't talk to you like this with the door open," she said. "Step inside and let me close the door."

Grudgingly, I did as she asked. The house smelled of some sweet, burning herb. Candles were lit all around her altar. Maybe I'd interrupted one of her devotions.

"Look," I said. "I went to the prayer circle of the Black Queen, thanks to your map. But she ended up catching me and locking me in a basement filled with snakes. I got out, but now she's haunting me. Last night, I poured a mix of black salt all around my house to keep her devils out, and around midnight, the whole place started rattling, as if a hundred hands were all pounding on it from the outside. Then this morning, I found this on my front stoop."

I pulled the silk note from my pocket and showed it to her.

Madeline's face split into a grin. "You really stepped in the hornets' nest this time," she said. "Charlaine Marie is not the woman you want to be pissed off at you. If I was you, I'd stick pretty close to home."

"I have to find her as soon as possible," I said. "Can you give me her address?"

Her eyes bugged out as if I'd just said that Martians had landed in Jackson Square.

"You're just going to drive over to her house and...do what exactly? Arrest her for sending demons to your house? Write her a cease and desist order?" Madeline shook her head. "I've helped you as much as I will. You know where to find her. You just have to stay alive until then."

"Can you tell me what part of town she lives in, at least?"

She began to laugh. Then she reached out and touched my chin with her forefinger. "You're cute, you know that? Why don't you come back downstairs with me? I can keep you safe here until Thursday. Or maybe you'll decide you don't want to leave at all."

I shrugged and opened the door.

"No," I said. "I'll take my chances out there."

She grinned. Like a shark.

"Good luck," she said. "You'll need a lot of it."

CHAPTER THIRTY

Thursday, September 12

Moon enters Pisces

On Thursday night, I drove to the swamp. While I hadn't found where the Black Queen lived, I did know where she conducted her rituals. I just had to avoid being taken prisoner again.

This time, I thought as I patted my service revolver, I was ready.

Once again, I pulled up in the driveway of the old house. And once again, nobody seemed to be around. I carefully made my way through the woods in the back, careful this time not to catch my foot in a hole.

Some things did not bear repeating.

It was almost 11 p.m., so I figured most of them should be there by now. I could smell the smoke of their ritual fire.

But as I neared the clearing, I realized that there were no voices coming from up ahead. No drums.

And as I stepped into the open space, I confirmed my suspicion.

No people.

But there were still traces of fire and smoke from the firepit. I walked across the grass slowly and bent down, holding my hand over the center of the pit.

The coals still glowed, and made the area much warmer than the summer night's air.

When I looked up at the altar, I saw that there had been a ceremony here tonight. Apparently, one truly befitting the title of Black Queen.

The front of the stone was splashed violently in red blood. And something rested on the top of the stone.

I stepped around the firepit to look closer. A pool of blood covered the surface of the stone, shimmering in the pale light of the moon.

In the center of it, a naked man lay silent and still.

The reason was obvious. The center of his chest had been carved open. He looked to be in his mid-forties, slightly overweight, pale in complexion...maybe in part because of all the blood loss. His mouth was stretched wide...because a mass of white and brown feathers – and pink clawed feet – stuck out of it.

Chicken feet.

They carved this dude open and stuffed half a chicken down his throat. What the hell?

Had they really performed a human sacrifice tonight?

Sure looked like it.

And why was it done so early? And why had they left the body?

I knew that their usual rituals were staged to culminate at midnight, the dividing point between night and day. Supposedly the moment when the division between the spirit and the physical world was weakest, and easiest to transgress.

I was about to walk around to the other side when a hand suddenly gripped me by the shoulder.

"Don't have any clues, is that what you said?"

It was Tarrington. And of course, Aubrey slouched right behind him.

"What are you doing here?" I asked.

"I knew you were holding out on us," Tarrington answered. "So we decided to follow you tonight after work. When you didn't head home, I knew we were onto something."

He held his hand out and gestured with a fresh cigarette at the altar and the firepit. "So what's the story? And where are the suspects?"

"I heard that they do voodoo rituals out here on Thursday nights, so I came to check it out. Obviously, by the time I got here, it was too late."

Aubrey nodded at the altar. "Apparently too late for whoever that was too."

"Clearly."

Aubrey had wandered across the clearing, toward the tree line.

"Do think there's a connection to the people who did this and the full moon disappearances?" Tarrington asked.

"I don't know," I said and pointed at the body lying on the stone.

"But there certainly appear to be some similarities. They went for the heart."

Aubrey suddenly yelled from the trees. "Hey you guys, get over here. You have to see this!"

I looked away from the altar, and saw Tarrington's partner waving from the trees. I followed Tarrington, who broke into a jog instantly.

When we arrived, I saw immediately what had excited him.

There were pale, white shapes hanging from the trees. Dozens of them. They stretched back, deep into the swamp trees. Moss cascaded around them like garlands, but didn't change the clear definition of what they were.

Skins.

Human skins, still intact enough to tell. They all had arms and legs and the deflated remains of faces.

"What the fuck," I whispered.

"Yeah, that's what I said," Aubrey answered. "Just like at Pernaud's Landing."

"How did you know?" Tarrington demanded.

"I didn't. But I also don't know what to do about it. We still haven't ID'ed the ones we found at the landing."

"We have to call this in," Aubrey said.

"Yes, of course," I said. "Our unsolved mystery file just doubled."

"Well, even without these, we have an actual body here," Tarrington said.

I nodded.

Aubrey started taking pictures of the ghostly things hanging like grotesque Christmas ornaments all around us. Tarrington walked ahead of him, brushing his hand against each skin and watching as it shivered translucently in the faint moonlight.

"I'm going to make the call," I announced, and walked out of the tree line and back into the clearing.

I pulled my phone out and thumbed through to the start screen. But just before I hit dial, my eyes strayed to the stone altar.

And I realized it was empty.

I slipped the phone back in my pocket and walked over to the altar.

The body didn't reappear the closer I got.

There was a pool of blood that now completely covered the stone surface, and a familiar organ graced its center.

A human heart.

How the hell had they grabbed the body while we were just a few dozen yards away?

"Tarrington?" I called. "Aubrey? You guys have to see this!"

I walked around the stone altar, noting the blood still dripping like fresh rain off the edges.

There was no answer from the tree line.

"Tarrington?" I called again.

Nothing.

The whole clearing was eerily silent.

I walked back to the area where the skins were hanging from the trees, and clicked on the flashlight app on my phone. I played it across the trees. The harsh light caught the skins and leaves in a weirdly bright reflection. I could barely see beyond them until I walked farther into the forest and shone my light on other hideous things hanging.

A cigarette lay just in front of me, still smoking on the ground.

"Tarrington?" I called again. Not quite so loud this time.

I moved to the end of the grotesque hangings, until there was nothing but dark forest branches ahead. And then I walked back toward the clearing.

I was nearly out of the trees when I heard a branch snap behind me.

My heart suddenly pounded louder than the tribal drums I'd heard here a week ago. I held my breath and pivoted, struggling to see deep into the trees. The branches kept all of the star and moonlight out, and I could just barely see the pale shimmer of the skins moving faintly in the low breeze.

"Aubrey?" I called, but this time, my voice was much quieter.

The swamp did not reply.

I began to back out of the woods again, toward the clearing. Something was wrong. I could feel it in the air. The body had disappeared. Tarrington and Aubrey had disappeared. All while I'd been standing nearby.

Another branch snapped somewhere down the path.

I bolted.

It was a relief to take a breath of fresh air back out under the canopy of the stars and not the trees. I stopped at the altar and set my hand on the stone. And then instantly pulled it back when I felt the wetness.

I stood there in the clearing for several minutes. I could hear my breathing.

And the low chirrup of bugs, celebrating the humid night.

There was nothing else.

Charlaine Marie and her minions had taken Tarrington and Aubrey. As well as the body.

I had no intention of letting her do the same to me.

I scoped out the forest that I had to walk through to get to my car.

Slowly, I walked in that direction. Just before I reached it, I flipped the flash on my phone on, and shone it ahead of me.

I saw only dark trunks and roots on the uneven ground.

There was nothing more to do but do it.

I ran.

PART FOUR
LAST CALL

CHAPTER THIRTY-ONE

Saturday, September 14

Harvest Moon

Tarrington and Aubrey did not turn up the next day. I needed to find Charlaine Marie. I had looked into the windows of the old house before I'd left the swamp and they were not inside.

She held all the keys. My last hope of finding her was Renee. The only trick was tracking Renee herself down. If I texted her, I'd not only put her in danger with her husband, I'd make her so angry she wouldn't help. I drove to Eleanor's Arcana and was excited to see the lights back on. Eleanor's husband still had to pay rent on the space, so it made sense that he'd reopened the store in her absence, at least for the short term.

There were a couple familiar faces inside. I walked up to one of them, a pink-haired girl named Penny, and asked about Renee.

"Yeah, she still's working here," she said. "But she don't do Saturdays. She'll be back Monday if you want."

Good to know. Only I didn't intend to wait that long. I thanked Penny and ducked back out onto the street. The night was just beginning, and you could still walk down the tourist part of the Quarter without having people stagger into you. That would change in a couple hours.

I retrieved my car and drove to Renee's neighborhood for an impromptu stakeout. I parked a few houses away, and then walked slowly down the sidewalk toward her house. The first step in tracking someone was to make sure they were actually where you thought they were.

My steps slowed as I approached their place. The lights were on, but nobody was in the front room. Glancing around to make sure nobody was obviously watching me, I turned off the walk and followed the fence line down the west side of their small frame house.

I was rewarded with a glimpse of Renee's hair in the kitchen window.

She was home.

But would she stay there on a Saturday night?

I quickly exited her yard and ambled back to my car to wait. I was going to find out. I knew that Renee rarely spent the weekends at home if she could help it. I was gambling my night that this night would be no different.

The thing about a stakeout is that you can't get anxious. You can't succumb to boredom. You have to put your mind in the right state. After days of stress and constant running around, a stakeout is a chance to just sit. Let your thoughts roam. Relax and enjoy the private time.

Of course, you can't take your eyes off the thing you're watching. But if you can find the mental space to enjoy the hours of doing absolutely nothing, a stakeout can actually be a rewarding mental experience.

I was not finding that positive mental space.

I shifted in my seat every five minutes and exhausted my thumb from scrolling down and down and down past pictures of cats and food and cartoons and people holding glasses of wine and beer.

There was nothing on Facebook or Twitter to hold my interest, and nothing happening in the front of Renee's house.

The neighborhood was pitch black now; the glow of the lights behind drawn shades illuminated odd shapes and shadows on each lawn. Some houses were completely dark, blank spots in a row of gentle murmurs. The distant voices of television chatter mixed with the thud of someone's stereo doling out an undercurrent of bass rhythm. And crickets.

My ass was numb when I saw the clock finally hit 10 p.m. I didn't know how long to stay with this; I wasn't sure how long I reasonably could. It was all I could do not to just march up her front walk and pound on the door.

But I restrained myself. Just barely.

And then, just as I was about to give up hope, I saw a sudden flash of light from the front of Renee's mostly dark house.

The front door opened.

Renee stepped out onto the front porch. She held the door a minute, and then yelled something back into the house. I couldn't make out the first couple words, but the last one was clear almost a block away:

"Asshole!"

She slammed the door, giving it and the man inside her middle finger. Then she walked quickly toward the curb. Her car was parked in front of the house and she unlocked and got inside. A moment later the running lights came on, and she pulled away from the curb.

I started the engine, and once she'd turned the corner, began to follow.

This might actually work out after all.

Renee wound out of the old neighborhood and drove about a half mile before pulling over and parking. I was careful to stay far enough behind that she wouldn't see she was being followed. Not that she would have been looking for it. But I didn't want to spook her.

She got out and headed across the street to a bar I knew well. I'd met her there in the past after she'd gotten off work at Eleanor's. It was midway between her house and the shop. The place was called Last Call because they stayed open later than any of the other places in the area. This was the last stop before people staggered home at 4 a.m. I wondered how long she planned on drinking there tonight.

I waited in the car for a few minutes before turning off the engine and getting out. It was suspicious enough that I was going to show up at one of her spots. I didn't need to walk in thirty seconds after her.

★   ★   ★

There were only a handful of people in Last Call when I stepped inside. It took me a minute to realize that, because the place was lit for making out. That's to say...not lit much at all. The back bar was crisscrossed in red Christmas lights. There were blue and green and yellow glows from the jukebox and a couple of neon beer lights. But no standard overhead illumination. Still, it was easy to spot Renee sitting at the bar, because nobody had hit on her yet. She was nursing a martini when I pulled out a stool and slid in beside her.

"Is this seat taken?" I asked.

Her face lit up when she saw me. "What are you doing here?"

"Lucky coincidence? I was hoping you might be out tonight."

"Well, you found me," she said. "I don't know that I'm very good company though."

"Bad night?"

She shrugged. "The usual. He's already half in the bag and took a swipe at me. I told him to go fuck himself and left."

"Just another Saturday night," I said.

That made her snort.

"So why are you looking for me?" she said after a sip. "After what you saw the other night, I didn't think you'd want to find me again."

"I figured I finally owed you that drink after you saved my life."

"Ah," she said. "So, this is payback? Don't feel obligated."

I put my hand on her shoulder. "Don't be like that," I said. "I really appreciate what you did. I know you risked your own safety to get me out. Have you seen Charlaine Marie since that night?"

She nodded.

"I'm guessing she's pretty angry that I got away."

That made her smile.

"She was not in best of moods, no."

"Does she suspect that you helped?"

Her eyes widened. "Oh hell no. She'd kill me if she did."

"I really think she has something to do with the full moon murders," I said. "And I think she knows what happened to Eleanor."

Renee frowned.

"I don't know," she said. "She does practice a lot of black voodoo, but...why would she hurt Eleanor? They knew each other forever. And I think they really respected each other, even though they practiced different kinds of magic."

"They were on opposite sides of the coin, though. Black magic is no friend to white." I took a sip of my beer. "Plus, Eleanor was helping me try to track down who was behind all of these bloody disappearances. I know she reached out to Charlaine Marie. And it wasn't long after that that she disappeared."

Renee didn't have an answer for that. Instead, she asked me for a dollar, then pushed away from the bar to walk over to the jukebox.

A minute later, 'You Shook Me All Night Long' was rattling the front windows of the bar. She returned and whispered something in my ear about what she'd like me to shake and I couldn't help but grin. Renee, I had learned, had a lot of energy when it came to 'shaking'.

We talked about the reopening of Eleanor's Arcana, and the increasingly violent mood swings of her husband, and the potential for the New Orleans Saints to actually have a decent season this fall. The jukebox moved from AC/DC to Lady Gaga to Billy Eilish's 'Bad Guy'. When Eilish sang-whispered about being on her knees, Renee mouthed along with the words, and then leaned over to bite my ear at the chorus. At just the right moment, she whispered along with Eilish, "Duh."

The bar got increasingly crowded as the night wore on, and Renee got increasingly flirty. Four martinis didn't hurt. Though they might in the morning. By the time it hit midnight, the place was close and loud. I was almost shouting to talk to her. When Renee asked me to save her seat so that she could go to the restroom, she nearly fell off the stool. Her legs had turned to rubber after a couple hours of drinking.

"I should take you home," I said when she came back. She was clearly unsteady.

"I don't wanna go home," she said. "I wanna go with you." She slurred just a bit, and I knew she needed to not sit back down on the stool, no matter what. I had paid our tab while she was gone, so I slid off my chair and took her arm. She leaned against me as we walked down the sidewalk. "I've really missed you, ya know."

"I know," I said. "But we've been through this before. You're married. We can't—"

"We can," she said. "I need to get away from him."

"Well, once you do—"

"But he'll kill me if I try."

I opened the door and helped her into the car. As I slid into the driver's seat, she began to cry.

"Please don't take me back yet."

"He's going to be looking for you," I said. "The later it is, the worse it's going to be."

She shook her head. "By now, he's passed out. Please, let's just go somewhere else? Can we stop at your place for a while?"

The pleading look in her eyes melted any resistance I had. Maybe it wouldn't be a bad idea to brew her a pot of coffee to straighten her out a little bit before I dropped her back in the viper's pit. Maybe it would even sober her up enough so that we could pick her car back up and drive it home later. I pulled out carefully and wound my way through the dark streets back to my neighborhood.

Renee grabbed onto me hard as I helped her out of the car and walked her up the steps. I hesitated for a minute when I pulled out my keys. What if Charlaine Marie and her hexes had somehow gotten through my protection barriers and left a trap waiting inside?

"I need some water," Renee said, leaning her head on my shoulder.

"Okay," I said, and took a breath as I turned the key. No way to find out but to go inside.

I flipped on the light as we stepped over the bannister, and noticed nothing immediately amiss. Renee collapsed on my sofa as I walked down the hall and flipped on more lights. I looked in the bedroom, not seeing anything beyond the outline of the bed at first. But I breathed an audible sigh of relief when the overhead light cut the gloom and the mattress appeared empty. Then I returned to the front room via the kitchen with two large glasses of water with ice. She downed hers in two gulps, and then took mine from my hand.

"You're supposed to do that in between the martinis," I suggested.

She grinned. "I know. I wasn't being good earlier."

Renee set the glass down on my coffee table and put her arms around my shoulders. Her hand slipped into and ruffled the hair at the nape of my neck. She pulled herself closer to me until I could feel the warmth of her chest pressing against my arm.

"I don't want to be good now either."

When she kissed me, I didn't pull away.

With all that had gone on lately, it felt like a long time since I'd been this close to Renee, and I missed her. After the last time, I'd tried to stay distant. I didn't want to be a reason that her marriage went south any quicker or worse than it already had. But I wasn't feeling strong this time. At that moment, I needed someone to hold me as much as she needed someone to hold her.

When I returned her kiss, she took that as an assent and pulled herself into my lap. I slipped my arms around her waist and lost myself in the heat of her kiss. Her eyes flashed brown fire as I met them, and her mouth moved from my lips to my neck and back again. The hunger in her was infectious. I slid my hands beneath her shirt and traced the smooth silken curves of her body. It had not been my intent when I'd sat down next to her, but five minutes later I had unclipped her bra and rolled her back to lay her head on the armrest as I held our kiss — a sinuous meeting of tongues and lips — while my fingers stroked the hard nubs of her nipples, teasing them to even more erect expressions of desire.

She moaned and tugged at my shirt until I broke our kiss and shrugged it off. As I did, she also shed hers, and then pulled me up from the couch to stand. She hugged me close then, pressing our naked skin together as if by pulling our arms tighter, we could become a single body, her chest melting and merging into mine.

We swayed that way faintly, her head on my shoulder, her breasts tight to mine, for several minutes before she broke the embrace, and took my hand to lead me around the coffee table.

Renee took me to my bedroom, and stopped when we reached the bed. She put both hands against my cheeks and smiled. I don't think I've ever seen her in a more perfect light than in that moment. She was earthy and dark but soft and sensuous in a transcendent way. An angel of sexuality and desire.

Her hands slipped from my face to my belt, and as she unzipped my pants, I was painfully aware that there was no way I could stop what was about to happen. I needed her as much as she wanted me. I stepped out of my pants, scooped her up in my arms, released her on the mattress and climbed on top of her. My lips kissed her from her neck to her toes. I wanted to taste her every pore. I breathed in the scent of her desire and kissed her wetly between her thighs before sucking one of her nipples and then losing myself again in a hungry, tongue-wrestling kiss.

We made love fast. And not because I was 'out of practice' and couldn't hold back. She was crying out in orgasm within a minute of me being inside her, and the two of us grabbed and kneaded every bit of the other. Her hands rubbed beneath my armpits and grabbed at the cleft of my ass. My fingers touched her breasts and her ribs, her hair and her calves. We flowed against each other like tide against sand, unstoppable and joining, pulling away only to grab and engulf again.

When it was all over, I lay next to her gasping for breath. Sweat ran down my neck and between my legs. The room smelled of our passion, and it was a scent more rich and exotic than any candle.

She ran fingers across the sweaty hair of my chest, and then ventured lower, playfully moving around the damp object that moments ago had moved inside her.

"I have something I have to tell you," she said. Her voice was a whisper. It almost sounded afraid. Small.

I slipped my arm tighter around her shoulders and pulled her closer. "What is it?" I said.

"I didn't want to tell you before, because you already probably think badly of me," she whispered.

"I don't," I said. "I think you're amazing. No matter what you've done in the voodoo circle. I just don't understand why you would go to Charlaine Marie when you were so close with Eleanor."

"That's what I wanted to explain," she said. "I've always been with Charlaine Marie."

She raised her head up off the pillow until her eyes met mine. There was a sadness there that alcohol and sex could not erase.

"Charlaine Marie is my mother."

CHAPTER THIRTY-TWO

"I can take you to her," Renee said as the next afternoon waned to evening. For us, it was still really the next morning. I'd called in sick to work and turned off the alarm. Hours later, I managed to stagger out of bed. Eventually, Renee followed.

We sat at my kitchen table, nursing swollen eyes and throbbing heads, as well as a desperate question: where could Renee go? I didn't dare take her home to her husband after she'd been out all night and most of the next day.

I didn't want to take her to her mother's if she had me in tow. That would only put her on the shit list of Charlaine Marie and also waste any 'ace in the hole' element I held by having Renee in my back pocket, so to speak.

"I'd rather you stay here," I said. "There's a protection barrier around the house. If I can pin down Charlaine Marie without visibly involving you…that's better for all of us. I do have one thing I have to ask, though."

"Sure," she said. "What is it?"

"Why did you work for Eleanor if your mother was the Black Queen? Isn't that like a stripper working as a receptionist for a convent?"

"Are you calling me a stripper?" She feigned offense.

"You know what I mean."

She leaned back in her chair, a sad look on her face.

"My mom wasn't always the Black Queen," Renee said. "She and Eleanor used to be pretty close. Eleanor babysat me when I was a kid, and I got my first summer job at her shop. My mother didn't run her own business like that, so it made sense for me to be working at a voodoo kind of store somewhere, even if it was white voodoo and kind of touristy. My mother hadn't talked to Eleanor in a long time when I took the job there, but she didn't stop me. A job is a job. And I really loved Eleanor."

"I don't think your mother did."

She frowned.

"Sorry," I said. Then I pulled out my phone and opened the map app. "Just tell me where to go to find her. The sooner I go, the sooner I can get back."

Renee grudgingly read me the address to plug into the map. And then an idea struck me.

"I'll be right back," I said. I walked back to my bedroom and opened the top drawer of the bureau. The locket I'd found at Eleanor's was there.

"Maybe you should wear this while I'm gone." I presented it to her and she frowned when she saw her picture in the charm.

"Where did you get this?"

"Eleanor's devotion tree," I said. "I've been wanting to give it to you. She really cared for you, you know."

A tear appeared at the edge of her left eye. "I know. She was like another mother to me. I can't believe that my real mother hurt her. But then again if I'm honest, I guess I can."

"Will it help protect you if you wear it?"

"Maybe," she said. "If that was Eleanor's intent in making it."

She slipped it over her head and tucked it under her hair.

"Promise me I don't have to go home to my mother *or* my husband," she said. "You'll let me stay here?"

"Do you really want to stay with me? Or do you just want to not stay with him?"

She smiled – the kind of smile that says, 'You are such an idiot.'

"Yes, I want to stay with you. Why do you think I've been trying to get you to buy me coffee for the past six months?"

"Because you're broke?"

She wadded up a napkin and threw it at my face.

"You can stay," I said. "But please do that. Stay. Don't leave the house."

★   ★   ★

The address she'd given me was far off the beaten path. No surprise. It was a good forty minutes' drive away, and not, honestly, too terribly far from where the ceremonial clearing was. I suppose that shouldn't have been a surprise. Why wouldn't she hold her rituals near where she lived?

The house was small and the siding faded. If you didn't know better, you might have thought the place was abandoned, another leftover remnant from Katrina. But I knew better. The last glint of sunset reflected off the slow-moving river that bordered the edge of the property. A large stone crucifix stood near the water. A cairn of stones surrounded the base, perhaps to hold it in place during floods.

The cross wouldn't have drawn my eye but for two things: someone had painted it black, an unusual color for a crucifix. And small dolls hung from its arms. They moved slightly, as if someone had just rushed past and dragged a hand across them.

Nobody was around.

The moon was already rising against the deepening blue of the horizon. I could see its faint glow above the high tops of the old cypress trees that had probably held down this border of the swamp for a century or more. The moon, of course, had seen many generations of cypress as it rose and waned, grew wide and diminished to a sliver. Tonight, it was full.

Full.

The import of that hit me. How had the month slipped by and around again? I'd put a calendar reminder for myself on my phone, but given the events of the past couple days, I hadn't paid attention. The beauty of the moonrise suddenly felt sinister.

This was, perhaps, a busy night for Charlaine Marie, if she was truly the person behind the bloody beds.

I walked up the weed-filled stone walk.

My goal for the next hour was to find out if she was, in fact, the person who had for some reason stolen away my wife and dozens more.

I raised my hand to knock on the aluminum screen door, but before I could bring my knuckles down, the door opened.

A woman wearing a head scarf and a checkered blouse leaned out via the opening.

"So you found your way here after all," she said. Her voice was rich, and lackadaisical. As if she had all the time in the world.

I didn't trust it.

This was possibly a case of the fly wandering right into the center of the spider's web.

"I'd like to talk to you," I said.

"I'm sure you have many questions," she said. "Come in."

She held the door for me and I stepped inside.

It was gloomy within, but the shimmer of an altar glowed from the sitting room next to the entryway.

The twisted horns of several ram heads, however, jutted from the wall behind, taking away the initial impression of holiness.

She gestured to a wooden chair. "Please sit, and I'll get us some tea."

I shook my head. "You are not leaving my sight until I've gotten some answers."

"As you wish," she said.

I followed her into a small kitchen. The walls were covered with paintings of horns and beasts and devils. On the kitchen table, a small statue of a man with a goat's head thrust himself between a woman's legs. It was not a depiction of consensual sex; her arms and legs were chained to posts.

Charlaine Marie pulled two mugs from a cabinet and then took tea bags from a black porcelain bowl.

That's when I saw the skulls.

There was a small shelf above her sink, just below the cabinets. And nine apparently human skulls lined up on it, grinning. How had she gotten them, I wondered. I probably didn't want to know.

I watched as she filled an old-fashioned bronze tea kettle and put it on the stove.

"Why did you leave the safety of your home to venture into the danger of mine, Mr. Ribaud?" she asked.

"I needed to talk to you. I have questions that only you can answer."

She smiled. "Of course you do. But the only real question is what do you hope to achieve by coming here? Putting your neck in the lion's mouth, as it were."

"You are the lion?"

"Perhaps."

She set a small carafe of sugar on the table and then reached into the refrigerator to pull out a carton of cream.

"Or perhaps I am the ringmaster, and I'm only biding my time before using the whip."

"Where are Officers Tarrington and Aubrey?" I asked. "They were with me at your ceremonial circle on Thursday."

"What makes you think I know?"

"I think you know everything that goes on in that space. And I think you were nearby when I discovered that you had performed a human sacrifice."

"What makes you think I performed any sacrifice at all?"

"Well, the blood for starters," I said. "And the body. And the mouth, stuffed with chicken's feet. Very Black Queen of you."

"Body, you say? Have you taken it to the morgue then, for identification?"

She smiled sweetly at me, awaiting the reply she knew I had to give.

"No," I said. "Because you took the body when I was looking for Tarrington."

"Ah, so you *think* you saw a body, but then it was gone. And you *think* you saw your friends, but then they were gone. Could it be, perhaps, that you might have been suffering from hallucinations, Mr. Ribaud? Had you been drinking, perhaps, prior to entering my ceremonial circle without invitation?"

The kettle began to whistle at that moment, and she turned to remove it from the stove.

"I know you know exactly what I'm talking about," I said. "Let's not play games."

She set the kettle on an unlit burner and reached up into a cabinet. When she turned to face me, she held a small doll in her hands. It was made of clay, but had the semblance of blue pants around its legs and a blue shirt around its chest.

She held a pin in one hand.

"Games like these?" she asked in a deceptively little-girl voice.

Charlaine Marie stabbed the pin into the doll's right arm.

My arm seized up. White-hot pain instantly pierced my biceps and shoulder. I wasted no time on the pain. Instead, I leapt up from the table and swung my hand at her. I knocked the doll from her grasp to the floor with so much force that my knuckles were stinging.

She laughed, while rubbing her hand.

"You don't want to play?"

"No, I very much don't. I want answers."

She nodded. "I'm sure you do. I'm not sure you'll believe the ones I have to give you."

"Try me," I said.

"Why did your arm hurt just now?" she asked.

"Because you stabbed that voodoo doll with a pin."

"Very astute of you. I was sure you were going to tell me it was a random muscle twinge."

She took a sip of her tea and then met my eye. "So you believe in the power of voodoo now? I was given to understand that you were a skeptic. Of course, you've recently begun putting guard spells around your house. I figured that was the work of a wife, or girlfriend."

I shook my head. "You killed my wife," I said. "And I want to know why."

Her eyebrows rose. "*I* killed your wife?"

"I woke up six months ago and the bedsheets next to me were wet with blood. There was a heart lying there in the middle of the mess. But Amanda was gone."

"Perhaps she cut herself while trimming her nails in bed," Charlaine Marie suggested. She turned in her chair and bent over to reach for the floor. When she sat back up, she held the doll in her hand.

I held a gun in my hand.

"Drop it," I said.

"If I stick this pin through the head of the doll, you will likely have a brain hemorrhage and die immediately," she said. Her voice was tight. Deadly serious.

"I promise you that I can pull this trigger before you can pin that Kewpie doll," I said.

"Standoff," she said. Her voice was deceptively calm. "How will you explain pulling a gun on a woman holding a doll?"

"I won't. I'm not here in an official capacity. This is personal."

She pursed her lips slightly. Then she dropped the doll on the table.

"Trust me," she said. "A clay doll is not my only weapon."

"And a gun is not mine. Tell me why you killed my wife. And Eleanor Trevail."

"I didn't kill your wife," she said. "Eleanor is a different story."

"So you did kill Eleanor." My voice betrayed no triumph in getting her to admit that. Only bitterness. "What about Flip Frenzie? And those people at Pernaud's Landing? They didn't die the same as all of those who disappeared on the night of the full moon. But there was certainly some black magic involved."

She shrugged. "People sometimes go where they shouldn't go."

"What about all those skins in the forest? Did they all go where they shouldn't?"

She smiled. "In one way or another."

"How did you remove their flesh without ruining their skins?"

"That's the beauty of voodoo, Mr. Ribaud," she said. "We have help. Very special help."

I looked her hard in the eyes. "Did you or did you not create a curse that is stealing the bodies of people every month on the night of the full moon?"

Charlaine Marie frowned. "Have you ever had someone hurt you, Mr. Ribaud? I mean really tear your heart out and crush it?"

I nodded.

"I gave him everything," she said. Her voice dropped to a husky whisper. "I called on the most dangerous spirits to fulfill his desires. I sacrificed years of my life to give him the pleasures he yearned for. I loved him."

"Who?" I asked.

"Walter Trask. My husband."

"The construction developer?" I asked.

"Yes, he owed the success of that business to me. Not to mention the bodies of sacrifices that rest at the bottom of the cement pilings of each of his high-rise buildings."

"Did you have him renovate the underground chapel of the Rivera family mausoleum?"

She looked faintly surprised. "I did. Why?"

"So your coven could meet there?"

"We are not a coven, Mr. Ribaud. But yes. The Lady of the Rose meets with her followers there, and there were floods that made it unusable for them. I had Walter renovate it for them, and in return, when the weather is bad and we can't meet for our devotions outdoors, we meet there."

"So there *is* a sisterhood in voodoo," I said. "Even with the dark side."

She said nothing.

"So what happened with your husband?"

She took a breath. Steeling herself. "I left one of our ceremonial circles early," she said at last. "It was a bad night. The initiate who was to bring our sacrifice for the ritual called after we were all there and said that she was not coming. She wasn't the only one. Half the group had issues: sickness, vacation, had to work late unexpectedly. Even my right-hand initiate, Cadence, the girl who helped me run all of our rituals, was missing. Everyone who did come seemed out of sorts.

"We ran through a short fire circle, but the energy was wrong. I ended it and sent everyone home early. I would not call the loa with such a poor showing.

"I was angry on the way home; I had not cancelled a circle night in years. But that anger was nothing compared to what I would soon be feeling."

She paused and took a sip of her tea. I could see a glint of fury in the spark of her eyes, just from recounting the memory of whatever it was she was about to say. When she continued, I could hear the bitterness edging her voice.

"The lights were off when I got home, which was odd because I was so early, I thought that Walter would still be up. I figured he must have had a difficult day and had gone to bed early, so I was quiet when I entered the house. I set my things down in the kitchen, and considered staying up to watch television. But I was frustrated and tired myself, so I decided to go to bed.

"When I walked into the bedroom, I saw that Walter was in bed. The sheets were rumpled and the comforter was balled up at the foot of the bed. His head lay on the pillow, his mouth facing the center of the bed. Facing the mouth of another.

"There was a woman lying in my bed."

Charlaine Marie closed her eyes and shook her head. "They talk about seeing red and losing yourself in a black cloud of emotion. I know what those things mean now. I knew the woman. She had been to our house before for parties. I had seen her the few times I went to

Walter's work. She was one of his managers. He had sung her praises a million times, and now I knew why."

She stopped and looked into my eyes. The piercing glare of pure hatred emanated from hers. "I did not scream or go to the bed to slap him. Oh no. I knew what I had to do. I went to my prayer room, and gathered the things I would need. Then I stripped off my clothes and knelt at the altar of Somis. He is one of the Midnight Loa, and most don't dare seek him out. But he had come to my aid many times before, and the anger in my soul called out for him now as it never had before. I took my ceremonial dagger and pierced both of my breasts. As the blood began to run down to my nipples, I whispered the prayer of the Milk of Death. I offered myself as always to him, and begged for one favor. Sometimes it takes minutes or even hours before you feel the touch of the loa. But on that night, my voice must have been strong. Somis brushed his hands against the nape of my neck like a lover. And then he took my hands and pressed them to my chest, smearing the blood and stopping its flow. When he released me, I stood up and returned to the bedroom.

"I said only three words. 'Wake up, Walter.'

"His eyes fluttered open, and he realized after a second of confusion where he was. And how badly he was compromised. He tried to turn, but he couldn't move. I held a very special doll of him in my hand. And I kept my hand squeezed tightly shut. I showed him my clenched fist and the small head that stuck out of the end, and his eyes grew large. He knew this was bad. Worse than anything he'd known, probably. I walked to the other side of the bed, and carefully tugged the sheet down. When the breasts and belly of his whore were fully exposed to me, I lifted my right hand and whispered an invocation. I offered this life to Somis, and then brought the dagger down hard.

"She barely struggled. The knife pierced her chest and her eyes opened wide in shock and her arms flailed about for a minute. She tried to sit up, but the blood was coming out of her fast. Her hands clenched at her chest and she looked confused when she held them up in front of her and saw blackness covering them in the faint light of the stars. When she saw me standing there with the knife by the side of the bed, her lips curled up and she shook her head and began to cry."

She paused again, sipped her tea, and looked for some reaction from me. I said nothing.

"Walter's whore turned to him then, begging him to wake up and help her. Blood poured through her fingers as she held her chest with one hand, and grabbed at his arm with the other. When she realized that he was awake, just not moving, she tried to scream for help. I stepped forward then and brought the blade across her throat. She began to gag. There was nothing she could do to hold back the blood as I called out to Somis and Beal and Nostras and more. There had been no sacrifice in the circle tonight. So I appeased their hunger at home.

"When she finally fell to the pillow, I moved to Walter's side of the bed. I shoved the sheets down and pushed him over to lie on his back before I straddled his waist with my knees on either side of his hips. His cock was still comically erect; men are foolish beasts, truly. Even as it rubbed against me, begging perhaps, for reprieve, I leaned forward and touched my dagger to his chest. 'You said that your heart was mine once,' I said to him. 'Well, I've decided to take it.' Those were the only words I said to him before I carved open his chest. I plunged the knife into him again and again and again until my face dripped with his blood. When I finally reached into his broken chest and pulled out that ragged organ he claimed was mine, I bit it and chewed. Then I spit it out in the face of the dead woman beside him. And took another bite."

Charlaine Marie fell silent then.

After a while, I broke it.

"Why did you kill my wife?" I asked.

She shook her head.

"That night, I vowed that nobody else should feel the pain that I felt. I knelt between the bodies of my husband and his lover, dripping with their blood, and I spoke with Somis. Together, we fashioned a curse upon all those who would dare to do what Walter had done. When the moon was full and looked down upon the earth with its best, cold eye, it would give power to my army. On that night, those who had been wronged would rise from their protected slumber in the swamps, and avenge those who had been wronged by an adulterer."

"I don't understand," I said. "If everyone who cheated was to be killed on the night of the full moon, half of this city would be dead by now."

"The curse's power is in the way it grows," she said. "Nobody has the power to strike down so many at once. But this expands with every full moon. Walter was the first. I took his heart...and so by the terms of the curse, he is reborn each month under the light of the full moon to go find someone else who has done what he did, and take out their heart to punish them for their transgressions against love. But it doesn't end with him. Every time he exacts his vengeance, that person must also rise again the following month to seek out an adulterer...and punish them for their sins against the heart. Each month, their numbers grow. They are my army. My vigilantes of love. They redeem their sins by punishing the sins of others."

"That's insane," I said. "If what you're describing is true, in a few months there will be hundreds dying every month and then thousands. You have no right to cast such judgments or retribution simply because your husband broke your heart. We're all weak. We all make mistakes and are lured by temptation. Yes, I know my wife cheated on me, but I would take her back in a heartbeat if I could."

Charlaine Marie laughed. "Would you?"

She bent her head then and stared at the table. I watched for a minute, wondering what her game was. Then I realized there was the faintest of whispers; her lips were moving. It was as if she were speaking to the table itself.

"What are you doing?" I demanded. She didn't answer.

"Look at me," I said.

The whispers stopped, and slowly, she raised her head to meet my eyes. She was smiling.

"What did you do?" I asked. My chest was suddenly tight. She had whispered some kind of spell, I knew it.

"Nothing you didn't ask for," she said.

There was a crash in the back of the house. The sound of glass breaking. I stood up fast. "What was that?"

She rose slowly, and turned to face the living room. But she made no move to go see what had broken. That only made me more nervous.

I followed her gaze. Something moved in the shadows from the other room. My eyes followed it, trying to make out the shape. And then it came into view. A woman with dark hair and a long, blackened nightshirt. Strands of algae hung over her shoulders, mottling her already stained covering. But I barely noticed that. I was looking at her face. At the deep-set brown eyes, and the thick lips covered with round sores of rot and decay. There were jagged pieces missing from her cheeks, and her hair was knotted and tangled with small branches and seaweed. Despite all of it, there was no mistaking who she was.

Amanda.

She staggered forward, moving into the kitchen. Toward me.

I felt frozen, not sure whether to run away or run forward. It was Amanda, the woman I'd courted and loved and married and missed with an unending hole in my heart for months. But she'd clearly been decomposing.

I stood still as she drew closer, step by painfully slow step. She was silent, but water leaked from the sides of her mouth, as if she were trying to speak. She rounded the table, closing me in. And then she held out her fish-white, wrinkled hands and slid them across my shoulders.

"Amanda?" I whispered.

Her eyes said she knew me. Her lips pressed forward, as if to make up for her long time away.

I was rooted in my spot. She didn't slow. The thin remnants of her nightshirt dripped on Charlaine Marie's kitchen floor, leaving puddles behind her.

Amanda's face moved closer, her intent clear. I tried to remember the last time we were together, the last time I wanted to kiss her. And all of the weeks and months I had dreamed of having one more chance to hold her. Those memories kept me still as her face loomed closer. I could see the black dots of swamp dirt speckling the pores of her face, and the ragged places where things had bitten chunks from her. The water of the swamp had leeched away any blood or pink of any kind.

She was more than pale; Amanda was corpse-white, her skin wrinkled from time apparently spent underwater. She smelled of the swamp and decay.

But I let her lips touch mine anyway. For a split second, everything in the world felt right again. Amanda was there with me. Showing me affection.

And then the bitter taste of rot and death filled my mouth and I couldn't stand it. I shoved her away from me with such force that she stumbled and fell to the floor.

Across the table from me, Charlaine Marie laughed. A horrible, cruel sound. Amanda struggled to rise again from the floor, grabbing onto a chair back for balance as she stood. Tears flowed from her eyes; my denial had wounded her.

"I'm sorry," I said. "But...."

"So much for the power of love, eh?" Charlaine Marie said. Then she mouthed some foreign words and pointed at the door to the living room. "Return to your rest," she said. And Amanda turned and disappeared through the doorway.

"You talk a big game, but you're just like every other man," Charlaine Marie said. "Love is not forever or without qualifications. Maybe you'd enjoy joining your wife in my army."

She rose from her chair, and her face looked evil. Gone was the playful Charlaine Marie who I'd met upon entering. This was a woman dedicated to retribution and punishment. I reached into my pocket and grabbed the most important weapon I'd brought with me. It wasn't a gun.

Charlaine Marie was already mumbling words that sounded ancient and cruel. I didn't know what she was saying, or what spirits she was calling, but I knew that they were not aimed at granting me a long and happy life.

I pulled the small bag of black salt from my pocket and dropped to a crouch. Carefully I emptied the bag on the kitchen floor, forming a full circle around me. I did it quickly, so that she wouldn't realize my intent, and then rose with my gun in hand once more.

"You have to stop the curse," I said.

"You're in no position to make demands," she said, interrupting her foreign words.

"Your curses can't touch me right now," I said. "I'm safe within this circle. However, I can still fire this gun. And your spells can't stop bullets."

"Are you so sure?" she said. "Your pitiful circle may protect you for now...but you have to leave it eventually. And perhaps I have my own protection from brute weapons."

I didn't believe that she could truly cast a spell to stop bullets. But I didn't completely put it past her either. We were in a stalemate once more. And she was right, I couldn't stand here in a small circle for long.

"Let Amanda go," I said. "Let all of them go. You're not simply punishing people who have made mistakes, or been weak. You're torturing them. How can they continue to live as their bodies rot away in the swamp?"

She shrugged. "They deserve it. They sleep beneath the water for most of the month. Only when the moon is full do they rise. If they have a personal connection to anyone who is a cheater, they wake with that knowledge and may go to that person first. They live half in our world, and half in the next, and so they can step between spaces. They can move from the swamp to the city in a heartbeat, and be at the bedside of the person they will punish in seconds after waking. And once they have completed their mission, they bring the bodies of those that they have punished back to the swamp with them in the same way. Their numbers will grow and multiply until only those with true hearts remain."

"You're insane," I said. And then something she said hit me. And brought back a memory of last night. An awful realization of what it meant.

"Your...vigilantes...you say they are drawn to go to people they know, as long as that person has cheated?"

She nodded. "If they had a connection to someone in life, and that person has cheated since the last full moon, they will be called to seek out that person in particular, and take their heart."

"Then you have to stop the curse now," I said. "Before midnight."

I looked at my phone, which said 8:33 p.m., as Charlaine Marie laughed.

But I cut her short.

"I slept with Renee last night," I said. "If you don't stop this curse now, there's a very good chance that after midnight, your daughter will be dead."

CHAPTER THIRTY-THREE

Charlaine Marie's face filled with panic.

"No," she said. "Renee wouldn't." And then the doubt set in. "How could you?"

"Did she know about your curse? Your army?" I asked. "She is in your circle."

She shook her head. "The curse is mine alone."

"Your husband certainly knew Renee," I said. "And my wife met Renee before too. Who knows what other of your zombies knew her? If this curse works as you said, Walter or Amanda or someone else is going to rise and rip her heart out tonight, and she'll be rotting in the swamp behind this house tomorrow. And it will all be your fault."

All her venom seemed to drain away. Charlaine Marie's eyes blinked rapidly. I could see her trying to find a way out. Trying to think of some way to save her daughter.

"Will a black salt ring of protection keep your vigilantes outside?" I asked.

"No," she said. "They are still physical beings. They won't be able to move through space to appear inside the house, but they can enter the yard. And they can break windows and doors and enter the house. Your protection barrier will not stop them. Is that where she is? Your house?"

I nodded. "I didn't dare take her home to her husband after keeping her out all night."

She raised her eyebrows. "No. I've wanted to do something about him for months, but she wouldn't let me."

Charlaine Marie turned away from me and opened three kitchen cabinets in a row. All were filled with jars. They were all clearly labeled with white paper and black marker. I could read some of them – herbs and plant extracts, but also tinctures and dried bits of flesh from both humans and animals. She was clearly trying to think of something. And coming up empty.

She turned around again with tears streaming down her face.

"How could you?" she yelled. "How could you do this to my daughter!"

"How could you do this to my wife?" I answered.

She glared at me, clearly considering whether I was more valuable to her at the moment dead or alive.

"It's your curse and your army," I said. "Can't you control them?"

"It's bigger than me now. It grows stronger and more powerful with every moon. I have to think…."

Charlaine Marie's face creased and frowned. And then she suddenly pointed at the door.

"Get out," she said. "If you care about her at all, go and take care of Renee. Don't go to sleep tonight. Don't let her go home; he'll be as dangerous to her as one of the vigilantes now. He's a jealous lunatic. I need time to find a way to protect her. I just don't know…."

I stepped out of my circle. Charlaine Marie was now preoccupied and did not appear ready to strike me down. On the contrary, she suddenly seemed smaller, shrunken. While she may have had the power to punish scores of people, she was now struggling to find a stronger power to allow her to save her daughter.

When I left the room, I could hear her mumbling to herself, perhaps having a conversation with the spirits who had helped her release the curse itself.

I drove the back roads at breakneck speed, praying that Renee had done as she'd promised, and stayed at my house.

CHAPTER THIRTY-FOUR

The moon hung bright and full over the trees as I stepped out of the car. For the first time in my life I hated the sight of those craters and valleys illuminated in the night sky. Because the higher the moon got, the more likely it was for Renee to be killed just as Amanda had been.

The house was dark when I walked up the steps. There was one light on in the kitchen, but when I stepped inside, Renee was not there.

Shit. If she had gone home, I didn't know what I would do.

But it was still too early for the zombies to be out. It was not even nine-thirty yet and the moon was not yet fully high in the sky. They wouldn't come before midnight, would they?

"Renee?" I called, and walked into the living room. I flipped the light on and kept walking. The bedroom lights were also out, and I could see the sheets rumpled in the bed. But was that dark spot in the middle blood, or a body?

My heart was pounding as I flipped on the light switch.

Renee stirred on my pillow, throwing an arm over her eyes. I breathed a huge sigh of relief.

"Hey," she said. "I was so tired, I thought I'd catch a nap while I was waiting for you."

She sat up, brown eyes blinking hard as she adjusted to the light. "How did it go?"

I opened my mouth to start telling the story, and hesitated. Did I tell her that her life was in danger?

"Good," I finally answered. "I think."

"Does she know what this curse is or how to stop it?"

I nodded. "She does. And tonight is the night of the full moon, so she's going to try to do something about it now. She told me to take a hike so she could try."

Renee smiled. "That's good. Now I just have to try to do something about that loser I call a husband."

She swiveled her legs out of the bed and hopped up, tilting her head to give me a quick kiss on the lips. She was wearing one of my old gray university T-shirts, and nothing else.

"You're going to stay here, right?" I asked.

"For as long as you'll have me," she said. "I don't ever want to be in the same room with that bastard again."

"I'll do my best to make sure you never have to be," I said.

She smiled and slipped her hand around mine. "Do you mind if we stay in tonight?" she asked. "I'm still really tired. I'd love to just watch a little TV and go back to bed."

"Sure," I said. "That'd be perfect."

A few minutes later, Renee was cuddled in against me on the couch. We sipped bourbon on the rocks and watched a couple episodes of *Cheers*. And then when we both started yawning, one infectiously setting the other off and vice versa, I set my glass down.

"Time for bed?" I asked.

She sat up and stretched. "Do you have a spare toothbrush?"

* * *

We made love again. This time slow and tender. Renee's face glowed afterward. I don't think I've ever seen her so happy. I hoped that it was because she was with me, and not simply because she wasn't with her husband.

Minutes later, she was asleep.

I...didn't dare fall asleep. The clock was inching toward midnight. I could hear my heart pounding steadily in my chest. Now and then, the house creaked in the dark, and I stiffened each time, staring into the shadows.

Once Renee was deep asleep, I slipped out of bed and turned the lights on in the kitchen and living room. I had my revolver by the bed, but would bullets be effective against Charlaine Marie's zombie vigilantes?

I had no idea. I decided to hedge my bets, and went to the utility room, looking for some kind of blunt instrument, in case I needed it. There was a shovel behind the door that I kept for the tiny vegetable garden in back. I shrugged and brought that back to the bedroom. A bat or an axe would have been better, but it was something.

Then I slid back into bed, trying not to wake her.

And waited some more.

Now and then, I reached out and fingered the gun.

I listened to her breathing.

I looked at the clock.

12:01 a.m. Maybe we'd be lucky, and they'd pass her by this time. There were no doubt hundreds of others who had cheated in New Orleans over the past month. Maybe Walter and Amanda and whoever else would be called elsewhere.

Glass shattered somewhere in the house.

Damnit. I heard the sound and grabbed the gun. I knew what it meant; there was no way that this was a normal break-in. It was a zombie. Charlaine Marie had not been successful.

Could I actually protect Renee? Could a man stop a curse?

A figure appeared in the doorway of my bedroom. An older bearded man; his hair was white, and his clothes ragged and blackened with the decay of the swamp. His arms were bare and rotten; ribbons of flesh hung from them as if he'd been flayed. I could smell the stench of decay enter the room with him. He moved slowly, but his aim was clear. Renee.

I held the gun out in front of me. My hands were shaking.

"Stop right there or I'll shoot," I warned.

The zombie continued moving toward the bed.

I didn't give him a second chance. I fired.

The bullet went right through his forehead. A dark pucker appeared, and his head wavered.

But he kept walking.

I fired again. This time the bullet ruined his cheek. Chunks of bone and beard exploded, hanging in gory, glistening strands down his face. But he continued moving. I fired twice more in rapid succession and his body shivered but continued to move.

Renee cried out next to me when she saw the zombie reach across the bedsheets toward her.

"Daddy?" she shrieked. "No!"

As soon as his blackened hands touched her, she fell silent. Instead of bulging out in fear, her eyes fluttered and then closed as the zombie ran a blackened hand across her forehead. Realization dawned and I finally understood one of the biggest mysteries in the disappearances. That's how they kept the victims from waking up. Their touch was like a sleeping pill. Or a tranquilizer dart.

I rolled over her body and pushed the reeking form away from the bed.

The zombie fell backward, but as it did, I saw that there was another one entering the room.

A younger, black man. Someone else she had known. And I saw movement out in the hall. There were more.

Oh goddamnit.

Walter reached for my leg, and as his fingers touched me, I suddenly felt a wave of exhaustion overtake me. I yawned, and started to close my eyes before what was happening hit me.

I threw myself to the side, breaking the connection. My limbs felt heavy as stone. I crawled around the bed as the zombie behind me stood up. The younger man reached the foot of the bed just as I reached the shovel propped against the wall.

I swung the thing like a bat, and the flat of the metal spade connected with the face of the second zombie. The force of the blow sent him three steps backward before he fell down completely. Renee's father was reaching for her again, and I aimed a swing at his already ruined face. The sound was wet and unpleasant.

A third zombie was now entering the room. I could see another form in the hallway beyond it.

Shit!

Renee's adultery had not drawn one vigilante. She'd drawn an army.

Renee began to wake again. "What's happening?" she cried.

"Your mother's curse," I answered, and turned to meet the new threat. My stomach clenched when I saw the woman crossing the room. Her face was very familiar to me. I'd seen her just a few hours ago and woken up next to her for years.

Amanda.

"Goddamn it," I cried, as she moved straight to the bed. I hesitated, but only for a moment. And then I swung.

The last thing I'd ever wanted to do was crush that once-beautiful face. But I hit her as hard as I could. Amanda went down instantly. Then I swung at the hulking gray-skinned man who had entered the room behind her. He staggered backward, but didn't go down. I was outnumbered. Three men were now focused on me. Amanda crawled along the floor nearby. Until they could remove the shovel from the equation, they couldn't do what they'd been brought back to life to do. Two of them reached out to touch me as I brought the shovel back to my shoulder for another swing. They ducked as the shovel shot through the air in one direction, and then came back again to try to hit what I'd missed.

I brought the thing around and knocked the younger man away, but when I began to swing it back in the other direction once more, Renee's father grabbed my arm, and my limbs instantly grew heavy again. Like jelly. I couldn't control them. The shovel's trajectory slowed and then the blade dropped to the bed. I couldn't hold it up. "No," I said, pulling back. But then Amanda got up again, and came straight for me, arms outstretched. I tried to raise the shovel, but found myself struggling just to remain standing.

Behind me, Renee started to scream. Her father's hand left me as Amanda took me in her arms. Half of her face was crushed in, but I could still see a glint of intelligence in the one remaining eye. She had come back to me from beyond death and wasn't going to take no for an answer again. I collapsed like a rag doll into her embrace. I was helpless to stop myself. The shovel clanged as it hit the floor.

And then Renee's screaming abruptly went silent.

I forced my head to turn away from the ruined bloody face of my wife, and saw Walter kneeling over Renee on the bed, a blade in his hand. He drew a line with the blade across the naked skin of her chest right between her breasts, and then another transecting it. A cross. I saw the red of Renee's blood pooling up after the knife passed. With my last conscious energy, I threw myself as hard as I could manage out from Amanda's embrace.

I had weight on my side, and my body toppled across the bed and hard against Walter's. He readied his knife in the air, clearly preparing for a fatal stab down into the center of the lines he had carved. I fell into him, my consciousness fading. I had a brief feeling of satisfaction as I saw him fall away from her, and then my head was lying on her stomach. Something warm and wet leaked down against my cheek, and I felt my vision going gray.

Just before the wave of sleep overtook me, I saw something strange.

Amanda and the two men stopped moving. They were standing around the bed and suddenly went completely still. Walter did not rise from where I had pushed him to the floor.

And then my eyes closed, and I saw only blackness.

CHAPTER THIRTY-FIVE

"Cork, wake up."

Hands grabbed and pushed at my shoulder. I tried to force my eyes open, but they didn't want to. It was as if I was swimming through the depths of the ocean. I could hear the voice calling, but it was so far away.

The hands, however, did not give up and finally I was able to blink and see again.

The first thing I saw was Renee's face and bloody chest. I was lying in her lap, looking up at her. She'd bent over me, shaking me awake.

Seeing her eyes sent a warm surge through my body. And then the last moments before I'd fallen unconscious flashed through my memory. I bolted upright.

"Where are they?" I asked. Before she could answer, I turned my head and took in the scene around us.

Walter lay beside the bed, still in the same place he'd fallen when I'd body-slammed him off of Renee.

Amanda and the other two men lay on the floor at the foot of the bed. Something black and liquid pooled around their faces. The wounds I'd inflicted were seeping. None of them moved.

"What happened?" she asked. "How did you do it?"

I shook my head. "I didn't do anything. They were winning. There was nothing I could do to stop them. I slowed them down a little but then they knocked me out. But just as I was going under, it looked like they just...stopped. Maybe Charlaine Marie was able to stop the curse after all."

Renee reached over to the nightstand and picked up her phone. Then she brought up her mother's contact and hit dial.

The phone simply rang and rang.

"Well, it *is* the middle of the night," I said.

"Yeah," she said with a frown. "I don't think she went to bed if she was still trying to undo the curse at midnight. We weren't out that long."

She redialed the number, and waited as it rang and rang. I could see her face growing increasingly concerned. Finally, she ended the call.

"Can we go over there?"

I didn't relish going back to Charlaine Marie's house, but I was curious myself. What had she done to stop them?

"Sure," I said. "But we should get you cleaned up first. Get some disinfectant on those cuts."

She nodded. "I'll take a quick shower."

★   ★   ★

I explained the full breadth of the curse her mother had created on the ride over. Renee shook her head in disbelief.

"I knew that she had done something to my dad. He just... disappeared, and she refused to talk about it. But, to do this...to hurt so many people...."

"Isn't that what the Black Queen does? Create curses and spells of harm and vengeance?"

"Sometimes," she said. "But only for people who deserve it. People came to her asking for help against abusive bosses, spouses, neighbors, you name it. That's what we did in the weekly circle – we drew power from the loa to create spells to help the people who came to Momma. You would call it black magic, but there was usually a good reason to use it. The happiness and love charms that white magic produces don't really work for what our clients needed. To take care of some things, you need the venom of snakes and power of fire."

It was after 3 a.m. when we pulled up in front of the house.

The glow of lights from the back of the house illuminated the swamp shrubs all around the place. So Charlaine Marie was still up.

I knocked on the door, but there was no answer. We waited a minute and then tried again.

Still nothing.

"I have a key," Renee said, and fished through her purse to find it.

A moment later, I stepped across the threshold and into the Black Queen's house for the second time in less than twelve hours.

"Momma?" Renee called, walking across the foyer and through the living room. I followed her into the kitchen.

"She's probably back in her workshop," Renee said. She led me down a hallway to the rear of the house. We went down three steps and she opened a door into a dark room.

Not dark from lack of light – there were candles set all around the place. But the walls themselves were all painted black. Ram horns adorned three of the walls, one set mounted just above the grand voodoo altar on the long wall. The statue of the Christ Child had been painted a dark purple. And around his neck he wore a necklace made out of a snake. The thing ate its tail to complete the circle.

The room was filled with obscene and ghastly things but none of those could draw and hold my eye right now.

Because in the middle of the hardwood floor, Charlaine Marie lay flat and still on her back. She was naked, except for a bone necklace. Her skin was painted all over in black symbols of the occult. Her hands still gripped the end of a long sharpened goat's horn, which protruded from her chest. There were puncture marks on her thighs and breasts. Blood had flowed from a dozen places on her body. But it was not flowing any longer. Her lifeblood was pooled and still around her.

"Momma, no!" Renee cried and ran across the room to kneel next to the Black Queen, who had been brought down by her own hand.

Renee cried and grabbed at her mother's shoulders, but Charlaine Marie's eyes did not move. Her limbs did not stir. She had probably been dead for a couple hours now. Since right after midnight, would be my guess.

"Why would she do this?" I asked, crouching down beside Renee.

That question only made her sob louder. I put my arm around her shoulders until she was able to bring herself under control.

Renee rubbed the tears away with the back of her hands and looked at me with a haunted sadness in her eyes.

"She did it to save me," she said. "Sometimes, the only way for a priestess to stop a very powerful curse is to sacrifice herself. She probably tried other things, but when they didn't work and the zombies rose from the swamp anyway, she did the only thing she knew how to do to stop them. She had to stab her own heart. That would be the only thing one of the Midnight Loa would accept."

"I'm sorry," I whispered. "Do you think that...it's really over then? You think the curse is completely stopped?"

She nodded. "Its power died with her."

"What happens to all the zombies that rose from the swamp tonight?"

Renee shrugged. "They can finally rest. They will rot away completely now. They were preserved and reanimated by the power of the moon and the Midnight Loa and Momma's curse every month. But now? There are probably dozens of them lying in bedrooms just like yours, all over town. I think she stopped them just after they began their work."

I shook my head, dreading the return home. Why couldn't they just disappear?

"That's going to make for some really strange dispatch calls in the morning," I said.

She had to smile at that. Then she touched her mother's face once more. Softly.

"I'm so sorry, Momma," she whispered. "For everything."

I let her have a moment. Then I drew Renee into my arms and hugged her as tightly as I could for a really long time. We rocked together there, bodies entwined on the floor, next to the Black Queen, both of us crying with both sadness and joy in the midst of her secret shrine.

I thought of all the bloody beds I'd seen, and of Amanda and Eleanor and Rowan. And I put all of those memories aside. I kissed Renee, soft and long. I surrendered my heart in that moment completely. I had lost so much. But I had also gained.

Renee was alive. And she was mine. Maybe that love potion she'd thrown me at Eleanor's Arcana had actually worked.

The curse was finally over. For the first time in a long time, I would be happy, not empty, as the morning sun rose. The next few days would not be easy as we buried the remains of her mother, and her marriage. But I was ready.

Let the dawn come.

AFTERWORD

Every book has a story behind the story. This novel really began when New Orleans cast a spell on me over twenty years ago. I first went there in the late 1990s for a week-long business convention, and I remember being entranced by the music, the food, the voodoo…. I remember dancing in a gothy skull-deco club that didn't even open until midnight. I have lots of lush pictures from when I took a street car to the Garden District, where I walked until I found Anne Rice's home. I barely made it back that night for the meeting's closing dinner.

Fast-forward a handful of years. I was going over the final edits on my second short fiction collection, titled *Vigilantes of Love* (an allusion to New Order, since several of the stories in the collection had a 'music' bent). As I was wrapping up the book I got an idea for a short story actually called 'Vigilantes of Love'. It was inspired by the title and the cover art of the collection, which was a collage of photos that I'd taken, one of which was from Marie Laveau's House of Voodoo in the French Quarter. I jotted it down in a night, and sent it to the editor, Tina Jens, who founded and oversaw Chicago's Twilight Tales writers' collective, as well as its book line. They'd been releasing chapbooks from local authors for years before I found them and started doing live readings of my stories at their weekly open mic nights. Tina liked the story, but said it was really just a vignette. Turn it into a real story, she said, and we could slip it in at the end of the book before it went to press.

I tripled the size and breadth of the story that weekend, and emailed it to her, anxiously hoping that it would get the green light. Tina told me again that she still thought it should be a longer story; there was more there to explore. But she liked it and suddenly my book had an actual title story. At that time, I never intended to expand the tale. But ten years later, after a couple more trips to New Orleans, I sat down one day and sketched out a novel-length idea about the 'vigilantes of love'. It was one of several book ideas generated during my tenure with New York's Leisure Books, though it did not get written during that period.

Fast-forward another handful of years. I had been in New Orleans a lot during the interim. The World Horror Convention was hosted there and during that trip, my editor, Don D'Auria, took me to lunch at what would become one of my favorite restaurants, Red Fish Grill. My family also passed through NOLA at the end of a vacation, and stopped at some of my favorite sites, including one of the eerie above-ground cemeteries. In the spring of 2019, I was there again for a week-long convention, and this time, I set up shop in the Turtle Bay bar to drink NOLA Brewing IPAs and work on ideas for my next novel. I've written chapters of several of my novels at different bars in New Orleans over the past decade, but Turtle Bay has become one of my favorite low-key places to stop and work at. As I was trying to brainstorm there, it occurred to me that I still had 'that idea about the vigilantes' on my hard drive. I pulled it up to remind myself of what I'd been thinking about... started making edits and adding to it... and an hour later, sitting in a bar in New Orleans, I decided to write a novel called *Voodoo Heart* that finally told the full story of Detective Lawrence Ribaud. Assuming my editor and publisher liked the idea (they did). And so it began...after a very long gestation period!

There are always pieces of me in my books. Each novel is written and edited over the course of a year, so for me personally, the prose is sprinkled with little keys to that year. There are always nods to places I've been and things I've seen during the writing. In *Voodoo Heart*, Turtle Bay and Red Fish Grill, two of my favorite spots in New Orleans play a role, as does NOLA Brewing (I wish we could get their beer in Chicago!). The 'Adventure Time' tattoo described in Chapter Thirteen is because I was writing at one of Stone Brewing's outdoor garden bistros one night in San Diego last fall and a woman sat down next to me with...a Jake the Dog tattoo. The snake named Kuma in Chapter Twenty-Three was named while I was writing that chapter at the awesome heavy metal-themed burger joint and craft beer bar Kuma's Corner in Chicago. I had to smile at all of those memories as I reviewed the final publisher's proof this month.

So real life and real places often inform and inspire the fiction. Hopefully, they help make the story feel more real, though it remains fiction. For *Voodoo Heart*, I name a few places in New Orleans, but know that I've still taken liberties with the geography to suit the story.

The journey of writing and editing *Voodoo Heart* was actually supposed to end, just as it began, in New Orleans this year. The initial copyeditor notes on the book were due to come to me from Flame Tree Press just before I was to go back to NOLA in March for another week-long meeting, and I looked forward to reading the edited manuscript at Turtle Bay and Red Fish on nights after work. Unfortunately, that perfect closure to the novel was stopped by the onslaught of the COVID-19 pandemic, as the meeting was cancelled two weeks before it happened. But I still look forward to going back someday. Maybe with a copy of the published book in hand.

So that's the story behind *Voodoo Heart*. There are many people to thank for all their support of this and my other novels, from my longtime editor Don D'Auria, to my publisher Nick Wells and Gillian, Maria and all of the great staff at Flame Tree Press. I have to thank Bucket O' Blood Books and Records in Chicago for hosting my last two novel release parties, and my hometown Naperville Barnes & Noble for their constant support. Thanks to my family, Geri and Shaun, for letting me disappear into my stories, to my writer cabal of Bill Gagliani, Dave Benton and Brian Pinkerton for always having my back, and to Mort Castle and Jonathan Maberry for their sage advice and career support. And thanks, most of all, to my loyal readers, who have stuck with me year after year, always asking for more twisted tales. I hope this one gave you both a chill in the bones and a warm heart for a place that I love.

And finally, thanks to New Orleans, for inspiring these dark dreams.

John Everson
Naperville, IL
June 2020

FLAME TREE PRESS
FICTION WITHOUT FRONTIERS
Award-Winning Authors & Original Voices

Flame Tree Press is the trade fiction imprint of Flame Tree Publishing, focusing on excellent writing in horror and the supernatural, crime and mystery, science fiction and fantasy. Our aim is to explore beyond the boundaries of the everyday, with tales from both award-winning authors and original voices.

•

•

Join our mailing list for free short stories, new release details, news about our authors and special promotions:

flametreepress.com